Evan

"Ever since *Moby Dick* we fear that the ocean treats human beings by its own rules. Marlowe, a worthy successor of Captain Ahab, was the only one who knew these rules."
- *Lufthansa Exclusive Magazine*

"A fascinating read."
- *Adelaide Advertiser*

Trial by Fire

"The fast-moving dialogue and fine sense of characterization keep the reader hanging on for the ride."
- *Publishers Weekly*

"Haunting, memorable...will be considered a classic in years to come."
- *Midwest Book Review*

"D.W. Buffa would be a household name in a perfect world. Meticulously plotted...with unforgettable characters. Very highly recommended."
- *BookReporter.com*

Breach of Trust

"Another well-crafted legal thriller from one of the genre's best practitioners."
- *Calgary Herald*

"Political intrigue abounds...a truly surprising end,"
- *Publishers Weekly*

DISCARDED From the Nashville Public Library

"Maddening suspense, captivating courtroom scenes, and a marvelously twisted ending"
- *Booklist*

Star Witness

"A great legal thriller. D.W. Buffa keeps readers engrossed in this fulfilling drama that ends in a way nobody could have predicted."
- *Midwest Book Review*

"Legal thrills...in the world of Hollywood- a world where make-believe and real life are so entwined that it's difficult to separate the truth from the dreams shown on the screen."
- *Houston Chronicle*

The Legacy

"A first-class premise... taut, well-paced."
- *Publishers Weekly*

"Buffa builds a compelling, suspenseful story... He combines a strong plot with more character development and a striking portrayal of San Francisco, its corruption and its opulence, its beauty and its mystery."
- *Booklist*

"As the whos in the whodunit roll out tantalizingly, Buffa expertly lays out the chessboard of the courtroom and its inhabitants who range from crusty to cunning. Bottom line: Add this to your docket."
- *People Magazine*

The Judgment

"Buffa can keep company with the best writers of legal

thrillers and courtroom dramas. Absorbing."
- *The Orlando Sentinel*

"If there's anybody who can mount a challenge to John Grisham's mantle...Buffa's the most sure-footed guy to do it. A crisp, first-rate read...a tightly wound thriller. A richly textured cast of characters."
- *Edmonton Journal*

"D.W. Buffa continues to show great intelligence and erudition. There's nobody else like him."
- *San Jose Mercury News*

"Littered with plot twists and land mines that explode when least expected...A novel with wide appeal. A fast-moving tale that jolts and veers enticingly off track, but also stays comfortably in sight of the main objective. Well-developed characters and a rich milieu add depth to this excellent thriller."
- *Publishers Weekly*

The Defense
"A gripping drama...made up of not just one but several exciting trials...More satisfying still, it ends with a couple of twists that are really shocking. And it leaves you wanting to go back to the beginning and read it all over again."
- *The New York Times*

"An excellent legal thriller."
- *USA Today*

"Stunning legal reversals...fine, flowing prose...[a] devastating impact."
- *The New York Times Book Review*

DISCARDED FROM THE
NASHVILLE PUBLIC LIBRARY

THE
SWINDLERS

D. W. Buffa

DISCARDED FROM THE
ASHVILLE PUBLIC LIBRARY

BLUE ZEPHYR

Published by Blue Zephyr
Copyright © 2010 D. W. Buffa

All rights reserved. Without limiting the rights under
copyright reserved above, no part of this publication may be
reproduced, stored in or introduced into a retrieval system,
or transmitted, in any form, or by any means (electronic,
mechanical, photocopying, recording, or otherwise) without
the prior written permission of both the copyright owner and
the above publisher of this book.

www.dwbuffa.net

ISBN-10: 146358377X
ISBN-13: 978-1463583774

THE SWINDLERS

CHAPTER ONE

It was our own Gilded Age, a time of excess and raw exuberance, in which the rich got richer and, instead of trying to hide the fact, did everything they could to make sure everyone knew just how much they had. The lavish display of wealth became an art form, a competition not so much over what things looked like but rather how much they cost. If there was a single winner, someone who defined the age, it was Nelson St. James, the man some considered a financial genius when he was making them staggering amounts of money, and something rather different when their profits began to turn into substantial losses. He had, when I first met him, houses everywhere, so many of them that it was hard to think he had a home. He visited them the way other people stayed a few days in a hotel. If he had a residence, a place he felt comfortable, a place he could lounge around in an old pair of sandals and a shirt bought somewhere off the rack, it was here, on his own private yacht that, as the rumor said, had cost as much as some countries spent on their navies. Blue Zephyr could sail in any ocean, go anywhere in the world, which meant that Nelson St. James never had to be in the same place twice, and, more importantly, never, even in his sleep, had to stop moving. It was that, and not any great love of the sea that made him spend so much of his time on the water; that, and perhaps the sense that out here he was more difficult to find.

I had come aboard in San Francisco, invited for a weekend cruise down the California coast. Where Blue Zephyr was going after I left it in Los Angeles I had no idea, and I am not sure anyone else knew either. The last thing anyone on the yacht was interested in was their destination. There were more than a dozen guests, and all of them, or at least those I had met so far, were there for no other reason than because they had been invited. No one turned down an invitation from Nelson St. James. There was too much money involved for that.

Standing at the starboard railing, I watched the evening sun turn a stunning reddish gold as it drifted down toward the sea and hesitated, hovering, as if just this once, playing havoc with human certainty, it might desert the western sky and go off in some new direction. Finally, as if instead of belonging to necessity the decision was now its own, it slowly melted along the line of the horizon and drowned in a shining flow of molten bronze. I felt a hand on my shoulder.

"I'm Nelson St. James. I'm sorry it took me so long to get away."

The voice was different than I had expected, softer, less sure of itself, almost diffident, as if he had to make a conscious effort to approach someone he did not know. But when I turned around and we shook hands, that first impression quickly yielded to a second. His eyes, a steady grayish blue, were eager, alert, the eyes of a gambler quick to grasp the nature of the game, and quicker still to take advantage. His smile was full of mischief. That was what caught your attention, what gave him an interest, that look of keen anticipation, a sense of what might happen next, because otherwise he seemed fairly ordinary, no more remarkable than any other middle aged man you might pass on the street.

He continued to make his apologies as he led me to the starboard side, explaining that he had been forced to spend all day in his cabin below, working on "some business thing I had."

I was still trying to fit the quiet, self-effacing voice of his with that bold and almost avaricious look he had. In some odd way he seemed aware of it, amused at the condition, as if his voice belonged to someone else, someone he used to know and whose sudden disappearance caused a puzzled smile to come to his lips. He spoke in fits and starts, the words never quite adequate to the thought he meant to convey; words being slow, heavy things compared to what, if the look in his eyes was any indication, was all the wing-footed calculation racing through his brain.

"You've met...the others?" he asked with a vague half turn toward the small crowd gathered at the stern.

I nodded, but made no other reply.

"They're not very interesting." He said this as if the point were obvious, but obvious or not, he waited to see my reaction, and when I said nothing, he seemed to approve. "You've just met them; I've known most of them for years. Trust me," he said, laughing under his breath, "dull as dust. All they know is money." Pausing, he tapped his fingers on the brass railing. "Actually, they don't know anything about that, either."

St. James, short and slight of build, gripped the railing with both hands and gazed at the coastline little more than a mile away. "There," he said presently, pointing toward the red tile roofs and white stucco walls of a massive estate clustered at the top of the hills, bathed in the solemn twilight colors of the vanished sun. "That's something worth seeing, not the way the tourists do who buy their tickets by the bus load and go gaping through it, but from out here, where it doesn't look any different than when it was first built."

His eyes, filled with a strange, vicarious pleasure, moved in a steady arc until he was looking straight at me. It was as if he wanted me to guess what he was thinking, some secret he had not shared with anyone and was not yet certain he wanted to share with me. It was one thing if I could figure it out on my own; it was another thing if he had to tell me.

"The Hearst Castle," I said, returning his gaze. "The only castle in the world named for the man who could afford to build it."

"Exactly. Hearst was not like Getty or Howard Hughes, hiding from the world, afraid of what other people wanted. He wanted everyone to know what he had, all the things he had taken, taken from all over the world, to fill up that castle and, some might say, the empty corners of his life. And America is the only place he could have done it, built a castle like that, dedicated to his own importance; because we don't worship royalty here, we worship money. We're a nation of thieves, Mr. Morrison; it's what we've always been. That's what makes this country great."

He laughed, but he was serious. Everyone took what they could, he seemed to suggest; some were just better at it than others.

"I'm glad you came." He glanced over his shoulder at his other guests, talking loudly in the shadows at the other end. "Dull as dust," he then muttered, shaking his head.

"You're the lawyer – right?" he asked with sudden interest, as if he had just remembered. "Morrison. You work with criminals. Some of them must be interesting. At least they've done something that isn't just like everyone else." He put his hand on my sleeve, and with a strange, almost malevolent sparkle in his eyes, studied me for a moment. "Or maybe they're just as dull as the rest. Maybe the only different is that the rich are just criminals who haven't been caught."

"In this nation of thieves you were talking about?" I ventured.

"Exactly, Mr. Morrison; exactly right. A lot of people think that about me, you know. But they're wrong." The sparkle in his eyes grew brighter, became more intense. "I've never done a dull thing in my life."

He stayed there, talking, mainly about William Randolph Hearst and the way he had lived, for another twenty minutes or so, and he might have stayed there even longer, talking about the past, if his wife had not come on deck to remind him that he had to change for dinner.

"Aren't you going to introduce us?" she said as he started to leave. But she did not wait. "I'm Danielle," she said as she offered her hand.

It was painful, so painful that for a moment I did not think I could breathe. It was the story of Medusa, told the other way round, a face so lovely that, if you were not careful, you might lose all sanity. She was younger than her husband, though by exactly how much I could not say, but her intelligence was certainly as quick, and just as instinctive. Her eyes were full of laughter, and yet at the same time, just behind the laughter, there was a kind of sympathy, as if she had become used to the effect she had on men, the awkward stammering, the loss of all confidence, the sudden blank expression, and wanted to offer at least a word of two of kindness and encouragement.

"You didn't want to join the others?" she asked, tossing her head in the direction of the voices that, loud enough a moment earlier, now seemed muted, distant and irrelevant.

My mind had gone missing. I felt a smile start to twist its way across my mouth. I tried to pull it back, but too late. She gave me a teasing glance, the way someone does who knows more about you than you do yourself.

"Is it because you're…shy?"

"No, I was there." I heard the words and only then realized they had come from me. "I had a drink…but then…" I kept looking away, and kept looking back, my eyes both sentry and traitor of what I felt. "And then the sun was going down, and I'd never been out here before, and I wanted to see it all – the way the light changed color, the way the sun…."

I shook my head and laughed, held what was left of my drink in both hands and studied, though it was barely visible, the planking on the deck. I laughed some more, struck by my own sudden incapacity. There was nothing to do but shrug my shoulders and admit defeat. I looked at her again and this time did not look way.

"And because after a few minutes, I didn't have anything else to say to them."

"Anthony Morrison, the famous courtroom lawyer, didn't have anything to say?" Her voice was warm and breathless, every word seeming a mystery with more meaning than anything it said. "But then I suppose it must be different, what you do in court, when you talk to juries and ask questions of witnesses sworn to tell the truth, and a normal conversation, like this one, in which two people who have never met before try to make themselves sound interesting by telling all the lies they can."

It was stunning how easily she made you want to believe her. Even when she told you that she was not telling the truth, you knew, or thought you knew, that she was telling you the truth about her. Taking my arm, she began to lead me toward the others. The sun had vanished completely, all that was left a few jagged streaks of deep purple in a scarlet colored sky. Across the water, on the distant shore, where Hearst had built his castle, lights began to appear.

"Don't worry," whispered Danielle, her breath close against my face, her fingers pressed tighter round my arm. "I'll take good care of you."

It had been difficult enough to keep my composure, difficult enough to think clearly, when she was moving among the shadows of early evening; it was next to impossible in the fevered atmosphere of wine and candles when we gathered for dinner and, protected by the anonymity of the crowd, I could watch her closely. Her high cheekbones and soft teasing mouth, her eyes that seemed to grow larger the longer they stayed fixed on you, her hair an auburn shade that rivaled dusk. But it was the small gestures, the subtle smile that added warmth to what she said, the eyebrow lifted in delight or surprise at something someone else had said, that made her so fascinating to observe.

She sat at the end of the long table, a table covered with crystal glasses and fine china, carrying on a conversation with one of those same men her husband had dismissed as uninteresting, drawing him out in a way that made him seem interesting at least to himself. It was a gift she had, an instinct for the vanity of men, making them believe by the questions she asked, the things she said, that there was no one with whom she would rather be, no one who could hold her interest in quite the same way.

"So if I should decide to murder someone, you're the one I should hire?"

I was still watching Danielle. The conversation around the table came to a stop, and I became aware that suddenly everyone was watching me. I turned and found Nelson St.

James, leaning back in his chair at the other end of the table, the crooked smile on his face growing broader as he waited for an answer.

"That's what you do, isn't it?" he asked with a friendly and, as it seemed, sympathetic glance. "Defend murderers, rapists, and thieves, and -"

"Well, that depends on who you decide to murder," I replied. I sat back and tossed my napkin on the table. The question had brought me back to myself, put me in a position in which I knew what I was talking about, put me in a position to say something which, let me be honest about it, might make Danielle St. James think I was something other than a tongue-tied fool. "I make a rule never to defend anyone who has killed a friend of mine." I studied the glass I still held in my hand and smiled back at St. James. "A close friend, you understand."

Gathered around that table were some of the wealthiest people in the country. Like St. James, who grinned his approval at what I had said, they tended to forget how much their own success had depended on chance, and believed instead that it had all depended on them, their ability to see the world as it was, a place in which everyone who knew what he was doing always looked to his own advantage.

"Yes, well, business is business," said St. James, casting a knowing glance around the table. But then, as if to raise a doubt, question the validity of what they thought about themselves, he turned back to me and asked, "Does it ever bother you? I'm told you don't lose very often – almost never." He searched my eyes, trying before I made one to measure my response. "No, that's a stupid question, asking if it bothers you to win a case you should have lost!" He shot a sharp, almost dismissive glance at a balding man with small, greedy eyes. "That's like asking Darwin here whether it bothers him when some financial scheme of his puts a few thousand people out of work."

Richard Darwin had the habit, which must have started when he was a child, one of nearly a dozen children in his family, of eating with both hands, and talking while he did it. His hands, his mouth, were in constant motion, and there was no set pattern, no accustomed routine; it was purely a question of expedience. If he used his right hand to butter a piece of bread, he used his left to shove it into his mouth; if the salt was on his left, he used that hand to season his soup while he ate spoonful after spoonful with his right. When he bit down on something, it was the only mark of punctuation ever heard in one of his endless run-on sentences. It was impossible to imagine him, even when he ate alone, ever being quiet. But St. James' remark stopped him cold. His face turned red and he clenched his teeth so hard his head began to shudder. He jabbed a stubby finger in the air.

"Some people may lose their jobs when I buy up a company; but more jobs are created. I make things more efficient," he went on, his raspy voice rising with each angry word. "Creative destruction, that's what capitalism is all about – the future is only possible when you get rid of the past!"

Far from troubled, St. James seemed vastly amused.

"Isn't that what I just said?" he remarked quite calmly. "You don't feel bad about it when you close something down."

This was too logical. It missed, for Darwin, the essential point.

"I do feel bad about it," he wheezed. "It's hard to put people out of work, even when you know that, overall, it has to be done."

"I'm sure it's difficult," said St. James, dryly, and then turned again to me. "But as I was saying, the question doesn't have relevance. Your job is to win. The real question is how you do it. What makes you better than the others? Why do you win cases they say almost anyone else would lose?"

"Look at him!" cried Danielle, laughing at the blank expressions she saw all around her, laughing because none of the others had grasped what to her seemed so obvious. "Look at his face. Who would ever think he could lie? When

8

he gets up to tell a jury – I've never been in court, so I'm just imagining – when he tells a jury that his client is innocent, don't you think, if they have any doubt about it, that they'll take his word for it and not what some grim-faced lawyer for the other side tries to tell them?" She turned to me and smiled. "If I were on a jury, I'd believe what he said."

St. James held up his empty wine glass, studied it with a pensive expression, and then signaled that he wanted more.

"But beyond that honest face of yours, Mr. Morrison, don't you have to have a ruthless ambition, a willingness to do anything to win?"

I wondered if he meant it literally, or, like most of us, meant it only in the sense of doing everything you could within the rules. I had the feeling that he was more interested in discovering what I thought about it, whether I recognized any rules I would not break.

"I learned a long time ago," I explained, watching the way he was watching me, "that the only way to win is to know the case inside out, know it so well that you don't make any mistakes of your own, know it so well that you're ready to take advantage of any made by the other side."

This did not answer his question, but that fact, instead of bothering him, seemed to tell him what he needed. He bent forward, another question, or rather another observation, on his lips.

"A lot of lawyers must go into court fully prepared, but they don't all come out winners the way you do."

I could not resist a retort, not after watching Richard Darwin stuff his mouth while he talked about the hardships of forcing other people out of work.

"A lot of people spend their lives working very hard, doing everything they can to get ahead, but more of them die poor than ever get rich. Sometimes, what happens is just a matter of luck." Caught up in my own argument, I pressed the point. "Trials are sometimes won, or lost, by the smallest things: the way a witness shifts his eyes, or the sudden pause as if he has forgotten part of the well-rehearsed lie he had wanted to tell. I've seen trials decided because a witness for the other side wore a dress that was too revealing. Anything can change the outcome, and the great thing, if you happen to like this kind of work, is that you never know when a trial begins what it might be."

CHAPTER TWO

I had too much to drink, and when I woke up the next morning my head beat like a hammer. I managed to get dressed and make my way up on deck, and into a blinding noontime sun. Even with dark glasses, the shoreline was a distant blur. A steward brought me a Bloody Mary and, clutching the railing, I tried to steady myself.

"She's really quite beautiful, isn't she?"

I had not heard Nelson St. James come up behind me. Nodding in dim recognition of what he had said, I tried to show enthusiasm as I cast a glance of approval at the sleek lines of his prize possession.

"Not the boat, Mr. Morrison – my wife! Danielle. You couldn't take your eyes off her last night. No! Don't be embarrassed," he laughed, slapping me with something like affection on the shoulder. "Danielle is one of the world's truly beautiful women. Only a fool, or a eunuch, wouldn't want to look at her."

He noticed what I was drinking. Smiling to himself, he kicked at the deck and then shook his head.

"You drank less than any of them, and you're the only one who feels the effect. All they do is drink. But then, who can blame them? If you were as dull as they are, wouldn't you try to forget who you are? Or if you had their worries," he added with a strange, enigmatic look.

"Then why...?" I blurted out before I could think.

"Invite them along? Have them as guests?" He leaned on the railing and stared out at the distant hills, rising and falling with the swelling current of the sea. "The cost of doing business, let's just call it that." He took a deep breath and held it for a moment before letting it out. "It's more than that. They have a lot of money invested with me. They're worried now that it might not be safe." A look of shrewd malice danced in his eyes. "We're out here on this pleasure cruise so I can convince them that if they take their money out they'll lose all chance of getting the kind of returns I've been giving them for years. That's what they really worry

11

about: not whether they might lose what they have, but that they might lose the chance to get even more."

A wind kicked up and started to blow in gusts. Short, choppy waves began to slap against the hull. The ice in my glass rattled in my unsteady hand. The wind got stronger, the boat cut deeper into the sea.

"I'm not much of a sailor, but there's nothing like it, being out here on a day like this." He pointed to the coast which, seen from this distance, looked like some vast, uninhabited place still waiting to be discovered. "You can almost feel what it must have been like, back at the beginning, when the Spanish, and then the English, came; when all this was there for the taking, for anyone who had the nerve."

A look, as of someone cheated out of what he should have had, fell across his dark, implacable eyes. He was genuinely distressed, irritated, as it seemed, for having been born too late, thwarted of the kind of ambition he might have enjoyed.

"A whole country waiting to be built, and now – what?" He turned to me, a rueful expression etched deep with a peculiar bitterness plain on his face. "What?" he demanded. "Make money – just keep adding numbers. It's the world we live in, the one we never made." Suddenly, he laughed and threw up his hands in mock frustration. "Even criminals lack all ambition!"

Still laughing, he took me by the arm and started walking down the deck. The hard, heavy wind nearly knocked me sideways, but St. James, more used to it, did not miss a step.

"You ever defend someone charged with embezzlement?" he asked, continuing his line of thought. "Wouldn't matter if they had stolen millions, would it? It would still be boring, compared to a single act of piracy."

He stopped and swung around until he was right in front of me, a question in his eyes.

"That's not crazy, you know. I can prove it. Think back over the last few years, all the rich guys – I knew a few of them – who went to jail because of the money they had taken out of the companies they ran, or the investors they defrauded. Doesn't that show you how utterly dull and without imagination they were?"

His eyes were alive with excitement, eager to show me he was right, and I still had no idea what he was talking about.

"They were tried and found guilty, and they went to prison. That's the way it works."

He patted me on the arm and started walking, but just for a few steps.

"Why did they go to trial? That's one question. The other question is why did they go to prison after they were found guilty?"

He started off again, but almost immediately stopped again. Clasping his hands behind his back he squinted into the wind.

"You're too close to it, too much a part of the system. But what would you do, if you knew you were guilty, and you had, as they say, all the money in the world?" He arched an eyebrow and let me know he could scarcely believe how stupid people could be. "All the money in the world, millions – no, billions – and they go off to jail like good little boys who have been told to go their rooms! All they had to do – any one of them – was get on a private plane and get out of the country. The question is why they didn't. Isn't that what you would do, faced with the choice between wealth and freedom in some safe corner of the world or twenty, or thirty, or forty years locked up in a federal prison? Can you imagine a pirate doing that? Do you know why they did it, just went to prison when they didn't have to? – No imagination, no courage; they were all a bunch of clerks; they didn't know how to do anything that wasn't part of a routine. That's why they did so well in business: they just did what everyone else was doing. Trust me, I know these guys. You could leave their cell doors open, all the guards could disappear, not one of them would think about escape!"

St. James shook his head in mockery, and then, as if to

apologize for his rant against the cowardice of thieves, gave a modest shrug and shook his head once more, this time with an air of resignation.

"Have another Bloody Mary. I have some dull business to attend to; nothing like the life of a pirate – it will probably take all afternoon."

He walked away, laughing quietly, and then, suddenly, shouted back. "Maybe that's what I should do: raise the skull and crossbones and sail the seven seas!" A large, irresistible, grin cut hard across his mouth. "But then I suppose they'd just track me down with a global satellite and take all the fun out of even that!"

I did not know quite what to make of Nelson St. James. The more time I spent with him, the less I understood. But despite my growing confusion, I was starting to like him. Perhaps because he had so much of it, he seemed to have no interest in money, and a barely concealed contempt for those who had. It was all a game to him, money merely the counters, the way you kept score.

I settled into a deck chair and watched the long white wake stretch out in the distance, the ephemeral mark of where we had been. After a while the wind subsided and the sea grew calm and the only sound was the quiet murmur from the engine room below. Two couples came up on deck to take the sun and, though I was not in the mood for conversation – my head still hurt too much for that – I decided I owed it to my hosts to mingle with the other guests.

"They're selling the place in the Hamptons," said Pamela Oliver as she rubbed lotion on her long, sleek legs.

I had met her the night before, but then she had clothes on and not a bathing suit. She had the air of a pampered sportswoman, more concerned with how she looked on the golf course or the tennis court than how well she played the game.

"And the place in Palm Beach," added the other woman in a biting, scornful voice.

Standing at the railing, like a store window

mannequin, Bunny Harper had short, shiny black hair cut sharp across her forehead and straight across her slender shoulders, bright red lipstick and brazen white teeth. She was about to say something caustic, from the way her lip had begun to curl back, when she noticed me.

"Have you known Nelson long?" she asked with a smile invented on the instant.

"We've gotten to know each other," I replied. "But you were about to say something, and I'm afraid I interrupted."

"You were going to say that they're selling damn near everything they own," said Pamela Oliver, still working on her legs.

Bunny Harper gave her an icy stare.

"I wasn't going to say anything. I heard something about the Palm Beach house, but that's probably not true, either; probably just more rumors."

There was an awkward silence. Townsend Oliver, Pamela's husband, offered me a drink, and when I asked for a Bloody Mary allowed that he could use one himself. Bunny's husband, Roger Harper, finished off what was left of a gin and tonic and asked for another. He was older than Townsend, with tired eyes and a grim, almost brutal mouth, and the voice of a worn out gambler on a losing streak. His family owned steel mills in Pennsylvania. Townsend, on the other hand, was one of the new breed of self-made men; not the kind that, in an earlier generation, had worked their way up with their fists, but the kind who came from affluent, upper middle-class homes, and went to Stanford on scholarship. He had a software company and, not yet forty, had more money than Harper and his family had ever dreamed of making. I had not met him before last night, but I knew people who had. There was talk he wanted to run for governor.

"Why would anyone want to have a place in the Hamptons, or Palm Beach, or anywhere else for that matter, if you could live on this?" I asked in all innocence. "There aren't many houses this size, and you can go anywhere in the world on it." I glanced at Bunny Harper. "And they're not selling this," I remarked with perfect confidence.

Though she tried to hide it, she was surprised that I seemed to know this. She tried to hide a great many things. Eye shadow, piled too thick around the edges, had begun to crumble into pieces, revealing all the effort that had gone into the failed effect. Her husband, nursing his drink, sat at some distance from her. He was not surprised at all.

"This is the last thing he'd sell. Morrison has put his finger on it. You can go anywhere on this, sail far away, places where the government has no jurisdiction."

"Careful, Roger! We shouldn't be talking about…!"

He ignored her. He took a long drink of his gin and tonic and signaled the steward he was ready for another. A shrewd smile settled on his mouth.

"Our good friend Nelson is involved in a great many things and none of us much cared what he did, or how he did it, because whatever else happened we could always count on him getting a good return. The market did well, but we did much better - didn't we, Townsend? Did you ever wonder how he did it, did so much better than anyone else, made us the kind of money that made us feel smart for talking our way into the deal?"

"And he's still doing it, isn't he?" replied Townsend with some irritation. "Some people are just better at doing certain things," he added with confidence. "Nelson knows how to invest."

The lines in Roger Harper's forehead deepened and grew broader. He looked at Townsend with the pity one feels for a fool.

"Is that what you think he knows – how to invest? I think he knows something more interesting than that; I think he knows how blind people can be, how eager they are to believe it whenever someone tells them that he knows how to make them more money than they've ever imagined. I think –"

"I think you've had too much to drink," said Townsend.

"Screw you, Townsend," said Harper with a caustic

glance. "What the hell do you know about anything? And screw Nelson St. James," he added when his wife started to interrupt. "Screw the whole lot of them."

He crouched forward, looking straight at me. There was a marvelous clarity in his eyes, the seasoned certainty of someone who does not care what anyone else thinks or says.

"When people find out what's been going on, when they find out what he did, how he did it, they'll be talking about it for years, wondering why no one ever caught on. Who knows, they may even start to wonder how people who always thought they were so damn smart could be so stupid!"

Bunny Harper was tugging at his arm.

"He's coming!" she whispered urgently as he started to resist.

"Come on everyone!" shouted St. James as he stepped up on deck. "Danielle wants a picture."

That evening Blue Zephyr anchored off the Channel Islands. The lights of Santa Barbara danced on the moon-covered sea and the liquor flowed freely and everyone acted as if they were the best of friends, all of them anxious to please. St. James glanced down the table to where I was sitting between Pamela Townsend and Richard Darwin's small, waspish wife.

"We were talking last night about -"

"Getting away with murder," interjected Darwin as he continued to eat. His eyes never left his plate. St. James looked at him as if the man were hopeless. "Getting away with murder," Darwin reminded him again as he reached for another piece of bread.

"Yes, and for some reason it suddenly seems a much more attractive possibility," said St. James as he watched Darwin wipe the bread into some gravy before shoveling it into his mouth. The remark was lost on Darwin, but his wife understood.

"Getting away with murder," she said in a small, reedy voice that seemed to hiss with resentment, "If you have enough money I suppose you might think you could get away with anything."

She meant to stab him in the heart, to do all the injury she could; St. James treated it as an intelligent suggestion that led to the very point he wanted to make.

"Money would be essential. Without it, you couldn't hire Morrison."

But Darwin's wife was not going to let it stop there. She did not like being put off. She was about to make another caustic remark when Danielle got everyone's attention by challenging her husband.

"But if someone wanted to get away with murder – thought about it in advance – why would they need to hire Anthony? Isn't the best way to get away with murder not to get caught in the first place? Isn't the only reason to hire Anthony Morrison and his honest face because you've failed, didn't plan it well enough?"

Darwin belched, and seemed not be aware of it. There was nothing left on his plate. Beneath their heavy lids, his sharp, rapacious eyes darted from one side of the table to the other, searching for something he might have overlooked. Vaguely disappointed, he slid back in his chair and folded his arms.

"That's worse than murder."

He was looking right at me, and there was nothing friendly in the way he was doing it. I knew what he was going to say - it was written all over his face, and I had heard it often enough before. I tried not to laugh.

"What's worse than murder?"

"What you do, helping someone get away with it; what a lawyer does when he tricks a jury into letting some murdering bastard go free."

"Is that what you think you would call it – 'murdering bastard,' 'a lawyer's tricks' – if you were charged with a murder you didn't commit? It's really quite amazing," I said, daring him to disagree, "how many people who always thought anyone who was arrested must be guilty, suddenly decide the police are idiots or worse and the whole system stupid and corrupt when they're the ones charged with a crime."

Richard Darwin was too used to running things, too accustomed to everyone agreeing with him, to consider me anything but offensive. His face turned several shades of red, but before he could sputter an angry reply, Danielle again intervened.

"What I want to know," she said, laughing as if Darwin was acting a part, pretending to an anger he did not feel, "isn't how you could defend one of those 'murdering bastards' Richard gets so upset about; what I want to know is how you, yourself – after all you're the only one here who really knows about this sort of thing – would go about it, what you would do to get away with murder. Yes, tell us!" she cried. "You've worked with all these people, tried all these cases – you must have thought about it," she purred. "What would you do if you wanted to kill someone and did not want to get caught? Tell us, Anthony Morrison; tell us how to commit the perfect murder."

I felt a strange sense of triumph. I could look right at her now, return her gaze, and not lose my train of thought.

"Three things: an alibi that is unbreakable, a weapon that is untraceable, and, most important of all, someone else to blame."

"Someone else to blame?" asked St. James from the end of the table.

"The jury has to believe that the real murderer is out there, still at large, and that if they don't vote to acquit the defendant, the real murderer, whoever he is, will get away with it."

"But we're talking about the perfect murder," he reminded me. "The killer never goes to trial because he never gets caught."

"It comes down to the same thing: There has to be someone else to blame. The police almost never look for a second suspect once they have the first. There's one problem of course."

I looked around the table, at Darwin, who was thinking about something else, and at the others, at

Townsend Oliver and Roger Harper and the women they had married, and at the other couples, all of them rich beyond imagining and certain that they were worth even more. The problem I had posed was obvious, but only if you had a conscience. None of them were willing to hazard a guess. If you could get away with murder, if it was as easy as I had seemed to suggest – an alibi, a weapon no one could find, and someone else to blame – what problem, if there was one, could rank in importance with the fact that it could be done?

"Instead of committing just one murder," I explained finally, "you would be committing two."

Everyone still seemed baffled, all except Danielle.

"You also kill the person who gets blamed. He gets arrested, charged with murder, and though he's completely innocent, all the evidence is against him; everyone thinks he's one of those 'murdering bastards' of Richard's elegant description, and he's convicted and either spends the rest of his life in prison or is executed for his crime. But why is that a problem?"

She said this in such a casual, offhand way, with such stunning indifference, that I wondered if she meant it, if for all her beauty she could be as cold, as heartless, as that. She saw the doubt in my eyes almost before I knew it was there. The smile on her lips became enigmatic, mysterious, and yet somehow full of understanding, as if instead of just having met we had known each other for years.

"If the real murderer is worried about that," she explained in a quiet, thrilling voice, "all he has to do is make sure the accused has someone who can save him, some like you, Anthony Morrison."

Dinner was over and the serious drinking began. Whether or not it was the tension brought on by the uncertainty of what was going to happen next, all those whispered rumblings about whether St. James was in trouble and what that might mean for them, the drinking, once it started, did not stop. It went the way of most gatherings of unhappy people forcing themselves to have a good time: cheap talk and brazen laughter, knowing looks and sidelong glances, a single meaningless word the cause of wild hysterics, a sudden dead exhaustion, a raucous shout, and then a call for another round.

St. James and his wife smiled politely, laughed softly, and, as I noticed, scarcely touched their glasses. The louder the others talked, the quieter, the more withdrawn, the two of them became. A little after midnight, St. James excused himself and said he had had to get off to bed. A few minutes later, Danielle announced she had to get some air. As she passed behind me, she touched my shoulder and quickly whispered, "Join me, if you like."

My eyes were fixed directly across the table on Bunny Harper, who was trying to tell me something above the noise, something that, when she finally had my attention, she could not remember. I waited a few more minutes before I slowly rose from the table, stretched my arms and wandered out of the dining room alone.

It felt good to be outside, away from the noisy chatter and the stale scent of alcohol. Across the moonlit water, the lights of Santa Barbara flickered in the distance and in the cool night air I realized what I fool I had been. She might be the most beautiful woman I had ever seen, but she was married, and that was always trouble.

"What are you laughing about?" asked Danielle in that haunting, breathless voice of hers. "How easy it is to get me outside alone?"

And then, before I knew what I was doing, she was in my arms and I could not think of anything but how much I wanted her.

"Danielle!" shouted St. James as he suddenly came out on deck. He was still looking the other way.

"God, if he sees us…!" whispered Danielle, clutching my arm.

I started to tell her that it was all right, that he had started in the other direction, but she turned and vanished into the darkness.

"Oh, it's you, Morrison," said St. James as, less than a minute later, he approached. He had removed his coat and loosened his tie. He held a drink in his hand. "I had to get out of there," he explained with a gruff laugh. "Can't stand people who can't hold their liquor. Besides, I had some work to do. Have you seen Danielle? I thought I heard her come up on deck."

I could taste the lipstick on my mouth. Danielle's scent was all around me.

"I just came out a few minutes ago."

A trace of disbelief, or so it seemed to my guilty eyes, edged its way across his face. He offered me a cigar.

"Oh, I forgot – you don't smoke. Neither do I - just these." He lit the cigar and with a practiced movement of his slender wrist made the match go out. "You say you haven't seen her." His gaze roamed the distant shore. "Must have been mistaken," he said as he puffed on the cigar. "Sound carries out here. She's probably down below." His gaze, shrewd, knowing, and, if I was not mistaken, sad with disappointment, moved slowly back to me. "Down below with one of my guests, probably in bed."

I felt an emotion I clearly had no right to have, a sharp twinge of jealousy, not because of what she was doing with someone else – I knew very well she was not doing anything – but the sinful, taunting knowledge that it was the kind of thing she had done before.

St. James puffed on his cigar, his eyes glistening with something very close to regret. He leaned both elbows on the railing and flicked away an ash, and then, a moment later, stepped back and threw his cigar as far as he could, watching as the faint red glow grew fainter still and finally died.

"She has that talent, you know; that talent some women have. Even when she's being unfaithful, even when you know it, she can make you believe that she still belongs to you." A smile that beneath its cynicism seemed oddly sympathetic drifted across his mouth. "You must have felt that, those few moments she was out here, alone, with you."

And then he turned and walked away and did not look back, and for the first time in a very long time I felt something close to shame.

I tried to blame it on the alcohol. I had not had that much to drink, but the others had, and the rules of conduct had been forgotten in the late night sensuality of men and women who could not think but only feel. It was the worst excuse I had ever heard, blaming my misbehavior on someone else's state of mind, like a burglar blaming his victim for leaving the doors unlocked.

The night was getting cooler. I pulled my coat close around my throat and started walking, trying to clear my head. The sky was full of stars, a shining audience to the brief drama – comedy or farce? – that had just unfolded: the husband with the faithless wife who, given half a chance, would be forever faithful to a man she had only just met; a man with whom, had the scene lasted just a little longer, she might have run away and never once had occasion to regret it. I felt a kind of triumph, not because I thought it might really have happened, but that I was capable of imagining it. She was married, but what did the rules mean to me? But then, why that feeling of a guilty secret betrayed when I realized that St. James had known?

Twice around the deck and I was through. Like an actor leaving the stage, I waved my hand at the watching stars and went below. The dining room had been abandoned, empty glasses scattered on the table, some of what had been in them spilled on the chairs. Gold-rimmed plates tumbled against one another, half-eaten desserts crushed and melted into shapeless blobs of sugar. The silence was everywhere, eerie and absolute, as if the passengers and crew, grown tired of the voyage and of each other, had left me there alone. But then, as I passed the door of the yacht's master suite, I thought I heard a muffled noise. I stopped still, listening intently until I was certain what I heard. It was St. James all right, shouting at his wife. I could not make out what he was saying, the door was too thick for that, and if Danielle was saying anything, none of it, not even the sound of her voice, came through. It was none of my business, I told myself, but the taste of her mouth was still on my lips, and I knew that they were arguing about me. I started to walk away, but suddenly the door opened and Danielle came running out.

"I don't care if I ever -!" she screamed over her shoulder just before she turned and saw me. The look of anger on her face changed to something close to panic. Spinning around, she faced St. James and cried in an injured tone, "Do you think I want to sleep with every man I talk to?" And then, closing the door behind her, she went back inside.

I thought about that question, that last thing I had heard her ask, as I lay in bed and tried to sleep; not whether she wanted to go to bed with every man she talked to, but whether she wanted to with me. If we had been somewhere else, where there was more privacy and where, with her husband gone, there had been more time, would it have happened, would we have forgotten everything except each other and what we wanted? It was no question at all. That kiss had answered that. I tried not to think about her, but I could not think of anything else. Laying there, in the middle of the night, I laughed out loud at how easily I could play the fool, mesmerized by a woman I could never have and, once this short cruise was over with, would never see again. Strangely, or perhaps not so strangely, I did not feel bad about it. It was vanity, and I knew it, but I liked knowing that for a few stolen moments Danielle had wanted me. In the secret recesses of my uninhibited heart I was Don Juan, but in heaven, not in hell. There may have been a smile on my lips when I finally fell asleep.

"Who's there?" I demanded as I woke up with a start. The shadow moving toward me moved more swiftly at my voice.

"Quiet, not so loud," whispered Danielle as she pressed her fingers on my mouth and sat down on the edge of the bed. She was wearing a silk nightgown that did not quite come to her knees. "He's asleep, but when he's angry….I'm sorry you heard that, sorry that -" But before she could finish I pulled her down to me and started to kiss her.

"No," she protested. "We can't – not here, not like

this."

I couldn't help myself, I wanted her too much, and I tried again.

"It's too dangerous," she said with a look in her eyes that seemed ready to chance it. "Too dangerous," she repeated as if to remind herself what she stood to lose. "You don't know him; no one knows him the way I do. He'd kill us if we got caught."

For a moment, neither of us said anything. In the moonlight, filtered through the window like a silver screen, her face was as lovely as any I had ever seen. It held me captive, unable, unwilling, to look away. She was almost too beautiful to want, a painting in a museum too beautiful to touch.

"I shouldn't have come," she said finally, gently stroking my hair. She smiled at the look of hopeful disappointment in my eyes. "I had to see you again, one more time alone."

The excitement, the confidence, the sense of being always at the center of things, watched by everyone whenever she entered a room, all of that was gone. In its place was something sad and wistful and far away.

"You don't remember me, do you? I knew it as soon as I saw you, as soon as we started talking. You didn't recognize me; you don't remember anything about me. And I was always so certain that you would."

Without another word, without telling me anything of what she meant, she kissed me on the side of my face and vanished into the night.

CHAPTER THREE

It made me a little crazy, trying to remember a face that was impossible to forget. I could not have known her, despite what she said. Perhaps we had met at some gathering, a large party, in San Francisco or New York, where I did not know anyone and, to hide my awkward self-consciousness, I had had too much to drink. But she had meant more than that, more than some chance meeting that had lasted only a few, brief seconds. We had known each other well enough that I would have remembered – should have remembered - things about her, not just her face. I lay there in the darkness, searching through my past, wondering why I could not find her, how she could have vanished. The next morning, when I went up on deck to join the others, I could almost hear the laughter in that silky voice of hers, telling me all about a memory I did not share.

The motor launch was heading toward the shore. Sitting next to her husband, Danielle, a white scarf whipping in the breeze, was looking back over her shoulder, trying, as it seemed, to catch one last glimpse of what she had left behind. I thought she saw me, and I thought she smiled.

"Mr. and Mrs. St. James had to fly back to New York."

I turned and found myself under the watchful gaze of Blue Zephyr's captain who immediately offered his hand.

"Mustafa Nastasis. We haven't met. I'm acquainted with the other guests, but this is your first time, isn't it?"

There was something out of place about him, something that did not feel right. His manner was too formal, too studied, everything too perfect. His dark gray hair was cut just right, his black mustache trimmed with precision. His double-breasted blazer gleamed like a dinner jacket, and his tailored flannel slacks broke at exactly the right angle across a pair of soft Italian loafers. He spoke English with the meticulous pronunciation that a native speaker never uses.

"Greek," he explained in answer to the question he read in my eyes. "On my father's side; my mother was from

26

Istanbul. They usually hate each other, the Greeks and the Turks, but my parents did not care for politics, only each other. They had nine children."

His eyes, shrewd and observant, moved past me to the motor launch, barely visible in the morning haze.

"Are they coming back?"

"To Blue Zephyr?" His glance was full of meaning, or rather the suggestion of one, because there was something enigmatic in his look. A smile of cheerful malevolence suddenly started across his mouth, but then he shrugged his shoulders and made the vague remark, "Always, but when, or where…."

"They decided to leave rather suddenly. They didn't say anything about it last night."

His gaze turned inward, as if to shut out the question, or any other inquiry about what Nelson St. James might be planning to do next.

"Tomorrow, in Los Angeles, a plane will take you back to San Francisco."

"That's very kind of Mr. St. James," I replied, "but it won't be necessary." With an expression as enigmatic as his, I added, "I have other plans."

I was telling the truth. I did have plans of my own, something I had been meaning to do for a long time. Tommy Larson was just about the only friend I had. Though we lived only an hour's plane ride apart, he never seemed to get to San Francisco and I almost never went to L.A. We talked on the phone once in a while, usually after I had won a case and he called to complain that, thanks to me, the streets were now less safe than they had been and all the women were in danger, but I had not seen him in nearly a year. A lot had happened and not all of it was good.

Tommy had moved out of Los Angeles, from Pasadena where he had lived for years, since shortly after finishing law school, to a small town an hour's drive north, not far from Santa Barbara and a dozen miles inland. Ojai was a place to grow oranges and avocados, and a place to hear yourself think. The Thatcher school was the other side of the orchards on the east end of town, and there were other shady private schools spread along the oak lined approach. Gurus and mystics, disciplines of eastern religions that taught the path to inner peace, had flourished here, and Aldous Huxley, back in the 1950s, had often driven up for long discussions about what it all meant. There was still some of that, though it more often took the form of classes on yoga and other, stranger, meditations, but now the famous people who came here were mainly interested in having a place to hide. Celebrities walked around, or sat in small restaurants, dressed in shabby clothes, and for the most part no one noticed. Tommy had been famous once, but that was not the reason he had moved.

I followed the long straight palm-lined street up into the foothills until I reached a one story Spanish style house that looked as if it had been here for years, since sometime in the 1920s when some now forgotten movie star had wanted a place where he could escape the prying eyes of tourists and, depending on whom he was with, a jealous husband or an overzealous cop. It was barely visible from the road, hidden behind a tangle of reddish orange bougainvillea and clumps of cactus with exotic purple flowers. Low rock walls, three feet thick, rocks piled by hand on top of each other, rocks taken when the land was cleared and the house was built, marked the boundary of the property and both sides of a long narrow drive. It was Los Angeles a hundred years ago, before the movies made it famous and anyone who was anyone had to live in a mansion.

Tommy was sitting on the front porch in a faded gray t-shirt and a pair of tattered khaki shorts. The straw hat on his head had seen better days and one of his leather sandals had a broken strap. With a familiar grin he watched while I parked the car, then he stretched his arms and slowly rose from the stiff-backed chair.

"As you can see," he announced as he ran his hand across the heavy stubble on his face, "I've gone to a lot of trouble getting ready for your visit. What are you laughing at?" he demanded with a gruff, half bent grin. "Hell, I even got dressed, sort of; not like you, all pressed and buttoned up, but good enough. At least as good as I ever do anymore." He clasped my hand and with his other hand held my arm steady. "I hate to say it, but it's good to see you. What's it been – at least a year?" He seemed dazzled by the thought of it, that that much time had passed. "Funny how that works. Wasn't that long ago, I saw you every day."

"College."

"Yeah, college. Best time I ever had."

He studied me, wondering if I agreed; but then he remembered the reason why things had not been – could not have been - the same for me. He was too good a friend to say it, so I said it for him.

"You were an all-American; I was barely good enough to play."

"You started every game our senior year."

"Only because the other guy got hurt," I laughed.

"I always thought you were better. Come on, let's go inside. It's cooler, and I'll get you a beer, and I'll tell you all the lies I've been saving up."

I watched him move, the easy fluid motion, the way that even standing still he seemed ready to explode, suddenly running at full-speed, faster, quicker, than anyone I had ever seen. He left me in the living room and went into the kitchen and brought us back the promised beer.

"We're not going to talk football and how great we were, how we were the best team Southern Cal ever had, how you won that Rose Bowl game after I ripped up my knee."

He tapped his bottle against mine and took a long slow drink. He smiled with his eyes.

"No, I don't wonder what would have happened if I had not got hurt, what kind of pro career I might have had. I use to," he admitted, "but what's the point? Tell you the truth, I don't much like the game anymore." He looked out the window next to him, out at the flower garden and the swimming pool the other side, out, I suppose, to what he still remembered of his life. "There are a lot of things I don't like much anymore." A moment later, as if he had just realized what he had said, he shook his head and laughed. "It's so damn quiet here, sometimes I start talking out loud just to make sure I still have a voice."

I had wondered how I was going to say what I knew I had to. I had thought about it, tried to think of a way that did not sound intrusive, but now I just stumbled into it.

"Why didn't you call me, Tommy? There must have been something I could have done. We've been friends for...."

He stopped me with a look.

"We're too good of friends for me to lie to you the way I did to everyone else. Divorce is a little like death; worse in some ways. Everyone wants to tell you how sorry they are. You can't exactly tell them that it's the best thing that's ever happened, can you? Tell them how thrilled – no, grateful – that she finally decided to leave. You have no idea what a relief it was." He gave me a quick, appraising glance. "No, you know. When you heard, you weren't surprised, were you?"

"No," I admitted, "I wasn't surprised, but that didn't change the fact that I was...."

But he was not listening. He was still caught up in the memory of what happened and, more than that, the reasons why, if he had only known it, had made it all inevitable.

"She was the best looking girl in school and she married an all-American, the great running back, Saturday's hero. It was always going to be like that, the guy that everyone is eager to be friends with, eager to do anything they could to help us. When I got hurt, when I couldn't play anymore, when I decided I better follow you and go to law school and learn how to do something, it never occurred to her that any of it would change, and for a few years it didn't. I was still the player, the college football star, everyone who saw us full of smiles. And when it all went away, she went with it; not consciously, not on purpose: she found other things, other people, more interesting. All that bright-eyed eagerness went away, all the fun disappeared. When we were first married she would run to the door when I came home; when I joined the U.S. Attorney's office, became a government lawyer on a government salary instead of joining some high-priced firm, she barely said hello at night. She never complained, never asked me to do anything different, but there was a look of disappointment, a sense that I had let her down, that she had made a mistake."

Staring straight ahead, he tapped his fingers briefly on the arm of the overstuffed chair.

"It's quiet here. I already said that, didn't I? It's true, though. That's why I came here, why I bought this place. I've never been alone before."

Suddenly, in that effortless way he had, he was on his feet. He stretched his arms and then put his hands on the small of his back and with a thoughtful expression stared down at the faded red tile floor.

"You never thought you were very good," he said, raising his eyes just far enough to meet my gaze. "That's why you were better than that other guy, that's why you're just about the best damn lawyer around."

"Things were easy for you," I reminded him. "You were born with speed and quickness, and you could see how things were going to happen before they did."

"Things were easy for you, too – you finished near the top of your class in law school. I barely made it."

"And you became one of the best prosecutors the government had."

"Not good enough to get the guy you just went sailing with."

"You didn't tell me that when I told you what I was doing. You were after St. James?"

He made a helpless gesture, a rueful smile that suggested that he wished he had had the chance. "I didn't know if you were about to represent him. Is that why he invited you – to ask you if you would?"

We were friends, but we were also lawyers, a prosecutor and a defense attorney, and I started to hedge my answer. He caught my hesitation.

"I'm not prosecuting anymore. I quit, remember?"

Tommy had left the U.S. Attorney's office shortly after his divorce. He had not given any reason, only the familiar phrase that he was leaving to "pursue other opportunities." He had not pursued any, so far as I could tell, unless you considered living alone somewhere outside L.A. among the many possibilities that vague phrase suggested.

"Quit for good, or just long enough to figure out what you want to do?"

With his hands shoved into his pockets, he twisted his mouth to the side and narrowed his eyes, as if the question had been written out on a piece of paper and he was studying it for an answer.

"Quit the government for good. Quit being a lawyer? I don't know. Maybe." He searched my eyes as if he thought he might find the answer there, but nothing in my own experience would help him find a way out of what was clearly a dilemma. "I like the courtroom. I like the action. But it isn't like football: it isn't a game. You don't just walk off the field at the end, you don't just add up another game to the number you've won or lost." He was bouncing up on the balls of his feet, his shoulders slightly lowered, his eyes focused straight ahead, but, just like when he was playing, seeing everything around him. "You ever lose a case where you know the guy was innocent, ever have to watch someone go off to prison for something he didn't do and there wasn't a damn thing you could do about it?"

"Is that what happened?" I asked, intensely curious. "You sent someone away for something he didn't do?"

"Not on purpose, not with what they call 'conscious knowledge.' In some ways it was worse. We were going after people we knew we could get. Drug stuff mainly, easy cases to win; not the ones in charge, the ones who manufacture, the drug lords – we'd go after them when we could – but possession cases. You get some kid, he's hooked on crack, and you send him to prison for ten, twenty years. He broke the law, you convict him. You do it over and over again, and then you start to notice that it doesn't make any difference.

The kid was a junkie, an addict; he needed help. But we aren't in the business of helping kids like that. So we go after people who are, some of them, the real victims, and we let a guy like St. James go around stealing billions and don't do anything about it because it's too complicated, too expensive, because it takes too much time to build a case you have any chance of winning."

He burst out laughing.

"Christ! Listen to me, sounds like one of those half-time speeches we used to have to listen to – We'd be up thirty points and the coach would be talking about how lousy we'd played." His eyes shined bright with the memory of it and he laughed again, quietly now, at his own nostalgia. "That was the problem, you see – running up the score. You can always have a winning record – hell, you can go undefeated – if you only schedule weak opponents." He turned deadly serious. "That's what we were doing, trying only cases we knew we could win. I quit because I got tired of beating up on people who could not fight back, kids who had never had a chance. What kind of system is it that says that if you steal a few hundred you do twenty years, but if you steal a few billion – if you steal the whole damn country – you get to make an apology and a chance to make amends?"

With a wistful expression in his clear blue eyes, Tommy scratched his head. A smile that could have meant a dozen different things moved slowly across his fine, straight mouth, and then, slowly, faded away.

"But I might have gone on doing it, told myself that lie we all tell ourselves, that I was just doing my job, if I hadn't suddenly found myself divorced and if they hadn't closed down the case I had against St. James."

This, though it made more sense than what he had said about it before, raised a different, and a more intriguing, question.

"You were good enough to get him, but someone wouldn't let you. Someone in the government didn't want St. James prosecuted?"

"You could say that, but it's nothing I could ever prove. The order came from Washington, said we had spent too much time on it, too much expense. They didn't say I couldn't prosecute, only that I didn't have any more time to build a case. That was no choice at all and they knew it. I didn't have a case, not yet, that I could win."

"He got to someone, got them to back off."

"Not like that, not the way you imagine. It's more subtle. No one gave anyone a bribe. No one transferred a few million into some Swiss account. Some Washington lawyer, someone who represents certain interests that St. James controls, would have met with the attorney general, a friend of his, someone he sees at social occasions, and mentioned that there were rumors of an investigation, that Mr. St. James had nothing to hide, but that this kind of publicity was harmful to the various enterprises on which a good many people depended for their livelihood. If the government had a case, Mr. St. James would welcome the chance to prove his innocence, but if not, well, perhaps the attorney general could look into it."

"And the attorney general did – look into it, I mean?"

"I doubt he looked into anything. He didn't have to. All he had to do was let it be known that we were there to try cases, not waste time building cases that we weren't sure would ever amount to a case we could win. It's a perfectly legitimate policy, nothing that you could use to argue that the attorney general had done something improper."

There was something he had not told me.

"So why did I ask you if he wanted you to represent him, if the case against him had been dropped? After I quit, I had a long conversation with a reporter I knew, someone who works for one of the financial papers. I told him everything I knew, everything I suspected. He started an investigation of his own, and now he has started to write about it. No one will be able to stop it now. St. James will be indicted. It's only a matter of time."

He went into the kitchen and got us each another beer, and we went outside and sat at a wooden table beneath a eucalyptus tree and talked about college and how nothing had ever been quite that good again. We remembered some of the others we had played ball with and talked about what had happened to them and the way that, for most of us, our lives were still defined by what we had been, whether we were still living in the reflected glory of the past or trying to prove to ourselves and others that we were more than a faded memory of a vanished boyhood dream. We talked for hours, and the years fell away, and the dismal, minor tragedies of our lives seemed like nothing, as vague and distant from the present as when, instead of being part of us, they still waited in a future we did not yet know. It felt good, the way it always did, when I was with him, talking like this, the words less important for what they said than all the other things they triggered; three, four words and a dozen different visions of what we had not just seen but felt at the moment, years before, when they passed before our eyes. We talked about women, the ones we chased and the ones who, because they did not know us, chased us, but more than all the others, the ones that, if we had been smarter, we would have chased instead. We talked and laughed and then the light was almost gone and the still night air turned cool.

"We need to go eat," said Tommy as he stood up and headed back to the house. "I'll change. It won't take a minute."

It took less than that. He put on a long sleeve shirt and we were ready to leave. He still had on the khaki shorts and the sandals with the broken strap. We drove into town, less than a mile away, a four block street that seemed deserted, and out the other end, through two miles of orange groves to a roadside café. The waitress knew Tommy by sight, and without waiting to be asked brought him a glass of red wine. She had broad shoulders and the large hands of a woman who had always worked, and the tired, friendly eyes of a woman who never complained. When I told her I would have the same thing, she nodded her approval.

We were halfway through dinner when Tommy again brought up St. James.

"He's going to be indicted, and he's too smart not to know it. That's the reason you were invited, wasn't it? Because he wanted to have a chance to get to know you, to decide if everything he had heard about you was true – he would have had you checked out before he ever thought about meeting you, of course, as he's that careful. He asked you, didn't he?"

"Yes, no…not exactly," I mumbled incoherently.

"Yes, no, not exactly? What kind of answer is that?" laughed Tommy.

"He told me that he might need a lawyer, but I'm not really sure anymore that it was his idea. I'm not sure it wasn't his wife's idea instead."

I told him what had happened, how she said we had met before, and the strange reaction she had when she realized that I did not remember, but Tommy was not listening; he was enjoying too much some thought of his own.

"No, I didn't!" I protested when I realized what it was.

"You weren't screwing around with Nelson St. James' gorgeous wife? You're going to tell me that nothing happened?"

We had known each other too long, known each other too well. His laughing eyes taunted me with what they knew.

"I kissed her, once – that's all," I insisted.

He raised an eyebrow and nodded eagerly, waiting, certain there was more and that I would not be able to stop myself from telling him.

"I shouldn't have done it, and I knew it, and it didn't matter: as soon as it happened, I wanted to again. It was after dinner, and there had been a lot of drinking, and she asked me to meet her up on deck. That's when it happened, and then her husband showed up and -"

"He caught you? What did -?"

"He didn't see us. That's what we thought, anyway. As soon as she heard him, she disappeared. Then he saw me, standing there alone, and he came over and started talking about his wife, how she was probably downstairs in bed with someone else, and then he let me know that he knew she had been there with me. I don't think he saw us; I think he was guessing, but guessing the way you do when you're sure of something, when you know it, when you can feel it. Then, later, she slipped into my room."

Tommy's blue eyes glittered in anticipation of what he was certain must have happened. I did not say anything and let him know by my silence that there was something unusual, unpredictable, about what had happened.

"She came to tell me that she could not see me again – nothing had happened, just that one, fugitive kiss. That's when she told me that we had known each other before and that she knew I did not remember. And that was all. She did not tell me where, or when, or anything. I've tried to remember. It doesn't seem possible. Who could forget her?'

"Maybe she just wanted to make you crazy. One thing's for sure: you'll never forget her now."

"You're probably right about that," I sighed. "I'll never see her again, but I won't forget her."

"You might see her again. St. James is still going to need a lawyer."

I reminded him that it was not the kind of case I took.

"I wouldn't know what to do in a securities case. I do simple things like murder."

Tommy tossed his head in silent laughter, acknowledging the point, and then rested his elbows on the table and pressed his fingers together. He became quite serious.

"What he's done is worse than murder, the lives he helped ruin. Though to give him credit, he's more honest than most of them, or maybe just more immoral. He's certainly more interesting than the rest of that Wall Street crowd."

He thought about what he had just said, then pushed back from the table and crossed one leg over the other. He sat at an angle, with his arms folded and a pensive, almost brooding expression on his mouth.

"I used to love this country; I'm not sure I do

anymore. I used to think there was a clear line between right and wrong, that those who broke the law got punished. I was not so naïve to believe that everyone who broke the law got caught, but I thought that even those who got away with something knew they had something to hide. And that's true, for ordinary criminals, the guys that break into houses, who steal money at the point of a gun. But these guys on Wall Street, guys who head up banks and corporations, the whole New York financial crowd – they don't give a damn about anything except the money. Money is the only measure and only fools and suckers care about the rules. They rigged the markets, made billions doing it and thought themselves shrewd investors instead of thieves. That's what makes St. James so damn interesting: He realized what America had become – what no one else could see – not a country, but a system of organized theft. None of the others understood what they were doing. They had no self-awareness, if I can put it like that. They were just doing what everyone else did: bend the rules a little, maybe even break them once in a while, because the rules weren't really that important: technical stuff mainly, rules about insider trading, that kind of thing, nothing serious. If you got caught you might get a fine, might even, in the rare case, go off to prison for a year or two, but even then it was still a civil matter, nothing like what real criminals do. You know," he said as a jaundiced grin ran sideways across his lips, "murderers, rapists, and thieves – least of all thieves. These guys could steal billions, cost thousands of decent, hardworking people – people who would never cheat anyone out of anything – their life savings, but that didn't put them in the same category as some guy who instead of growing up in Greenwich, Connecticut did not know his father, and instead of going to Harvard did not finish the tenth grade, a guy desperate for a few bucks grabs a woman's purse and gets caught in the attempt. That's the real lesson about what kind of country we've become: steal from one person, go to jail; steal from thousands, hundreds of thousands, steal from millions – say you're sorry and start a charity."

Tommy's eyes were solemn, remote, with a look of grim remembrance etched deep within them. A rueful smile, the silent echo of something he had once believed, a shattered faith, twisted down the corners of his mouth.

"It was hypocrisy, pure and simple," he went on. The words came more slowly now. He was trying to explain as clearly as he could what he had been thinking about for months, trying to summarize in a few short sentences what he had only begun to understand. He narrowed his eyes and clenched his jaw, and began to wag his finger back and forth, like someone determined to correct the mistaken judgment, the false assumptions, not of other people, but of himself. "Hypocrisy, but necessary to their own sense of who they were; hypocrisy, but they never knew it: they could not afford to know it, to admit it. They had to think they deserved all the money; they had to believe that they were the ones who made everything work, that without them the markets could not function and the economy could not exist. They had to believe that it was only because they controlled the financial system that this was the wealthiest country in the world. They did not have the courage, the strength of will, to look things in the face and admit that they were only doing it for themselves. They needed a country to believe in, a country gullible and greedy enough to believe in them, a country dumb enough to let them think themselves heroes, admired and envied and respected for what they did. That's why St. James was so successful, more successful than any of them: he knew it was all a lie. He doesn't believe in anything: that's the key to his success. He'll take advantage of anyone and never give it a second thought. He'll do anything, and that's what makes him so dangerous, and, in a certain way, admirable."

I nearly fell off my chair. Admirable would have been the last thing I would have expected him to say about the man he had just described.

"I mean it," he assured me. "St. James doesn't pretend to be anything other than what he is. He doesn't make excuses or insist that he's only doing what everyone else is doing. You'll never hear him talk about the system, and how much depends on people like him; he gives none of those chamber of commerce speeches about the virtues of the free market. I said he doesn't believe in anything. I meant any of the things that act as a restraint on how far we're willing to go to get what we want. He believes in money, that the only thing that's important is that you have it and that you keep getting more. Those others, the ones that always talk about how much they've done for the prosperity of the country – St. James doesn't have a country, he has that ship of his. Everyone talks about a global economy – what better place to run it than a ship that can go anywhere in the world?"

I remembered what one of the other guests aboard Blue Zephyr had said.

"Where the government can never reach him. We had an interesting conversation," I explained. "He made a curious point, how so many of the people who get indicted, men with more than enough money to go off to some country without an extradition treaty, just stayed and went quietly to prison."

With a knowing look, Tommy gestured emphatically with his hand.

"That's what I've been trying to say. Most of them are too respectable to think about getting away. They go to trial, or take a plea, and go off to jail without a protest. Someone charged with murder – they'd run like hell if they had the chance, wouldn't they? They know they're criminals; they don't feel any obligation to do what's expected. St. James is like that. He's an outlaw in the classic sense, someone who rejects the rules, who won't do anything he doesn't want. There's a certain strength of character in that. When he finally goes to court, when he's finally convicted, you won't hear him say he's sorry. And you sure as hell won't hear him asking anyone to forgive him for what he did."

We finished dinner, but there was still wine to drink and so we stayed and talked some more, a rambling conversation that moved in fits and starts from one subject to another, one of us suddenly remembering something we had wanted to say. Tommy had become quieter, more introspective, but at the same time less guarded in the way he expressed himself. He was the best friend, perhaps the only real friend, I had, but we had not seen each other in a while and there had been some major changes in his life.

"What I said about… that look of disappointment in her eyes; that wasn't really fair. I think she was more disappointed for me. I liked all the attention, I liked the crowd; I was used to it, all the cheering, the way that everyone looked at you when you walked across campus, the way everyone waited for you after the game. I wanted a pro career. I did not want it to stop. I went to law school because I didn't know what else to do. That look of disappointment, that was not her, that was me. Maybe that's why, despite my better judgment, I can't help but admire St. James a little. He's like what I was – what you were, too – in college. We didn't follow anyone's rules but our own, we were better than the game. Everyone wanted to know us, get close to us. We could have anything we wanted and we never thought there was anything wrong with it. We could have any woman we wanted and I married the best looking girl in school, and he married damn near the best looking woman in the world."

"Danielle is all of that," I agreed.

"That's not her real name, you know," he remarked quite casually. It was nothing important, a minor fact he had picked up along the way, something anyone who conducted a criminal investigation, or simply followed the New York social scene and knew something about the world of high fashion, would have known. "'Danielle' was the name she used as a model. Just that one word. Clever, when you think about it; different, easy to remember. The most famous model in New York, the face that for a while was on practically every magazine cover any woman cared to buy. She was beautiful, and St. James was rich and good looking. So now she's Mrs. Justine St. James, and along with her husband, is about to lose everything she's got."

"Justine? Is that what you said?"

"Justine Llewelyn, that was her real name."

"Justine Llewelyn, who grew up near San Francisco, the other side of the bay?"

"As a matter of fact, she did. Why? – Oh, I see. You did know her then."

I was shaking my head in disbelief. Justine Llewelyn. I had not seen her since her older sister, the girl I wanted to marry, had broken our engagement.

"Justine was all of about sixteen, skinny as a rail and plain looking except for her eyes. A nice, quiet, shy kid. She felt sorry for me, after what her sister did, and she told me that she would marry me, when she was old enough. I remember laughing and telling her that she could do much better. And now she's Danielle, and I didn't remember a thing about her."

CHAPTER FOUR

Though it had been more than a dozen years since I had last seen her, Carol Llewelyn greeted me as if I had married into the family and had been gone only a few weeks.

"It's been a long time," I remarked.

"I've followed your career," she said with a brief smile. "I always knew you would do well."

Opening the trunk of her car, she reached for the metal sign. I started to help, but she swung it free on her own, joking that it was the only exercise she got. She carried the bright red and blue open house sign to the bottom of the driveway and placed it in front of the stone pillar on the right side of the open iron gate. She stood there for a moment, her eyes full of hopeful calculation, as she looked first at the house she was trying to sell and then down the curving narrow two lane road. Trying to guess what effect the searing summer heat might have, she squinted up at the sky. There might not be many people out looking on a day like this; on the other hand, the ivy covered house, set back from the road under the shade of a massive spreading oak, promised a welcome refuge from the blinding mid-day sun. With a quick glance that said she thought things were fine, she started up the drive, the staccato sound of her high heel shoes cracking the silence of the burning air.

The sun was not kind to Carol Llewelyn. Her make-up was too thick; her lashes too black and too brittle. She was in that inadmissible part of middle-age, when the vanity of youth has been reduced to the sad and useless lie that she was only forty-nine. The dress she wore, though perfectly pressed, was a little frayed, and a little out of fashion; and the silver-blue Mercedes she drove, though clean and polished to a shine, was almost ten years old. It was easy to imagine her, after a grueling day of smiling through the inane remarks of prospective buyers who did not know what they wanted, and could not afford it if they did, going back to her small condominium and kicking off her shoes, lighting up a cigarette and tossing down a beer.

"Last year, wasn't it?" she asked as she unlocked the front door. "You were on television, on all the time – some trial that had everyone's attention. You won, didn't you?"

She gave me the look of someone who wished things had turned out differently, not the trial, but what had happened with her daughter. It was what she had told me at the time, when the engagement had been broken off.

"You were too serious for her. You were starting law school. Jean wanted to have a good time, and, well…you remember. I told her she was making a mistake."

Her eyes brightened with encouragement, the same look she had given me the last time I had seen her, just after the engagement ended and I did not think anything would ever be any good again.

"And I was right," she went on. "You've become everything I thought you would be, and Jean's now been married and divorced and married again."

She took a picture from her wallet and handed it to me. Jean, the girl I had fallen in love with and wanted to marry, was standing with her arms around three small children. The carefree look had gone from her eyes and even her smile seemed solemn.

"Three kids and a couple of husbands will do that to you," said Carol, who, when it came to her daughter, had always been able to read my mind. "Are you married?"

"Me? No."

"Close?" she asked, eager to know.

I laughed and told her that I had not felt about anyone what I had felt about Jean.

"You'll say hello for me?"

"Of course. She asks about you. She won't say it, but she wishes she had it to do over."

She left the front door open and led me into the kitchen in back. Pouring a glass of water from the tap, she took a sip and sighed with small pleasure. She tossed the rest in the sink, wiped the glass dry and put it back in the cupboard. Opening the refrigerator, her eyes lit up.

"Here," she said, handing me a cold bottle of beer.

"They won't mind. After standing outside, waiting for me in that heat, you deserve it."

We sat down at a table next to the window and I took a drink, and then I took another. Carol watched me, waiting for me to tell her why I had suddenly called and asked to see her. A car stopped outside. Her eyes darted down the hallway to the front door, but the car started up again and with a shadow of disappointment her gaze came back to mine.

"I'm sorry I couldn't see you earlier, that I had to ask you to meet me here," she started to explain. "It's too warm in here, isn't it? I better check the thermostat."

She disappeared down the hallway, her steps a hard echo on the gleaming hardwood floor. A few moments later, she was back, nodding to herself as she made a mental note.

"They had it set too high. A big, expensive house – and they're trying to save a few dollars on the electric bill. Everybody's desperate now, trying to sell in a market like this," she mumbled. Suddenly, her eyes brightened, and she bent forward, wondering, from the delighted expression on her face, why she had not thought of it before. "Have you ever thought about living out here? Thought about getting out of the city? This would be a wonderful place for you, perfect for someone who likes his privacy." She turned her head toward the window, making sure my eyes would follow. "Look out there: a pool, a tennis court, and with that vine-covered fence you don't even know you have neighbors! I can get you a very good price," she promised confidentially.

After years of selling real estate, it was what Carol Llewelyn had become, her identity. Saying no was a little like telling her that you preferred someone else. Even if she had not been the mother of the only girl I had ever really been in love with, even if she had not always been so remarkably kind to me, I still would have felt an obligation to let her down gently, to make it sound as if I was not saying no at all.

"I like living in the city," I said, feeling foolish and defensive; "but if I ever change my mind…."

She filed it away, another name, different because of the minor part I had once played in her life, but another name on the list that grew longer every week, names to remember, names to call again. I lived in San Francisco, and I liked it there, but people change and, even if they don't, no one stays in the same place for very long.

"This week has been just impossible: new houses to see, buyers who have to be taken around, buyers who usually have to wait until their own house sells." Something caught her eye, a drawer that had not been completely shut. "Anyway, you're here, and this isn't a bad place to talk." She shut the drawer on the other side of the kitchen and came back. "I was a little surprised when you said it was something about Justine."

I told her what had happened; not all of it, of course. I did not tell her what had happened on the deck of Blue Zephyr late at night while the other guests were getting drunk down below and how close we had come to being caught; I did not tell her that Justine had slipped into my bed hours later, after she and her husband had quarreled. I told her only that I had not recognized Justine, that I had no idea that Danielle was the kid I used to tease when I was going out with her sister.

"Half-sister," said Carol Llewelyn. She turned away, as if there was something not quite right about it, something she would have preferred to keep hidden, and then, reaching across the table, gave my hand a squeeze. "I didn't do a very good job of things. The girls had different fathers. At least I was married to the first one." Crossing her arms, she leaned back and fixed me with a warm, steady, glance. "He was gorgeous, Jean's father: blonde, blue eyes, with tight fitting jeans and a summer tan, nineteen years old and he stole my seventeen year old heart, along with my virginity. I was pregnant before the summer ended and married in the fall."

She paused, and then laughed quietly at her hesitation even now to discuss what she thought the failures of her life. The laughter died away and her mouth began to tremble, but she stopped it with a smile, brave and sad and determined.

"I always liked it, when you and Jean were engaged, how easy everything seemed, how I never felt I had to hold anything back, whenever we talked. It must be those honest eyes of yours. I knew that whatever someone told you, you would not think less of them because of it. I've never told anyone what I just told you. God, it was so long ago; I was so young, so....It doesn't matter now; I can't go back and change it. We were married in the fall, and he left a few months later. He told me he was going, that he just couldn't settle down, stay in the same place, work a regular job. He said he knew it wasn't fair, but he couldn't help what he was, and so he left me and I cried for weeks, praying he would come back and knowing he never would. He only married me because he thought he had to, and then, before he could see the child he fathered and maybe feel something that might make him stay, he ran away. Maybe that's where Jean got it, the blonde good looks she had, the refusal to take life on anyone's terms but her own, the way she only wanted to think about today and never tomorrow, the only thing important having a good time. That's why you fell in love with her, isn't it? – You were always so serious, and she could pull you out of that, make you think about nothing but her. Justine was not anything like her."

The doorbell rang. Startled that she had not heard the car, she jumped up from the chair and went to greet the young couple that had just arrived.

"Take your time; look around. If you have any questions, just let me know. I'll just be in the kitchen. I'm helping someone write up an offer."

When she came back to the table, I raised an eyebrow.

"It wasn't exactly a lie," she whispered with a mischievous grin. "I'm still hoping you'll change your mind."

Her gaze drifted toward the window, out to the trees and the close cut grass and the kidney shaped pool and the tennis court, out to the ivy covered fence that guaranteed the privacy of anyone lucky enough to live a privileged life in which money and the cost of things were never an issue. A soft, wistful smile played at the corners of her aging mouth and she put aside the brandished aura of busy efficiency.

"Justine's father – I would have married him." She looked at me with a quizzical expression, as if wondering what my reaction was going to be, and then she told me, quite without any sense of guilt, that she had not been able to marry Justine's father because, "He was already married."

I had always liked her, and I knew she had always liked me, and I was old enough now to have a better understanding of what makes people do the things they do. There was, so far as I was concerned, nothing to condemn in what she had done or how she had chosen to live her life.

"You haven't had very good luck with men, have you? And I haven't had very good luck with women."

"Depends on how you look at it," said Carol with a good-natured laugh. "I was in love twice, and both times I got a daughter. Worse things could have happened." A shrewd, worried look came into her eyes. "And you fell in love with both of them, didn't you? First Jean, and now, unless I miss my guess, Justine."

I started to deny it, but I could not; not entirely, anyway.

"No, I didn't fall in love with her; I probably could have, though, if she hadn't been married, and if there had been more time, if…." I threw up my hands in frustration. I did not know anything, what I felt, why I was even here, asking about a woman I was never going to see again. I was curious, that was all; curious about how Justine had become Danielle, how the kid I had known, the girl no one noticed, had become the woman every other woman wanted to look like and every man who saw her wanted to have.

"That's the funny thing," said Carol. "She never had a date in high school; no one ever asked her out. She wasn't bad looking; she just wasn't obviously pretty."

"Obviously pretty?"

"I could see it: what she was going to look like. It was all there: the perfect structure of her face, the large, green blue eyes, the soft luster of her hair; but she was skinny and, worse yet, much too serious for her age. I don't really remember a single time she laughed." Reminded of something, she shook her head. "She laughed at her sister," she said, staring at me as if this almost forgotten fact had a new significance. "Laughed when she found out Jean had broken of her engagement; told her - she was only sixteen, her sister twenty-two – that she was a fool and that one day she would regret it. That was the difference between them," added Carol with a thoughtful gaze. "Justine always knew exactly what she wanted; with Jean you never knew what she was going to do."

The young couple that had been wandering through the house looked around the corner to say goodbye. Carol would not hear of it.

"Not before you see the pool!"

It was fun to watch. She was on her feet, walking toward them as if the pool were some prize possession of her own, one she shared, when she shared it at all, only with her closest, most trusted friends. I had seen some of that in Justine, the way she had made everyone feel important. It was a gift, an instinct for playing a part, playing it so well that it was not really playing at all, but, for the time they were doing it, what they really were. I watched now, seeing the daughter in the mother, as Carol Llewelyn led the young man and his young wife through the French doors onto the stone patio where, under the shade of a eucalyptus tree, long strips of tan bark peeling from the trunk, she made them feel what it would be like to live here in the quiet dry heat of a long summer's day.

"They'll be back," she said with an air of satisfaction after she waved goodbye from the front door. "They want it. I could see it in their eyes. They'll go someplace, a restaurant, sit across a table and talk it over. They can't afford it, but they're young, and they come from money. Did you see what they're driving? The market is down. This house would have gone for twenty, thirty percent higher a year or so ago. It's a good time to buy. That's what they'll tell themselves." A shrewd, knowing grin cut across her mouth. "He's still in love with her; he'll take it as a challenge. Sweet, really; men always love women more than they are loved back – while it lasts, that is," she whispered as she went to greet another, older, couple at the door.

Another car stopped outside, and another one after that. She met each new arrival before they could take a step inside, saying their names out loud to make sure she remembered them. Soon there seemed to be people in every room, poking their heads in closets, trying door knobs, looking all around. A man in his sixties wanted to know about the security system and whether the gate at the bottom of the drive could be closed electronically from inside the house. Whatever the question, she not only had an answer but gave it as if she had been waiting all day for someone smart enough to ask something as sensible as that.

Afraid of getting in the way, I went outside and walked around the pool. Standing in the shade of the eucalyptus tree, the same spot where Carol had invited the young couple to imagine the life they could have, I began to wonder about the same thing myself. It was easy to imagine the blissful quiet and the clean, sun-drenched air, away from the city and all the crowded noise. Maybe it was too late to think of doing something else, something other than what had become the settled routine of my solitary life, but for a brief moment I remembered how I felt, with Danielle in my arms, that night on Blue Zephyr, and thought how good it would be if I could live in a place like this and come home every night to someone like her.

"It's like a zoo in there," said Carol Llewelyn, smiling at my distraction. "The owner will be happy." She looked back across the pool to the rambling stucco house and the muted conversations going on inside. "I didn't mean to abandon you." She peered down at the lawn, cut as close as a putting green. "What's he like, the man she's married to, Nelson St. James? I've read some things in the papers, but…."

It seemed incredible, but she insisted that she did not know him, that they had never met.

"I wasn't invited to their wedding. I don't know what she told him about me; nothing, I imagine. I never heard from her after she left for New York."

"Never heard from her?" I asked, stunned by what she was telling me. "Why would she have done that? Did something happen?"

"You mean, did we have a fight, did I throw her out – something like that? – No, nothing like that at all. I told you she always knew her own mind; that doesn't mean that she ever told me what she was thinking, or anyone else that I know of. Maybe it was because she didn't have a father; maybe it was because I wouldn't tell her who he was. She resented me for that; and of course there was the way we lived, always just barely getting by. She was smart, a straight A student. Everything came easy to her. She could have gone anywhere to school – Stanford, Cal, one of those schools back east – but she was not interested. The only place she wanted to go was New York. She knew she had the kind of face they were looking for, knew she could become a model. No one else seemed to think so, but I told you she was smart. And so she went to New York and became Danielle, invented herself and forgot who she had been."

She lapsed into a long silence, remembering, no doubt with regret, but also with unmistakable pride, what her younger daughter had done.

"I did hear from her once, after her baby was born. She called from the hospital, happier than I had ever heard her. She told me she was sorry for what she had done, sorry that she had stayed away so long, sorry that she had cut me off. She blamed it on her own selfish ambition, the way she had created a new identity and become the woman the world wanted to see. She said that until she had a child of her own she hadn't known what it was like to have someone that you love no matter what, someone you would do anything to protect. She was crying at the end – the first time I had heard her cry since she was a little girl. She promised that things would be different, that she wanted me back in her life."

A small choking sound rose from Carol's throat. She

did not need to say that despite Justine's promise she had not heard from her again.

"Why? – Do you know?" I asked with all the sympathy I felt.

"Things are easier the second time. She had left once; she left again. She may not even have remembered that she called. Isn't that what happens in a state of euphoria? – We say things, do things, we don't remember…or don't want to remember."

With a look of impatience, a well-dressed woman in her early thirties beckoned from the open French doors. She had a question. Carol looked right through her and then turned back to me.

"Is she in some kind of trouble? I've read things about her husband. But even if they're true, she wouldn't have been involved in anything like that, would she?"

Carol Llewelyn was still greeting new people when I left, all of them come to see whether this was the house about which they had always dreamed, the place that would finally and forever make them happy. As I drove back across the long double-decked span of the Bay Bridge, watching the city dance in all its colors through the golden haze of a summer afternoon, I knew I could never live anywhere else. San Francisco was still a mystery, the way it drew everything toward it, as beautiful, as close and as distant, as any look Justine – Danielle St. James – had ever given anyone.

CHAPTER FIVE

The telephone was ringing, but it was either too early or too late and I just wanted it to stop; but it did not, and I groped around in the dark until I found it.

"What is it?" I barked.

"It's me," said someone who sounded positively delighted that he had woken me up.

"Me?" I asked, turning on the lamp. The clock next to it read 6:45.

"Yes, me – who else would it be? You don't have any other friends."

Whoever this was, he was too cheerful, too full of life, too eager to - "Tommy!" I laughed, suddenly wide awake. "What are you doing, what's going on?" I swung my legs out of bed and sat up.

"Have you seen the papers?"

"I'm in the middle of a trial. I don't read anything," I started to explain. "You mean this morning? You just woke me up! Why, something happen?"

"St. James. I told you it would happen. He's been indicted."

Holding the phone, I walked into the kitchen and started the coffee, listening while Tommy took me through the details of the various charges that had been brought. The far flung financial empire that Nelson St. James had built and controlled was, according to the grand jury, nothing more than a criminal conspiracy that had corrupted not only individuals but entire governments.

"He's going to call you; he's going to ask you to handle it. Don't do it. Don't get involved. He's hurt too many people."

"He won't ask me, and I could not do it if he did. It's what I told you before: I wouldn't know what I was doing. And even if I did…."

I started to tell him about Justine's mother and what she had told me, but I realized that she had not really said anything that had any bearing on whether Justine's husband

53

was someone I would have wanted to defend. It was just a feeling, a sense that St. James and his wife were two selfish people who cared about nothing but themselves.

"He won't ask me, Tommy; and I won't do it if he does."

Tommy seemed almost relieved to hear it; not, I knew, for the reason he gave me – that I was the only lawyer who might be able to get him off – but because he did not want to see my reputation tarnished by a too close connection with a man Tommy had come to despise.

Even though I was in trial, I began to read the papers, following the story with the rest of the country, if with a peculiar interest all my own. I could not get out of my head what Danielle's mother had said: that whatever the son-in-law she had never met might have done, her daughter could not be involved. Behind the apparent assurance with which she had said it, there had been the bare glimmer of a doubt, the hint of a possibility that, given everything else she had done, how easily she had turned her back on the past, she might after all be capable of even something like this. But there was no mention of Danielle in any of the printed stories, nothing beyond a passing mention that Nelson St. James had after a messy divorce married the famous fashion model four years ago.

The stories were all about him, and at first they followed the usual, predictable pattern. He did what every rich man does when he gets caught, claimed that he was innocent and promised in a public statement that when he had a chance to tell his story in a court of law everyone would know that the only conspiracy involved was the one of which he had been made the innocent victim. Then the pattern changed. There were no more statements. He simply disappeared.

It was astonishing, how swiftly the rumors spread and how quickly they changed. Nelson St. James became the most famous fugitive in the world, Blue Zephyr a phantom ship that could be in two places at once. On the same day he was seen in Singapore, drinking gin and tonics in a bar, and also observed having a heated discussion with a suspicious looking man in the lobby of a Sydney hotel. He was seen in Paris, he was seen in Rome; Blue Zephyr was somewhere in the middle of the Atlantic, Blue Zephyr was anchored somewhere deep in Egypt, far up the Nile. For weeks there was a flurry of speculation, and then, gradually, with every rumor spent and not one thing proven true, other, different, stories crowded St. James and his pirate ship out of the papers and off the screen. Months went by, and then, after those who still remembered had finally given up and declared with utter certainty that St. James was living somewhere in South America where search was meaningless and extradition did not exist, Blue Zephyr, as new and shiny as the day she was christened, sailed beneath the Golden Gate and into the San Francisco bay. But Nelson St. James was not on her.

St. James was dead. He had been murdered, shot to death, his body lost at sea. That was the headline in the morning papers, but it was the picture beneath it that drew my attention and held it there, the photograph of Danielle – Justine, when I had known her, when she was the young girl no one noticed twice, the girl who in her adolescent imagination had thought she was in love with the still young man nearly twice her age who had been engaged to her older sister. The picture in the paper, the picture in my head, two pictures that looked nothing alike, and yet, remembering the wistful disappointment in her eyes when she told me that I had forgotten her, two pictures that merged as one: the face of the girl and the woman she had become. What I could not put together, what seemed impossible, was what the paper said had happened: that Danielle St. James had killed her husband and had now been charged with murder.

"Are you going to do it?"

I did not need to look up from my corner table in the courthouse cafeteria. Philip Conrad had been a court reporter for almost twenty years when I first started practicing law, and in a strange way we had become friends; strange, because we never saw each other outside of court. I knew him the way we all know people with whom we spent part of our time at work. If I had been asked where he lived or what he did on weekends, all I could have said was that he lived somewhere in the city and that he probably spent most of Saturday and Sunday typing up the trial transcript some lawyer needed for an appeal.

There were things I knew about him, however, that others did not. He had taken an interest in me from the first trial I had in which he was the reporter, and he used to tell me, a young lawyer who could not find his way to the clerk's office without help, stories about the legendary lawyers he had known years earlier. A few years after we first met, he told me that he had married the girl from the neighborhood where he had grown up, the girl he had known ever since he was just a boy, how he married her after he came home from Vietnam, a twice-wounded veteran of the war, how they moved into a small two-bedroom house out on the avenues where he still lived. He had an old-fashioned way of talking, especially when it came to things that were by any measure personal and deeply felt. In a single sentence, spoken with the kind of restrained emotion that only makes you, the witness, feel how much another man has suffered, he told me in a firm, quiet voice that she saved his soul every day he lived with her, and that when she died, a year and a half later, struck by a car on her way home from the store, the best part of him had died as well. He kept her picture on the bedroom dresser, and year after year went through the motions of his life, and never once, in that regrettable phrase which treats all tragedy as a temporary inconvenience, thought of 'moving on.' Modest, self-effacing, with a pleasant round face and gentle eyes, he was, so far as the world knew, a generally cheerful man.

"Are you going to do it?" he asked again as he settled into the chair on the other side of the plain plastic table.

"Do what?" I asked, though I knew very well what he meant.

He nodded toward the newspaper I had just put down. "Defend her."

"I haven't been asked."

"You knew them, didn't you?"

Beyond the fact that I had spent a weekend on Blue Zephyr, I could not remember how much I had told him.

"I met them; I couldn't really say I got to know them very well."

His eyes raised a question, seemed to suggest a doubt. He had been the reporter in so many trials, listened to so many lawyers, that he knew by a kind of instinct not just when someone was lying, but when, in that more subtle form of deception, they were leaving something out.

"You should have been a prosecutor," I observed. "You ask a question, hear the answer, and then just sit there and wait for something more. There isn't," I tried to assure him, but then, because I could not ignore that somber, unrelenting gaze of his, I had to qualify it. "Nothing important."

A prosecutor – any cross-examining attorney - would have smiled at this admission, but Philip Conrad, with his mute insistence, did not care about making a point, he only wanted to hear the truth. The only change in his expression was a slight movement of his thinning eyebrows as he discovered a deeper meaning in what I had said.

"A woman that beautiful, there's always something more."

"I suspect you're right about that," was my vague response.

"Are you going to do it, defend her? You haven't been asked. I know. But you've met her; she's met you; and even if you hadn't met, who else would she ask? Everyone who gets in trouble wants you for their lawyer."

There was something he was not saying, something he was holding back.

"You don't think I should, do you?"

He hesitated, as if he were not quite sure what he thought.

"It might be one you can't win. A jury won't like her. Married to a man with that much money, a woman who looks like that – a jury won't trust her. Would you?"

Conrad did not wait for an answer; I suppose because he thought the question answered itself. He was right, of course, if you had to make a judgment based on who she married and how she looked. It was in its own way one of the great ironies, that everyone thought they knew all about her when they knew those two things - all that money and that stunningly beautiful face - and that a dozen years earlier no one could have imagined that anyone with money would ever have wanted to marry her. That still left the question whether, whatever a jury might think, I could trust her if I had to, and the answer was that I did not know. When I knew her as a girl, I had never had any reason not to trust Justine to tell me the truth, but Danielle was a woman whom I barely knew at all. Justine could not have hurt anyone; Danielle, for all I knew, had done exactly what they said she had, murdered the man she married, the father of her child. Of course it did not matter what I thought. I had not heard from her and I was certain I never would. Some high profile lawyer from New York was no doubt already preparing a defense. I would not have to struggle with the question of whether Justine had really committed murder and what could be done about it.

But I was wrong; I would have to struggle with it, a struggle that would be much harder than anything I had imagined. Danielle was waiting for me late that Friday afternoon when I got back from court, the trial that had lasted weeks finally over.

"I seem to be in some trouble," she said in a soft, silky voice that floated breathless in the air. She rose from the chair, a faint smile of nostalgia and regret on her lips. "I was hoping you could help."

Though it scarcely seemed possible, she was even more beautiful than I remembered. I led her into my private office and watched, half-mesmerized, as she slid into the chair on the other side of my desk and started taking off her gloves.

"If I had come here a week or so after that weekend on Blue Zephyr," she asked as she pulled five slender fingers out of the second black glove, "what would you have done?-Perhaps invited me out to lunch?"

I felt too stupid, too confused, to talk. She seemed to enjoy how easily she had reduced me to utter incoherence. But there was more to it than the knowledge of the effect she had. For a brief moment, behind the laughter in her eyes, I thought I glimpsed the secret triumph of revenge. She tossed her head in what appeared to be defiance, not just at the memory of what she had felt as rejection, all those years ago, but at what was expected of a woman in her present, unfortunate, situation.

"Where do you think we would have gone?" she persisted in a mocking, teasing voice. "One of those busy places near the Ferry Building with a view – or a restaurant in some small hotel where we might have left before we ordered anything and taken a room?"

I was not sure what to say or even what to think. All I knew for certain – and if I had had any doubt about it before, I was sure about it now – was that I could not help her and she needed to find another lawyer. But then, before I could tell her, she shrugged her shoulders and with the quick, furtive glance, of someone who knows you share her secret, gave a rueful laugh.

"This is like one of those old movies, isn't it? – The widow accused of murdering her wealthy husband, the window in the black dress, the dress that suggests a great many things, though mourning isn't one of them, walks into the office of the only lawyer who might be able to save her and tries to seduce him into doing it."

In her quiet, pleading glance, something of the young girl I had once known came back, and I could not just tell her to find someone else.

"I'm sorry about the trouble you're in, Justine."

Her large eyes brightened with what seemed almost gratitude.

"You remembered."

"You changed, and it was a long time ago, at least a dozen years, and you were very young and I was nearly thirty, and…."

"And you were crazy about my sister and I was just a kid; and what I said to you, when you broke up, about marrying you – that must have seemed like some adolescent fantasy." She waited until I smiled, admitting the truth of it, before she added, "But even then I knew what I wanted, and I wanted you."

Something caught her eye, or perhaps she wanted to change the subject by the fact of distance. She got up from the wing back chair and went across to the window where her glance moved down the narrow, busy street to the Bay Bridge, to the hills on the other side and, beyond them, to a place she could not see, the place where when she was growing up no one seemed to notice her or pay her any attention.

"I always like San Francisco. I used to come out here, to get away from New York. Just for a few days, then I had to get back…. New York is like that, you know." Her voice was distant, wistful, and full of mystery. She kept staring out the window at the bay shining silver bright in the summer light below. "You think you'll go mad if you don't get away from all the people, all the noise; and then, even if it's only for a weekend in the Hamptons, you have to get back, afraid you might miss something if you don't." With an expression that suggested the vanity of things, she looked over her shoulder. "Or afraid that if you stay away too long, no one will miss you. But then, after I married Nelson, things changed, and we were always on the move, going wherever we felt the urge."

She came back to the chair and sat down again. For a long time, she stared at me and did not say a word. The silence became complete.

"Will you help me?" she asked, finally.

"I better not."

"But why?"

"You know why," I said as gently as I could. Her eyes cast too great a spell, and I looked past her to the window. "I knew you when you were still…, I almost married your

sister. I knew your mother," I said as I brought my gaze
back to hers. "I saw her just a few weeks ago." There was
no reaction, nothing, not the slightest interest. "I might have
been able to represent Danielle; but you're Justine."

"No, I'm not," she said quite seriously, as if I had made
some kind of mistake. "That's who I used to be; I'm not her
anymore."

"There are other lawyers, eager to take a case like this.
I can give you names; I'll even make the call."

"I don't want anyone else; I won't have anyone else!
You're the only one who can help me. Don't you understand?
– You're the only one I can trust. I'm in trouble, a lot of
trouble, and if you don't help me, no one can!" She was
trembling so hard she could barely finish.

"I'm sorry," she said, as she took a handkerchief from
her purse and tried to dry her eyes. "I couldn't trust anyone
the way I trust you; I couldn't tell them half the things they
would want to know. You knew me when – that's what you
said – when I was just a kid, but I knew you, too; knew you
better than you know. I saw what you were like, I saw how
much it hurt when my foolish sister did what she did. I would
have done anything for you then. I always believed in you,
knew that, no matter what, you'd always do the right thing –
I still believe in you. I know you'll help me. You have to. It's
the only chance I have."

The decision, like all the decisions that change our
lives forever, had already been made, made somewhere deep
inside where a voice insisted that only a coward refused
a challenge, even when the danger was almost certain
self-destruction.

"If I'm going to help you," I told her after a long pause,
"there can't be any secrets. I have to know everything; you
can't hold back anything."

She promised to tell me everything, swore she would
be the best, most cooperative client I had ever had, and I
believed her, not just because I had known her long before
she became the famous face so many people thought they
knew, but because she knew I meant it when I told her that

the first time she lied to me would be the last, that even if we were in the middle of the trial she would never see me again. When she asked me what I wanted to know, I started at the beginning, or what I thought was the beginning. I asked her why she had married him. I did not doubt it was all about the money, but I wondered if there had been something more, if not love, then at least a feeling. Though the question could not have been simpler, it seemed to catch her off guard. Apparently, she had thought I was going to ask about the murder, of what had been called murder, her husband's death. She had an answer for that; there would have been little else she would have thought about, coming to ask a lawyer to take her case, but she had not thought about this.

"Why did you marry him?" I asked again.

"I'll tell you; I'll tell you everything, though I wonder what you'll think of me when you know. But I want you to know one thing first: marrying Nelson St. James was the worst mistake I ever made. I wish I'd never met him, I wish…." Shaking her head in despair, she bit her lip and looked away.

"Take your time," I told her, watching the way she seemed to recoil from even the bare mention of her dead husband's name. "Start at the beginning. Tell me how you first met him."

Her head snapped up. She glared with what seemed anger, but, as soon became clear, it was directed, not at me, but at the memory of what had happened, of what, as it turned out, she had done to make it happen. That look of anger quickly became one of derision.

"It was in an office, an office rather like this," she said, with an expansive gesture of her hand. "It was larger, of course, much larger; but furnished in the same impeccable manner, the understated look of someone who knows the value of things. Whatever else Nelson did or did not know, he knew that."

Resting an elbow on the arm of the chair, she draped her thumb and forefinger around her chin and gave me a look catlike in its luminous intensity.

"He wanted to see me," she began, speaking slowly, making sure I understood the hidden meaning, the real truth, of each word. "Nelson St. James, the mysterious and always elusive Nelson St. James, wanted to see me." Her eyes flashed, her chin came up a defiant half-inch. "I was not invited, I was summoned. He owned everything – half of New York - , more than that, I suppose. Nelson St. James wanted to see me, a young fashion model with ambition. Why wouldn't I go?"

She bent forward, closer, a strange excitement coming over her as she began to tell me what had happened.

"He said he admired my work; he said he wanted to talk about my future. He said a lot of things about how my career would be managed and how famous I was about to become. I listened, I waited, I did not say a word; and then, when he was finished – after he had told me all the great things that were going to happen – I told him that was not the reason he had sent for me, and that he should have just told me at the beginning what he wanted. And then, before he could even think to say anything more, before he could start on that stale, practiced seduction he must have used on a thousand different women, I let him have me, right there in his office, an office just like this. When it was over, when he started to ask about the weekend and the places we could go, I laughed, and then I left. He started calling, of course...."

'Of course' - She pronounced that phrase without a shade of arrogance or conceit. Everyone wanted her, the woman she had become.

"I didn't take his calls," she continued; "and I wouldn't call him back. I made him wait a week; then I called him and asked him not to call again. He started writing letters, sending flowers, apologizing for what had happened as if it had somehow happened without my consent!"

It seems ludicrous, bizarre, but I tried to make excuses.

"You had second thoughts; you realized what you had done had been a mistake?"

I could have been sixteen, a young boy - an innocent

at heart - for the look she gave me.

"I did exactly what I had planned to do, and he did exactly what I had expected. Nelson had everything, all the money in the world, but he could not have me, not after that one time. He might have forgotten all about it, if I had said no at the beginning. I understood that, let him have me – part of me, anyway – and then I wouldn't let him have me again. He thought that I had wanted him, that day in his office, and that I didn't want him anymore."

She searched my eyes, letting me know that she trusted me in a way that she had not trusted anyone before.

"It's worse for a man, isn't it – to have a woman once who doesn't want you again – than not to have her at all? It makes you feel inadequate, undesirable, a little like what a woman feels when she's been cast aside for someone younger and more exciting. It was a new experience for Nelson. He didn't like it."

Danielle lowered her eyes, a secret on her lips. Her long, slender legs were crossed and bent to the side. She held her hands in her lap, barely visible behind her knees.

"What happened then?" I asked, despite myself intrigued.

"The letters, the flowers – that finally stopped. I waited another week. Then I called and told him I had not returned any of his calls because I had been busy at work. We both knew it was a lie. That was the reason I told it."

She waited to see if I understood, if I could fully appreciate the artful maneuver, the shrewd calculation, the way she had twisted everything to make it come out the way she wanted. It made me wonder about her estimate of me, what she thought my limitations might be. I had spent years examining the sometimes insidious means by which ingenious and unscrupulous people went after what they wanted, and she seemed unsure whether I could understand what she had told me without some further explanation.

"Because it was only if he knew, not just that it was a lie, but that you knew he would know it was a lie, that he would know you were interested, but only on terms of your own. Yes?"

"Yes, but can you guess the terms?" she asked as if this were some game she had now decided she wanted to play. "Will you be shocked to learn that having spent one short afternoon as the whore of every fantasy he had, I insisted on the same conditions that any proper virgin would impose?"

"Marriage?"

"If you want me – want me ever again – marry me! It was as simple as that. It was only complicated because it took him so long to understand it, to believe that I would never sleep with him again, never do much more than kiss him goodnight, until I became his wife, Mrs. Nelson St. James."

Justine – Danielle – laughed at her own temerity, and then, commenting on her own performance, threw me a glance that suggested that it had not been any great achievement.

"Nelson did what everyone does when there is something they don't have and think they need: he fell in love with me. Marriage became his idea. The thought of it made him happier than he had ever been. The night he asked me, he looked ten years younger. He took me to his favorite restaurant in Manhattan and gave me a diamond ring bigger, brighter, than anything I had ever seen. The whole evening was perfect. I said no."

"You said no?"

"I didn't want to get married."

"But you just said…?"

"That he couldn't have me again unless we were married. He made the same mistake you did: he assumed I wanted to marry him."

She rose from the chair and stood next to the window, thinking back to what she had done and whether she was really prepared to keep her promise and, without holding anything back, tell me everything. She turned and looked at me, but still kept her silence. Her eyes seemed to widen and grow softer; a smile, strange and ambiguous, full of a meaning I could not yet fathom, moved slowly across her mouth.

"I told him that when I met the man I wanted to marry, I would know right away."

She kept looking at me, reminding me that long before she had become Danielle, she had been Justine. And then, finally, she moved away from the window, but instead of coming back to her chair, she walked idly about the room, dragging her fingers on the furniture she passed as she glanced at the different pictures on the walls.

"That was cruel, to tell him that," she said as she stopped in front of a photograph taken years earlier on my first day in court. "Cruel, but necessary; or so I thought before he showed me how seriously I had underestimated him."

She spun on her heel and strolled back to the window. When she turned around and faced me, her eyes were all aglow.

"I thought he would be devastated. Does that shock you? - That I did it on purpose, that I was so determined to get what I wanted that I didn't care what I did? Have you ever felt like that? – wanted something so much you didn't care anything about the rules?"

"You wanted to marry him? You wanted to be Mrs. Nelson St. James?" I declared in a voice that surprised me by its harshness.

"Yes, Mrs. Nelson St. James. I didn't want Nelson, I wanted what he had!" The eager defiance with which she said this seemed an incitement, a wish – no! a compulsion - to confess, to admit what she had done and why she had done it. "I said no because I thought he would ask again, and that he would want me even more when he did. I had not counted on his sense of self-respect, the sense he had of his own importance." She paused just long enough to emit a slight, self-deprecating laugh. "The very reason I wanted to be married to him, and I didn't understand what it meant!

"I said no, and do you know what he did? – He smiled and told me that he hoped that when it happened – when I fell in love with someone the first time I saw him – that I would be as much in love as he was with me. He took me home, kissed me on the cheek, and left. A few days later, I read in the papers that he had gone to Europe on an extended vacation. It was the honeymoon trip he had planned for us. Two months later, he came back, engaged to some vaguely titled woman from a country and a court that no longer exists."

I could not pretend to sympathize for a plan that had so obviously deserved to fail, but I was interested in what she had felt about it and, of even more importance for the purpose of grasping something essential about what kind of woman she had become, what she had done about it, how she had managed to make her plan finally work.

"And how did you feel?" I asked, staring at her in a way that let her know I would not settle for some vague, inconsequential response. "What did you do when you thought he was going to marry another woman?"

"I knew he wouldn't marry her; he was only back a week before he took me out to dinner and asked me again."

She had not felt anything, certainly neither jealousy nor doubt; nothing but a cold, almost brutal calculation. But then, as I remembered, however much St. James may have thought he was in love, he had also seen certain other advantages to a marriage with her.

"He talked about you, that weekend on the yacht, as if you were one of his possessions, something he owned. He told me there wasn't any point being married to a beautiful woman unless you could show her off."

"He married me because he wanted me," insisted Danielle, thrusting out her chin. "But Nelson never wanted anything unless it was something everyone else wanted and could not have. Nelson was a bastard; I knew it, and I didn't care. I made my bargain and I kept it. I made him three promises and I kept each one of them."

There was something in the way she said it, something in the otherwise inscrutable look she gave me, that told me that what she was about to say would change everything, and that, however I remembered Justine, I would never be able to think about Danielle the same way again.

"What three promises did you make?"

"I promised that I would be faithful, and I promised I would have his child."

"And the third promise, what was that?"

Danielle pulled back her shoulders and did not blink.

"I promised that I would kill him, and I did."

CHAPTER SIX

Danielle had a talent for confusion, a way of making things sound completely different than they were. She had killed her husband, shot him after he had finished with her in bed, a fact she had not even admitted to anyone until she admitted it to me, and she had not admitted it to me all at once. She told me the day she came to my office that she had killed him, but, strange as it may seem, not the meaning of what she had done. That third promise, the promise to kill him, the promise she had carried out, had not meant at the beginning anything like what it meant at the end. St. James had said it, made her promise she would kill him, in a way that was playful and nothing serious. Perhaps he said it, after what they had done that day in his office; to convince her that he would never do anything against her will. Perhaps there was not any reason at all, perhaps he was just in a mood to make a noble sounding gesture, when told her that he thought that men who mistreated women ought to be taken out and shot, and, while he was still laughing about it, made her promise she would kill him, shoot him dead, if he should ever treat her like that.

It had been, as I say, a lover's gesture, whose only meaning was as a pledge of gentle treatment and devotion, a promise that, having served its purpose, they would both certainly forget, a promise there was no reason to remember until she began to hate him and wish he were dead. Then the words, with a new and bitter meaning, came flooding back, and with a kind of vengeful pride that long forgotten promise became the definition of betrayal and a justification for what she did.

And that was the problem. Her justification was no defense. She killed him, the fact was indisputable, and however she might insist that she had good reason to have done what she did, it was, by any definition, still murder. I had looked at it every way I knew how, examined the question from all sides, read every reported case that appeared to have even a remote connection with the issue, and there was nothing, nothing that would allow a woman to kill her husband for breaking the vows he had made. The law was all on the side of the prosecution. Danielle St. James was guilty of murder and there was nothing I could do about it, nothing I could do to save her. The only chance she had was luck, and the only thing I knew for certain was that I could not let her testify. If she told a jury the truth about what happened, not even luck could save her. I could not let her testify and I had no other witness I could use, no one who could help persuade a jury of her innocence. The only chance I had, and this had happened to me more than once in a trial, was to use the witnesses of the prosecution to prove, not her innocence, but a doubt, a reason to question whether, despite its best efforts, the case against her was sufficient.

It was easy to know what you had to do; the trick of course was how to do it, and the night before the trial I still did not know. I had gone through the police reports and statements of the witnesses, everything the prosecution had, dozens of times; I had gone through them so often that I only had to glance at the first line on the page to know everything that was written there, but it had not helped. I was going to have to challenge everything the prosecution did, seize on any inconsistency, no matter how minor, wait for the other side to make a mistake; but there were no inconsistencies, no mistakes, nothing that had been left out in anything I had read. The only hope was the trial itself. A witness on the stand was a different creature than a witness on paper, easier to trap in a lie, easier, if the truth be told, to make seem a fool.

I lay on the sofa in the living room of my Nob Hill apartment, staring at the ceiling, driving myself a little crazy each time I tried to think of some flaw in the prosecution's case against Danielle St. James. I hated nights like this, the night before a trial, when no matter how hard I tried, I could not think of anything except the trial and all the unexpected things that were almost sure to happen. It was never easy, the night before a trial, but this night was the worst one of all, because I already knew I had made a mistake, and it was too late to do anything about it. I had known almost from the beginning that I should never have taken the case, that I should have done what I had meant to do and told Danielle to find another lawyer. The words of Philip Conrad, the court reporter, kept echoing in my over cluttered mind, that a jury would not like her, that they would not trust a woman that was so beautiful and rich.

I suddenly remembered that I had wanted to remind Danielle to wear to court in the morning something simple and understated, and wondered if I had. Then, in my confusion, I remembered that though it was nearly eleven, I had not eaten anything. At least that was something I could do something about. I got up and was headed for the kitchen when the telephone rang. It was the doorman, calling to tell me that 'Mrs. St. James' was there to see me.

"I thought you might have some last minute things you wanted to talk about," said Danielle.

Her voice had none of the anxiety, none of the trepidation, expected from someone about to go on trial for murder. She walked through the marble entryway and into the wood paneled living room as if, despite the late hour, this was nothing more than a social visit. Hesitating, not quite sure where to sit, she settled on a pale blue easy chair across from the sofa where I had spent half the evening and next to the fireplace I had never used. She seemed in no particular hurry, glancing around, making herself familiar with the room. Pushing her legs farther out in front of her, she sank lower in the cushioned chair. The gray silk dress, made by some designer especially for her, inched up above her knees.

The easy certainty, the sense, not exactly of entitlement, but of utter confidence that she could do whatever she chose to do; the way that with a single lifted eyebrow, the bare beginning of a smile, she thought she could command my attention; the very things that made her so damnably attractive, were now, with the trial just hours away, the source of as much irritation as I had ever felt. I was not sure if I was angry because of the way she was, or because, despite those solemn promises I had forced her to give me before, against my better judgment, I had agreed to become her lawyer. In a strange way it was funny.

"You're on trial for murder, I still don't know how I'm going to save you, and you come over here with that 'I don't give a damn attitude' of yours, as if nothing can touch you! Why? Because you've always been able to lie your way out of anything?"

Her reaction was immediate. She sat straight up, a look of icy contempt in her blue-green eyes, and with slow precision parted her red painted lips, ready on the instant with some withering reply. But I was past the point of caring what she thought or what she felt.

"Every time I ask you to tell me what happened that night," I shouted over her, "there's always something missing, something you've left out. You haven't told the same story twice - and you think I'm so stupid I don't notice it?"

I was standing a few feet away, staring at her with all the built up frustration of months of what seemed useless effort, a search for the truth that had only gone in circles.

"You swore you'd never lie to me, and that's damn near all you've done!"

Her face turned white, her eyes were wild with rage. She was on her feet, starting for the door, determined not to listen to another word. I grabbed her by the wrist and would not let go, and the harder she tried to get away, the tighter I squeezed.

"You…!" Her eyes burned with a proud, defiant intensity, daring me either to take her, or let her go. "At least Nelson knew what he wanted and how to get it!" she shouted with naked candor into my face.

Everything - all my hard-earned resolution, all my honest, well-meant intention to treat Danielle St. James like any other client and think only about the case, - went the way of all illusions. I wanted her, and nothing else now mattered. I kissed her, but she twisted away, a look of triumph in her eyes. She had won, taught me that whatever else I thought I wanted, I wanted her. And then she kissed me back and my hand was off her wrist, moving down around her waist, while her long arms curled around my neck and her lithe body pressed against my own. We stumbled blindly toward the bedroom, tearing at each other's clothes.

We were wrapped around each other, just about to start, but I had to see her, I had to see how she looked. I raised my head, and in the moonlight, streaming through the window, that gorgeous face of hers, bright and shining, was staring past me, her mind on something else. Swearing under my breath, I rolled away.

Danielle's face was a study in confusion.

"I thought you wanted me."

"You didn't want me back."

"I thought you wanted to make love."

"I would have been having sex alone," I said with a cold stare. "This was a mistake."

I got out of bed and started putting on my clothes, disgusted with everything, and especially myself. Propped up on one elbow, Danielle seemed puzzled by how abruptly I had changed my mind. It was a rare, and for all I knew, unique experience, one she did not know quite how to handle, a seduction that had failed in the last moments.

"Why did you come here tonight?" I asked while I buttoned my shirt. "Did you think you had to sleep with me to make sure I'd do everything I could to win? I've won cases for a lot of people charged with murder, and, believe it or not, I didn't sleep with any of them!"

Her knees were pulled up, the sheet tucked under her chin. Something I had not seen before, a wounded, frightened look, entered her eyes.

"I've watched how hard you've worked these last few months. I wanted to give you something before the trial began, before it ever goes to the jury, before they come back with a verdict, so you'd know it wasn't out of gratitude for what you had done. I wanted to give you what I thought you wanted, and I thought you wanted me."

It almost did not matter that she looked the way she did, her voice alone was irresistible, something you did not so much listen to as feel, like a soft warm wind in the evening of a perfect summer day, reminding you of every good day you ever had and, more than that, all the good days you had somehow missed, the days you wished you had had and never did. That was what drew you toward her: not just the face that graced the cover of so many magazines, but the promise of things you had not known and had never quite thought possible. She was the girl you saw in a crowd, the girl you never met, the one who could have made everything right, who would have made you happy with the life you had, made you forget forever the restless search for something new and different. She was the girl with whom sex would be the beginning, and not the end, of what you felt, what every man was looking for and felt foolish to admit.

"You were never in love with him, were you? Ever?"

"Nelson? No."

"You've never been in love with anyone, have you?"

A bashful smile slipped unbidden across her soft and girlish mouth, and she bent her head to the side.

"Not since I was sixteen, no."

Finished with the last button on my shirt, I did not bother with socks or shoes, but barefoot and disheveled left her in the bedroom and padded out to the kitchen, threw open the refrigerator and looked for something to drink. It was after midnight and I had a trial in the morning. Angry with myself, angry with the world, I muttered a few mild obscenities, slammed shut the refrigerator and made a cup of coffee instead. If I was not going to be able to sleep I might as well try to work.

I had told Danielle to get dressed, that she had to leave, but when she came into the kitchen all she had on was one of my abandoned shirts, a shirt she had not bothered to button. She sat across the table, holding a cup of coffee next to her mouth, waiting for me to say something, but I would not look at her. I took a sip of coffee, but, still too hot, it burned my mouth. Already too much on the defensive, I ignored the pain, crossed my arms and, finally looking at her, tried to assume an attitude of indifference.

"I don't want you. It was a mistake. It isn't going to happen again."

She ignored me.

"I wasn't in love with Nelson, but that didn't matter to him. He thought I'd never been in love with anyone, and that I never would be." Raising her head, she gave me a significant look. "He thought I wasn't capable of loving anyone more than I loved myself." A smile that seemed to know everything moved bright and golden across her lips. "I imagine a lot of women have fallen in love with you, besides me, when I was sixteen. Have you fallen in love with any of them – other than my sister?"

I did not understand what she was saying, where she was going with this. I was not kept in the dark for long.

"Tell me the truth: with all the women you must have slept with, have you always wanted them as much as they wanted you? Are you going to tell me that you never slept with a woman you weren't in love with but who was in love with you?"

When I did not answer, her eyes glittered with vindication at this brief summary of my life as a failed romantic. She bent forward, eager to press her advantage.

"Are you going to tell me that you never made love to a woman and for just a quick, passing moment, thought about something else."

"Or someone else," I reminded her in a cold, determined voice.

"I wasn't thinking of someone else," she replied, quick to deny it; but then, just as quickly, she changed her mind. "Or maybe I was. But not because I was wishing I was with someone else. It wasn't that at all. Tonight was the first time since...."

Her eyes clouded over, and in a brooding silence struggled with her emotions, the conflict she felt. Staring straight ahead, a pensive expression darkened her brow. Finally, after what might have been only a few seconds but seemed like a very long time, she turned again to me.

"Tonight was the first time I've been near a man since the night he died."

She said this without remorse, without regret, without, so far as I could tell, the slightest sense of responsibility or guilt. I understood what she wanted, understood it as clearly as if she had taken the time to explain it: She wanted to know if I believed her, believed what she had told me about what happened the night she killed her husband. She kept looking at me, searching my eyes, too proud to ask and, beneath it all, perhaps too scared not to want to know.

"I suddenly remembered," she started to explain. "I suddenly saw it all over again: the way he felt, hard up inside me; the way his body tensed the moment he finished – started to finish. That look he had in his eyes, the look that was there every time he did it, every time he had me; that look that said -"

Her eyes were wild with – I was not sure what: anger, fear, excitement? – Or all of them at once, the long suppressed reaction to what she had done.

"He did that, he always did that – that look that said he owned me, that no one else could ever have me, that he was better than everyone because of it. They say that men rape women to show they have power over them. He had sex with me to prove he had power over other men."

More than with resentment, she said this was something close to pure hatred. She fed on it, took pleasure in it, the thought that what he had done to her was as bad as rape, and maybe worse.

"You could have made love to me, but you didn't, because you thought I didn't want you as much as you wanted me, because you wanted something more than sex. Nelson didn't want that, he didn't want to make love. He didn't know what that was. Nelson wanted what we did that day in his office: he wanted to fuck! That's all he knew. Beneath all that money and charm and that handsome face of his, beneath all the expensive clothes and private school manners, all Nelson cared about was what he owned. Nelson in love with me? – It's what he told you that weekend on Blue Zephyr: the only thing he loved was the knowledge that everyone else wanted what he had. Make love with me? – All I was to him was a dressed up whore!" she cried, becoming more agitated with each word she spoke. "And that look he had on his face! I couldn't stand it anymore. That lie he told me before we were married, that there was nothing worse than a man who mistreated a woman! That promise he made me make that I would never let him mistreat me! I wonder if he remembered all that when he looked at me like that again that night and I pulled out a gun and shot him."

She began to cry, hot, bitter tears, and I held her close and did what I could to comfort her until, finally, she told me she was all right and with a brave smile said I better get some sleep. I waited while she dressed in the other room, and then I walked her back to her hotel the other side of Nob Hill. We stood just outside the entrance, away from the doormen with their whistles and all the noisy cars, and she kissed me on the side of my face and said she knew that everything would work out the way it should. And then I walked back and tried not to think about what was going to happen in the morning when we started the first trial I had had that I knew I could not win.

CHAPTER SEVEN

Intrigued by the marriage of money and beauty that had ended in murder, reporters came from all over the country, and as far away as Europe, to cover the trial. Sex and violence always sold papers, and brought higher ratings to television, and never in such numbers as when power and celebrity were involved. In the tabloid mentality of the age, it was a simple question of a woman's greed. From the time Danielle St. James was arrested it was all about the money and nothing else. It was obvious, plain on the face of it, that she was guilty as charged. The morning the trial started, the always impartial Philip Conrad, waiting patiently at his machine, may have been the only one in the courtroom who had not already reached that conclusion. The first words out of the prosecutor's mouth only repeated what everyone claimed to know.

"She murdered him for the money, it's as simple as that."

Robert Franklin struck a combative pose. With small, pudgy, grasping hands, thick black hair plastered to his skull, and small, black, impenetrable eyes, he had at times the look of a fanatic. Shrill and insistent, he rose up on the balls of his feet, jabbing the air to emphasize the crucial importance of what he was saying.

"This was not one of those so-called crimes of passion, an act of violence when an argument got out of hand. This was cold-blooded murder carried out for gain. Nelson St. James was one of the wealthiest men in America. With his death, his widow inherits everything he had."

Franklin turned slowly toward the table where Danielle was sitting next to me. Pausing for dramatic effect, he raised his arm and pointed.

"She murdered him in cold-blood, and then tried to blame it on someone else."

Robert Franklin had the habit of precision, an addiction to taking each thing step by step. This gave his argument a relentless, logical quality, but it also narrowed his focus to what was right in front of him. He was about my age, perhaps a few years older, and like most lawyers of our generation, much of what he knew of courtroom dialogue had come from movies he had seen, and much of what he knew of courtroom theatrics from all the television he had watched. Though a seasoned prosecutor, the murder trial of Danielle St. James was the most important case of his career, a chance to make a name for himself. Anything would be possible after this: a seat on the bench, elective office, things he had dreamed about since law school, if only he did everything right. He must have rehearsed his opening statement for days, or even weeks, gone over it so many times he could give it backwards in his sleep. He was flawless, every word, every gesture, exactly the way he had planned it, and then, five minutes into it, he suddenly stopped. The next word, the next phrase - which from the look on his face was going to be the most devastating thing he had said so far – had somehow, unaccountably, vanished from his mind, and what came after that he did not know. The silence became uncomfortable and then embarrassing. Philip Conrad looked up from his machine.

"'Then tried to blame it on someone else,'" I said in the bored voice of a director forced to remind an actor of his lines.

Robert Franklin blinked and, in his dazed condition not certain where the voice had come from, looked around. His mouth began to twitch nervously and his black, tiny eyes, smoldering with resentment, grew smaller still. His hands, held down at the level of his jacket pockets, tightened into a pair of useless fists. He stared at me, puzzled because he had not quite understood what I said, then with open hostility when he heard the courtroom laugh. He wheeled around and faced the jury, ready to redouble his attacks on the defendant and the evil calculation of what she had done.

He forgot what he was going to say.

"She killed him," he mumbled, buying time. "Killed him, and we're going to prove it." Head down, his hands clasped behind his back, he began to pace in front of the jury box, but before he had taken two steps he stopped and looked up. "I mean, the People are going to produce evidence that will show that...."

He could not remember what came next, and without that he was lost. His short, squat neck bulged over his stiff white shirt collar; beads of sweat formed a thin necklace on his forehead. The harder he tried to think, to remember all those well-rehearsed lines with which he was going to drive a stake into the heart of the defendant before the trial was an hour old, the angrier and more embarrassed he became.

Others might feel sorry for Robert Franklin; I could not afford to show mercy. If he made a mistake, I was there to take advantage of it. Sitting at the counsel table, less than ten feet from the jury box, I leaned forward.

"This is usually the place where the prosecutor says something about meeting the burden of proof," I said in a whispered shout.

Franklin went white with rage.

"Your Honor!" he cried. "This is my opening statement. The defense doesn't have the right to interrupt!"

One of the youngest trial judges in the city, Alice Brunelli was also one of the best. Tapping a pencil in a slow methodical cadence, she gave Franklin a look that was anything but sympathetic.

"You're no doubt familiar with the phrase, 'Nature abhors a vacuum,' Mr. Franklin? It's your opening statement – if you can make it. And while I'm not sure Mr. Morrison really meant to be helpful," she went on, with a quick, warning glance in my direction, "you'll have to admit that what he suggested might perhaps be exactly what you ought to do."

Never in a hurry when trying to teach a lesson, the judge removed the thick horn-rim glasses that reinforced the no-nonsense, scholarly impression she would have made even without them, breathed on the lenses and then wiped them clean with the hem of her robe. She held the glasses up to examine them, and after a close inspection, put them back on and immediately turned her attention to a document she had on the bench in front of her.

"The floor is yours, Mr. Franklin. If you can keep it," she added, her sharp gray eyes still fastened on the page.

Franklin had suffered what was tantamount to stage fright, the temporary inability to remember what he was supposed to say, but he was not an empty headed fool who could only recite lines someone else had written. He had written them himself, written them in long hand on the pages of a long yellow legal pad left on the counsel table with his other things. With a new air of self-confidence, he looked them over as if he were only now about to begin.

Keeping to the facts, the concise litany of what the prosecution intended to prove, Franklin was capable, efficient, and completely persuasive. The jury of seven men and five women, the majority of them middle-aged or even older, followed with steady, believing eyes the simple, straightforward narrative of what had happened. He was not up on the balls of his feet any longer, his arms were not flying in the air; he had given up those theatrics. He stood flat-footed a step or two from the railing of the jury box, his hands plunged deep down in his pockets, speaking in a normal, conversational tone and, though it must have cost him an effort, sounding almost pleasant.

"The defendant in this case, Danielle St. James, was married to the victim, Nelson St. James, for a little more than five years. They lived in New York, among other places, but they spent most of their time on his yacht. You have probably heard the rumors about Mr. St. James and his financial dealings; you have probably read in the papers about the trouble he was in. His difficulties have some bearing on this case."

He paused to let the jury consider for itself the link that might exist between one of the great financial scandals of the century and the murder of the man who had, if you believed half of what was written, swindled half the country out of what it owned.

"Shortly after Mr. St. James was indicted, they left New York and disappeared, though they did not disappear all at once. Before they set out to sea again – that last, mysterious voyage of theirs – they flew out here, to San Francisco, where the yacht was waiting. They were heard arguing from the moment they stepped off his private plane, they were heard arguing that night at dinner. They were still arguing the next day. The arguments became so heated that the defendant walked out of the restaurant where they were having dinner the second night and got into a cab alone."

Again Franklin paused, but this time, instead of watching the jury and how they reacted, he looked out at the courtroom, jammed with spectators eager to see what would happen next. He was glad to have an audience for this, his biggest, most important trial. His dark, deep-set eyes registered his approval, but then, almost immediately, he remembered another face. It was astonishing how he tried to hide it, the way he narrowed his eyes and tightened his jaw, preparing to look at Danielle without appearing nervous or unsure of himself. Because there she was, on trial for murder, and no woman had ever looked more desirable and less like a killer. She wore a simple, pale blue dress, something that, for the first time in years, she had bought off the rack, and, even in that dim, windowless courtroom, her hair was like summer sunshine and her eyes lit up the room. Like a teenage boy peeking around a corner at a girl he had a crush on, Franklin finally turned and looked, and then immediately looked away. No one, not even the prosecutor who was determined to send her to her execution, was immune from the spell she cast. It was there in his voice, the tell-tale catch in his throat, as he faced the jury and tried to pretend the face of the defendant was no different than that of any other women he had ever prosecuted for a crime.

"They argued all weekend – at one point the hotel had to send someone up to their suite to ask them to stop. They checked out of the hotel early Sunday morning and left San Francisco on their yacht, and, as was widely reported at the time, disappeared. We now know that they were sailing around the south Pacific, stopping at different places but without any apparent destination. The arguments never stopped, and if anything, got worse; got so bad in fact that she finally moved out of the cabin she shared with her husband and slept alone. And then, a short time later, she killed him."

Franklin was back in stride, reciting the elements of the crime with the kind of certainty that makes doubt seem impossible and even absurd. He was good at this, better than most prosecutors, better than most lawyers. The main point was that he was not afraid of the courtroom, was not afraid to stand up in front a dozen jurors and a watching crowd of strangers and give it everything he had. He made mistakes, forgot a few of the things he wanted to say, but that was not going to stop him. He had the great advantage of believing that everything he said was the truth.

"This is not a complicated case, once you get beyond the celebrity of the people involved. It is as cut and dried as any murder case can be. If the way she did it does not seem particularly inventive, murder, despite what you see on television, is seldom well-planned. They had an argument, a fight – they had been going at it for days. She had a gun, and she used it."

He hesitated, quite on purpose, just long enough so everyone could wonder if it could really be that simple and guilt that obvious. And then, to make sure a doubt like that never arose again, he showed that it could.

"You will have evidence," he said with a glance that warned that this went right to the heart of their obligation as jurors, "that the bullet that killed Nelson St. James came from the gun she was still holding in her hand after he was shot. You will hear evidence that the gun belonged to them, Nelson St. James and his wife. I say belonged to them both because you will also hear testimony that Nelson St. James bought it because his wife, Danielle St. James, the defendant, wanted a gun for her own protection."

With both hands, he leaned on the jury box railing, eager and tenacious, looking from one juror to the next, searching their eyes, daring them – daring anyone! – to disagree.

"It was her gun, and her fingerprints were all over it. There was no one else who could have done it. She shot him dead and he fell overboard into the sea. There was blood on the deck, blood on the railing, and – make no mistake! – the blood was his."

While Robert Franklin went on about the witnesses who would testify about the murder weapon and the fingerprints found on it, I tried to project an air of unshaken confidence, to act as if nothing he said would in the end have any consequence. I turned to Danielle, put my hand on her arm, and whispered in her ear to look at me and smile back. Then, nodding to myself, like someone in complete control of things, I scribbled a brief note, an illegible scrawl that meant nothing, but that, seen from the distance of the jury box, might be thought significant. There was only one point in this masquerade, one reason only for this mimic's dance, and that was to create by any means I could the impression that what the prosecution was promising it would prove would turn out to be nothing like as damaging as Franklin wanted them to believe.

"The question isn't whether the defendant murdered her husband," insisted Franklin, assuming his own conclusion. "The question is why did she do it, what was her motive? She was angry – they had been arguing for days – but the defendant isn't charged with manslaughter, she's charged with murder in the first degree, and that means that she killed him with 'malice aforethought,' that she intended to do it before she did it; that she didn't just fly off the handle and kill him in a fit of rage, but that she thought about it, decided she was going to do it, and then did it, murdered him in cold blood."

With one hand on the jury box railing and the other on his hip, Franklin arched an eyebrow and shook his head in scorn.

"She may have killed him during an argument, but she did not pull the trigger in a moment of uncontrollable anger. She had a motive that did not depend on rage, one of the oldest motives there is: money, more money than you or I could ever imagine."

Franklin walked to the end of the jury box closest to the empty witness stand and turned, until, with the jury on his left, he was facing the crowd.

"Rufus Wiley was the personal attorney of Nelson St. James. Mr. Wiley is a witness for the prosecution. He will testify that the defendant signed a pre-nuptial agreement under which she would have been left, in the event of a divorce, what most of us would consider a very wealthy woman, with a house in the Hamptons and a million dollars a year."

A thin, malevolent smile edged its way across Franklin's narrow pinched mouth. He stood there for a moment, and then another, saying nothing, letting everyone consider for themselves the meaning of the phrase, 'what most of us would consider,' and the implication that what most of us might think did not even begin to measure the extent of certain other people's greed.

"A house in the Hamptons and a million a year," repeated Franklin, his voice venomous and sarcastic. "What was that, compared to the hundreds of millions – the billions! – that would be left to her if she was married to him when he died. But there was a problem. Nelson St. James wanted a divorce. He had told his attorney, Rufus Wiley, to draw up the papers. That is what they were arguing about, the victim and the defendant: he wanted a divorce, and that is why she killed him: to make sure it did not happen!

"All that money at stake, all that money she wouldn't have! What was a million dollars compared to that?" he asked, slamming his hand on the jury box railing as he lunged forward. "A million dollars! – That's probably less than she spends a year on clothes!"

I was on my feet, shouting an objection.

"Your Honor! First he forgets his opening, and now he thinks he's in the middle of his close! Worse yet, the argument he seems to be making is pathetic! He's attacking the defendant because she happens to look rather good in well-made clothes?"

It had to have been one of the strangest objections ever made, but I was not interested in how the judge would rule on it; I wanted to make Franklin seem the real villain, a man who would taunt a woman for how she looked. Whether or not it worked on the jury, it worked on Franklin.

"It's part of the People's case!" he sputtered, as bits of saliva went flying. Lifting his hooded eyes to the bench, he pled the importance of the point. "The difference between what she would have gotten and what she would have lost."

Peering over the tops of her glasses, lowered halfway down her lengthy nose, Judge Brunelli pursed her thin, white lips.

"This is the time to give the jury an outline – a brief outline – of the prosecution's case. You can argue your point later, after all the evidence is in. Now let's move on, shall we?"

Franklin had been too much in court to make the mistake of arguing anything with a trial court judge. As soon as Brunelli finished, he turned to the jury and without any change of expression picked up where he had left off.

"A million dollars a year, when she could have had it all! What better motive for murder?" He cocked his head and struck a pose, as if a question of some considerable importance had just occurred to him. "What better motive for murder?" he repeated in a pensive tone, the question no longer rhetorical. "Other than that other motive, at least as old: sex. Yes, that's right, a double motive was involved, sex and money both. Nelson St. James was going to divorce his wife because, as Rufus Wiley will testify, his wife, the defendant, Danielle St. James, had been having an affair. That was the reason she killed him, because it was the only way she could have both her lover and the money, too."

Someone might as well have kicked the chair out from under me. She had been having an affair and the prosecution could prove it, and this was the first I had heard about it! Franklin had not called his first witness and I was already certain we had lost. I wanted to turn to Danielle and tell her what I thought, dare her to try to explain why she had never told me. And I might have done it, too, if Franklin had not chosen that moment to end his opening statement. I watched as he sank into his chair at the other counsel table, farthest from the jury box, a brazen look of self-satisfaction on his face.

Judge Brunelli checked the clock and then peered down at me.

"Mr. Morrison, do you wish to make an opening statement at this time?"

It was the routine, formal request, the moment when the defense attorney gets to his feet, reminds the jury that they have not yet heard any of the witnesses whose testimony the prosecution had just described, and, with all the false honesty he can invent, tells them that when they do they will discover that rather than proving guilt beyond a reasonable doubt, the evidence will prove instead the necessity of an acquittal. You did not have to believe it when you said it, but it was always good to have at least the hope.

I got to my feet, but instead of starting toward the jury box I looked at the judge.

"With the court's permission, the defense would like to reserve its opening statement to the close of the prosecution's case."

"Permission granted." Brunelli penciled a note, reminding herself of the agreement, and then, folding her arms, sat back and glanced toward the other counsel table. "The prosecution will please call its first witness."

Franklin did not hear her. A smile, cold and vengeful, was playing at the corners of his mouth as he stared down at the floor, lost in the recollection of his own achievement, an opening statement that, if it had not gone perfectly, had gone well enough.

Alice Brunelli had no patience for those who made her wait.

"Mr. Franklin," she said sharply. "Please call your first witness!"

Shocked out of his daydream, Franklin looked at the judge with a stunned, bewildered expression.

"My first witness?"

He seemed surprised to see me sitting at the counsel table instead of on my feet, heading toward the jury box. The color rose above his stiff shirt collar and spread like fire along his cheek. He realized what Brunelli had asked, what he had not heard, and that was only the beginning of his embarrassment. Springing forward, he tore at a thick binder and started thumbing through the pages, searching for the list of witnesses that would remind him of the name he wanted to call first.

Alice Brunelli watched these clumsy antics with an icy stare. She had a way of looking at you that reminded you of the least favorite teacher you had ever had, the one who could make you feel invisible, as if, of all the pupils she had ever taught, you were the one great failure of her long and otherwise distinguished career.

"Never mind, Mr. Franklin," she said with weary impatience. "We'll start again in the morning." But she could not leave it there. She shot him a last, withering glance. "Perhaps by then you'll have some idea how you want to try this case!"

He stood there, straight as a board, like a soldier facing discipline, holding his breath, forcing himself to keep his silence, while she gathered up her books and papers and, rising from the bench, walked briskly out of the courtroom and into her chambers. When the door swung shut behind her, when she was finally gone, his shoulders slumped forward and he could breathe. He began to collect his things, but then, with his hand on his tan briefcases, he turned his head slightly to the side, just far enough so I could see the anger in his eyes.

CHAPTER EIGHT

Robert Franklin had only himself to blame, and I was, in any event, scarcely in a mood to sympathize. I had my own reasons to be angry, and they were far more substantial than some hurt feelings caused by a judge whose only concern was that you do your job properly. Franklin's problem was his own vanity; my problem was my client.

Muttering to myself, I tossed my suit coat on the chair behind my desk and stood at the window, peering into the dark gray dreariness of the late November day. Thanksgiving was a week away and the Christmas decorations were already up, the merchants doing everything they could to create the mood, continue the illusion, that you could still buy happiness, if only you could afford it.

"You did not tell me," I said in a grim, determined voice that echoed quietly in the silence of the room.

"It isn't true."

I kept looking out the window, watching the people on the street, wondering what it would have been like to be married with children, someone with a regular job, and not have to spend every day sorting through all the lies I was told.

"That was the second promise, wasn't it – or was it the first? Give him a child and -"

"Have a child," she said, insisting on a distinction I did not understand. "Not give him one. Michael is more my child than he was ever his."

"And stay faithful," I reminded her. I turned just far enough to see her. "That's the promise we need to talk about."

Danielle raised her chin, the way she did whenever she was challenged, in her mind unfairly. With calculated belligerence, I stared back.

"It isn't true," she insisted, now adopting a tone of indifference, as if it did not matter if it were true or not. It was astonishing how distant, how utterly detached, she could become when there was something she would have preferred to ignore.

"All those months getting ready for trial, all the times I asked you if there were anything – anything at all! – you hadn't told me; and I have to hear it first in the prosecution's opening statement: that your husband was about to start divorce proceedings and that you were going to lose all that money!"

She would not respond a third time to what she considered the same accusation. With the limitless arrogance of a woman who has better things to do, she sat there, silent and beautiful, staring past me.

"Does this bore you?" I asked with a cynical indifference that quickly yielded to disgust. I picked up my jacket and settled into the comfortable security of my chair. "Is there some place you would rather be? It must be difficult, having to go through all this, when you could be back in New York, going to parties with all your wealthy, famous friends. It must be inconvenient, being charged with murder, having to sit all day in the drab surroundings of a courtroom with nothing to talk about except the evidence that may very well cost you your life, forced to listen to someone like Robert Franklin, compelled to -"

"Franklin is an ass!" she cried, all the indifference, all the belligerence, now concentrated in her eyes. She bolted forward. "Who is going to believe anything he says, after what you did to him? He could barely remember what he was supposed to do!"

My eyes full of warning, I bent closer.

"You think he isn't any good, because he made one or two mistakes? He'll be up all night getting ready for tomorrow, making sure he won't get caught like that again. This isn't just another case to him; it's the biggest case of his career. He's been dreaming about this since the day he got to law school. You think he won't learn from what happened? You think he isn't serious? Didn't you see the look in his eyes just before we left?"

"No, why would I look at him? I saw the way he looked at me before."

Like most of the rest of us, she only understood what she knew, and there was one thing she understood as well, or better, than anyone.

"I imagine that's a look you've seen a lot," I said, drawing back. Folding my arms, I watched closely her reaction to that basic fact of her existence. Her first response was purely conventional.

"I try not to notice."

"The effect you have on men?"

There was a flash of impatience in her eyes. The answer was obvious, the question, worse than unnecessary, almost obscene, an inquiry in which the truth could only be stated with apparent conceit. This time, however, the question had nothing to do with the modest good manners society required of its more fortunate members.

"What Franklin did – that stupid gawking look on his face, like some teenage kid who had never been out with a girl before – couldn't have been more effective if he had planned it in advance."

At this, Danielle seemed curious. Her attitude, the reluctance bordering on open refusal to listen to anything more I had to say, disappeared. She waited for me to explain.

"Everyone on that jury thinks they know why you married your husband. They've seen the pictures: the gorgeous young model who marries a man ten or fifteen years older, a man who just happens to be one of the world's richest men. You've lived too long in a cocoon of money and privilege; you've forgotten what it's like to have to settle for whatever you can get and work at something you hate. No one thinks it's fair, that you should have all that: looks and money, too. Most of the people on that jury – all of them, for all I know – never had anyone look twice at them and have to struggle just to get by. And now," I went on in an ominous tone, meant to tell her that what they felt, those twelve random jurors who were watching every day in court, would be every bit as important as the evidence they heard; "now they have a way to make it all even out. You killed your husband and, as Franklin just finished telling them, you did it for the money, something that none of them, with their average looks and their average lives, would ever think of doing. They want to believe you're guilty – want to believe it in the worst way, though they would never admit it, even to themselves – because if you are, if you murdered your husband, it means that instead of being better than they are, you're not nearly as good! They want to convict you – don't you understand that yet?"

She heard me, took in every word, but she did not believe me. It is one of the failings of rich men and beautiful women to think that everyone likes them for themselves. After all, everyone they come in contact with is always so nice to them.

"No one feels sorry for the rich. Why should they? The rich buy themselves out of trouble. Don't you know what most people – the kind who do jury duty – think of all the famous, beautiful people like you? - That you're all spoiled and stupid and only worried about yourselves."

It had no discernible effect. Nothing disturbed those perfect mannequin eyes, and I began to wonder if anything ever could. Philosophers and gifted artists may live within their minds, indifferent to what the world thinks important; Danielle, and people like her, lived at the center of the world's attention. Men had always wanted her; women had always wanted to be just like her – Why would anyone ever wish her harm?

I got up and began to prowl aimlessly around the room, glancing vaguely at the pictures and the books and the few articles I had kept as memorabilia from other trials. Perhaps something would remind me of some forgotten tactic or strategic device that might make the jury begin to see her in a new and different light, see her, not as some remote celebrity, a face in the papers, but as someone more like themselves.

"There isn't anyone sitting in the first row behind us to show support. Your mother would come, if you'd ask her."

Danielle fairly bristled at the suggestion.

"If she had wanted to be here, she would have been."

She said this with a cold, implacable expression, as if we were talking about someone she barely knew but did not like, instead of the woman who had raised her.

"I haven't seen her in years," she added, studying her nails. "I certainly don't want to see her now." She threw me a measured glance, and then stood up, ready to go.

"There is one other thing we could do…," I remarked in a cautious, tentative voice. We had talked about it before, or rather I had talked about it and she had listened, but always to no result. Nothing, not even, it seemed, the chances of her own survival, would change her mind. On this point, she was adamant, and the truth was I respected her more for refusing than I would have had she, with whatever reluctance, agreed. Ironic, in that by refusing to do the one thing that might help to make the jury more sympathetic, she proved the jury wrong in their assumption that, rich and beautiful, she cared only for herself.

"No, never," she declared emphatically. "I'll do anything you want, but not that. Michael isn't going to be dragged into this. Think what it would do to him, listening to how his father was murdered and all the reasons his mother did it! And besides," she added with a shrewd insight into how really desperate I had become, "wouldn't the jury just decide that I must be really awful, exploiting my own child like that?"

Exhausted, out of ideas, I sank into the tall leather chair in which I seemed to spend half my life and fell into a long silence. I gestured toward the other chair, but Danielle remained standing, searching my eyes, trying to guess what I was thinking. Whether she had a rare instinct for anticipation or I was just too easy to read, she guessed right.

"It isn't true," she said finally.

My gaze, which had drifted away, swung back; my mind, which had become lazy and confused, was suddenly clear and on point.

"What isn't true? – That you were having an affair, or that Nelson was going to divorce you because of it."

Her eyes grew wider, a mark of interest in the way I

had posed the question; but if there was any emotion behind them – fear that she might have been caught in a lie, anger that she had been accused of something she had not done – I could not find it. A brief smile, an acknowledgment of the logical precision with which the issue had been framed, and then the same studiously blank expression, the only visible sign of what she felt, or rather did not feel, because with her, as I was learning, there was always something missing.

"It isn't true that Nelson was about to start divorce proceedings because I was having an affair."

She could have run for public office, the way she appeared to answer a question while she was evading it. There were not many lawyers as quick to produce a simple statement with a double meaning; nor many actors as able to fashion a smile as ambiguous as Mona Lisa and as enigmatic as Machiavelli. Holding her confident and inscrutable gaze as close as I could, I tried, and failed, to penetrate it with a searching gaze of my own. The game continued.

"He was going to start divorce proceedings for another reason? Or he was not going to start divorce proceedings, though he knew about the affair?"

A smile, similar but even briefer than the first, shadowed her mouth, and then vanished as quickly as it came. She stared down at her hands, held with elegant indifference in her lap, in search, as I thought, for another, more Byzantine, path away from the question. But when she raised her head and looked at me again, I found in her eyes something that seemed more a recognition of defeat, than any sense that she had discovered a new way out.

"Nelson was going to start divorce proceedings as soon as he stopped running from the government, but it was not because I was having an affair. He was having an affair."

I did not believe her. The words were as much a lie as the look of pleading vulnerability that had suddenly come onto her face. It was impossible. Why would Nelson St. James – why would anyone - want another woman when he could have her?

She seemed amused by my stunned reaction.

"That's right: Nelson was going to leave me for another woman. And he would have, too, if he had not been indicted, if he had not had to leave the country and get away. I wasn't surprised; I'd been expecting it."

"Did you know about this – the affair – before he asked for a divorce?"

She looked at me in disbelief, and then laughed out loud.

"Asked? Nelson never asked for anything. He told me he was getting a divorce. He didn't have to tell me why. I knew about the other women; I knew it was only a matter of time."

She had been all day in court, forced to pretend that she was oblivious to the prying eyes, the constant, relentless scrutiny of countless strangers come to look and pass their own private judgment, and now, for nearly an hour, here in my office, questioned again about the same things she had been asked dozens of times before. She was all wound up, tight as a drum, and now, suddenly, she could not do it anymore. Her eyes began to move erratically, darting from one place to the next, and then, without warning, she slapped her hands on the arms of the chair and jumped to her feet.

"I told you I killed him!" she shouted fiercely. "I told you how it happened; I told you why. It was that look on his face, that look that said he owned me and that he could do anything he wanted and there was nothing I could do about it."

She marched to the window, and when she got there spun around on her heel.

"Do you know why I went to bed with him that night, why we had sex? Because after days of telling me that he was going to get a divorce, days of telling me that he would get one even if he could never go back to New York, he told me that evening at dinner that he had made a mistake, that he was sorry for all the things he had said, sorry for the things he had done. And then he said that for the sake of Michael, we should try to make it work."

A strange self-doubt came into her eyes, as if even

now she could not understand how, knowing what she did about her husband, she had let herself be used.

"For the sake of Michael," she repeated, ghostlike, in the failing light that beat a pale reflection on the glass. "There isn't anything I wouldn't do for Michael, and so I went to bed with Nelson and was every bit the uninhibited whore he wanted me to be; and then I saw that look, and I knew that it was all a lie, and that he was going to shove me aside and divorce me after all. He had used me. That was all right; I had used him, too – married him because of who he was and what he had - but that night, that was unforgivable, using Michael, our son, just to have me again. That look told me everything. That look - I couldn't stand it! Something happened, something I can't explain. Something broke, snapped inside. I'd never hated anyone, but that night I hated him!"

Her face went ashen, and a tear started down her cheek. She stood there, staring at me, waiting helpless for me to tell her what to do, and there was nothing, absolutely nothing, I could say.

"All I could think about was Michael, and how he shouldn't have to have a father like that."

It was curious, when I thought about it as a lawyer, how little sense it made. It was not self-defense: she had not acted to save her own life; it was not, according to any legal standard, any defense at all; but it was hard to think that Nelson St. James had not gotten what he deserved. If it was a crime, what she had done, it was a crime of passion, committed in the heat of the moment. But should it be even that? She had been lied to, told by her husband that he had changed his mind, that he did not want a divorce after all. For the sake of their son he wanted to try again. And then, when he was nearly finished with her, finished using her for his own enjoyment, she had seen in his eyes the awful truth of what he had done. She had killed him, but what woman with any self-respect would not have wanted to do the same thing? It was manslaughter, not murder, but under the circumstances should it even be a crime, should a woman be sent off to prison for doing what Danielle had done? The question assumed, of course, that she was telling me the truth, that she had killed her husband for the reason, and in the way, she said she had, but even now, watching her wipe away a tear as, in a wretched halting step, she came back to her chair, I still was not sure.

"But what about you?" I asked quietly in the eerie calm that had descended on the dark, shadowed room.

She ran the back of her fingers a last time across her tear-stained cheek.

"What about me?"

"You said you had known about other women. Had you started seeing other men? Nelson seemed to think so, from what he told me."

She did not ask me what Nelson had said, but launched instead into a bitter attack on his lawyer.

"Did I do what Rufus Wiley is going to say I did? – That evil little bastard with his greedy eyes. He should know all about that pre-nuptial agreement! He's the one who insisted we have one. Nelson did not care. He was embarrassed; he didn't like the way it made him look, like he wasn't sure of what he was doing – or that he wasn't sure about me. He blamed it all on Rufus; or tried to, because in the next breath he was telling me that Rufus was only doing his job, that he had been hired to do what was in Nelson's best interests even if Nelson objected. Nelson could explain away anything. That was part of his charm, the way he made whatever he wanted sound like something you thought he should have."

The tears were gone, her eyes were dry, and there was nothing missing of their former clarity and force. She might have killed her husband, and given all the consequences she had already had to endure she might have felt some regret about that, but there was certainly no remorse. She talked about him and his lawyer as if they were a pair of ruthless conspirators whose only aim in life had been to take advantage of her.

"Rufus knew how to look after Nelson's interests, all

right; because he knew how quickly, once Nelson had what he wanted, Nelson could change his mind. The pre-nuptial agreement might have been Rufus Wiley's idea, but he knew that Nelson would eventually thank him for it."

She shook her head, but not in anger, or even disappointment. There was more to the story, a final chapter that would nullify what the two of them, Nelson St. James and his lawyer, had tried to do.

"That agreement isn't as important as that Mr. Franklin seems to think it is," she said as she rose from the chair and prepared to leave. "He doesn't know about the changes to the will."

"The will?" I asked, realizing that it was not just the prosecution that was in the dark. "What about the will – what changes?"

But she was already thinking about other things.

"I have to go; I have to get back to the hotel. It's three hours later in New York and I have to call Michael to say goodnight."

It was only after she left that I remembered that she had not answered my other question. The one about other men.

CHAPTER NINE

Robert Franklin was hunched over the counsel table a few feet to my left, holding a pencil with both hands, testing it with his flat thumbs to see how much pressure he could apply. His thumb nails dug in opposite directions two irregular grooves into the yellow sides. The pencil began to bend, ready to splinter in half, but as if he knew its exact tolerance, he stopped, let go of one end of it and starting tapping the eraser in a sharp staccato.

It was quiet. Courtrooms, even one as packed as this one with cynical reporters and thrill seeking spectators, usually were; but never as quiet as when someone was on trial for murder and the likely punishment was death. A trial at this level, murder, a capital case, brought with it a sense of solemnity, a reminder of finality, the feeling you might expect to have if, somehow, you could watch someone's funeral in advance. I had not thought about it before, but now it came to me all at once, the way all these strangers, men and women who had never met her, would glance at Danielle, sitting next to me, and then immediately look away. It was not what Franklin had done, look way because he was afraid what his look might show; it was not that at all. They looked away for the same reason we find it hard to look at someone we know is going to die. Death is the one obscenity we still avoid.

Franklin kept tapping the eraser, beating time, measuring the wait. Philip Conrad, the court reporter, sat at his machine like a well-trained and proficient musician just before the moment when, the orchestra ready, the conductor walked on stage and, with a single motion of his baton, started everything into motion. Danielle, in the chair closest to the jury box, not ten feet away, stared straight ahead, lost in thoughts of her own.

I leaned back in the curved wooden chair, chipped and scuffed from years of use, turned away from Franklin and the murderous rhythms of his impatience and looked out at the sea of faces on the chance there might be someone I knew. I was not sure whether it happened to other lawyers, but it was always easier, when I had a trial, to be in the courtroom than home at night worrying about what was going to happen the next day or the day after that. It started the first trial I had. I had not been able to sleep, my mind full of a thousand different possibilities - questions I could ask, answers that might be given – nothing ordered, nothing in its proper sequence, just the jumbled noise of my own helpless incoherence. In the morning, when it was time to go, it got even worse. I had to force myself to get dressed, force myself to leave the safety of home. When I climbed the courthouse steps I learned what it felt like to attend your own execution. And then I opened the door to the courtroom and entered a different world. All the thinking stopped; everything slowed down, everything was easy. I knew what I was doing and, though it may sound strange and even demented, watched myself do it. I did not know what I was going to say before I said it, everything happened on the instant, and there were no second chances. I was like an actor in a play, and though all the lines were different, scarcely ever room for repetition, they came - the way, I'm told, they come to someone on stage - as if of their own volition. I could not get enough of it; the only thing I did not like was the fact that at the end of every day we had to quit.

Franklin stopped tapping the eraser end of the pencil. Holding it between his hands, his fingers pointing forward, he twisted it back and forth, the way campers without matches use the friction from a twig to start a fire. Suddenly, the door at the side flew open and the wraithlike figure of Alice Brunelli blew into court.

Other judges might take their time, look around the courtroom, nod at the clerk or the bailiff or some other familiar face, climb the few short steps onto the bench with slow, deliberate effort, and then settle into the heavy leather chair like someone getting ready to watch a movie; Alice Brunelli came in like a whirling dervish, a tornado, a harsh, bitter wind. The court clerk, out of habit, placed her hand on the stack of papers on her desk when Brunelli passed to keep them being blown onto the floor, and then touched the back of her head to make sure her carefully combed hair was still in place. Alice Longworth Brunelli did not hold her head high - that was not the kind of pride she had - she held it in the way of a prize fighter who cannot wait to get in the ring. She bounded up the three steps to the bench and almost before she hit the chair flashed a quick, razor thin smile and welcomed the jury back to court. Then she glanced at me, but only for a moment, and only to let me know she knew I still existed, and turned immediately to Franklin at the other table.

"You may call your first witness."

Franklin shot straight to his feet. The much abused pencil flew out of his hands, struck the table, ricocheted onto a floor bent and misshapen under the weight of a thousand useless arguments, and then rolled under his abandoned chair. Franklin did not notice. With his shoulders thrown back, he stood there, his gaze squarely focused.

"The People call…."

He hesitated, and everyone remembered what had happened yesterday when, asked to do the same thing, call the first witness in the trial, he had drawn a blank and made to seem a fool. He stared down at the case file, and the needed witness list, open on the table in front of him.

"The People call…."

A sly look, a smile that grew broader and more confident across his face, and suddenly everyone, and especially the jury, knew he was doing it on purpose, reminding them of what he had done, showing that, like them, he could laugh at his own mistakes. There were not many lawyers who could have pulled it off, made a temporary weakness into a permanent strength, taken a minor error and turned it into a major advantage.

"The People call Mustafa Nastasis," he announced in a clear, powerful voice.

The captain of the Blue Zephyr, the captain who, when I first met him, the morning I watched Danielle leave with her husband, had struck me as somehow out of place – What was he going to testify?

Instead of moving close to the witness, from where he could ask questions in a conversational tone, Franklin stood in front of the counsel table, nearly twenty feet away. He had a good voice, moderately deep and unusually vibrant, and, more importantly, a voice that carried into every corner of the room, a voice that held your attention from the sheer sound of it. And he knew it. You could tell from his eyes, the look of pleasure each time he spoke. Too much pleasure, as it seemed to me.

"Mr. Nastasis, you're employed as the captain of the yacht owned by Nelson St. James – Is that correct?"

I was on my feet before the witness could answer.

"I wonder if Mr. Franklin would mind repeating the question, your Honor? I could not quite understand what he said."

Franklin clenched his teeth. In a louder, and slightly rigid, voice, he asked again, "Mr. Nastasis, you work as the captain of the St. James Yacht – correct?"

I bounced back up.

"Objection! Leading."

Alice Brunelli did not look up from what she was reading.

"Sustained."

Franklin was fuming. He knew what it meant to lead a witness, but what difference did it make with a question as routine and commonplace as this? Rolling his eyes to show the jury that the defense lawyer's objection was not only time consuming but stupid, he asked the same question the proper, textbook, way.

"How are you employed, Mr. Nastasis?"

Mustafa Nastasis sat on the witness stand calm and alert, his manicured hands folded in his lap. A shrewd smile stole across his mustached lip, as he watched the brief exchange between the lawyers. His dark, hooded eyes widened with a kind of grudging admiration at the way the judge, a woman, took control. He waited, in no hurry, after Franklin asked the question, glancing past him to see if I was going to again object.

"I am the captain of the yacht – Blue Zephyr – owned by Mr. St. James before his death," he replied finally in a smooth, even cadenced voice.

I remembered his voice, the way he pronounced each word with grammar book precision, and I remembered what he had told me, that strange, enigmatic remark that wherever else they might go, Nelson St. James and his wife always came back to Blue Zephyr. Now St. James was dead, but Nastasis, still vague and unfathomable, did not give the impression that he was burdened with any great grief over the loss.

"Would you tell us what happened that night, what you saw when you were out on deck, the night that Mr. St. James –"

Objection!"

Franklin wheeled around. "Objection?"

"Yes, that's what I said," I replied, returning his look of incredulity with a brief smile of massive indifference.

Alice Brunelli removed her glasses and bent forward, a slightly puzzled expression on her rather long, angular face.

"Objection, Mr. Morrison?"

I raised an eyebrow, as if the point were obvious.

"He asked the witness how he was employed."

"Yes, and…?"

"He asked him how he was employed at the present time; he did not ask him how he was employed then. It may be interesting to know that Mr. Nastasis is today the captain of the St. James yacht; it tells us nothing about how he was employed the night in question and how he happened to be out on deck."

Alice Brunelli did not change expression. Her eyes moved to Franklin. First one interruption, then another; he could barely contain himself.

"It's implicit!" he insisted with ill-concealed contempt.

"What is implicit?" I questioned with all the innocence I could pretend.

"That he was employed then the same way he is now, that he was working there, that he went out on deck, that - !"

"All that because he works there now? That was months ago." With a sidelong glance at the witness, I continued, "Maybe Mr. Nastasis was on board as a guest; maybe he liked it so much he decided he wanted to be there all the time and hired on. Maybe – well, maybe a lot of things," I said, looking Franklin right in the eye, "but we'll never know unless you ask."

Franklin was about to shout that this was mindless, a complete waste of time, but he saw from the stern expression in Brunelli's watching eyes that when it came to the rules of evidence it was not going to be a question of convenience. He threw up his hands in frustration.

"Okay, I'll ask. Tell us, Mr. Nastasis, how were you employed the night you went out on the deck and found the defendant, Danielle St. James, holding a -"

"Objection!" I cried, springing at once to my feet. "The prosecution is again leading the witness."

I could have stopped there, but I wanted to do more than state my objection: I wanted to annoy Franklin, harass him every way I knew, do anything I could to throw him off, make him lose his temper. I had to attack his vanity, lecture him on the finer points of the law, treat him as I knew everything and he knew nothing. I had to drive him crazy, if I could.

"The witness has to describe what, if anything, he found," I explained in a tone that suggested this must be news to the prosecution. "It isn't the prosecution's place to tell him."

Franklin began to protest, but Brunelli had had enough. She waved him off and in almost the same motion crouched forward so she could better see the witness and the witness could see her.

"Mr. Nastasis," she began, "were you employed as the captain of the St. James yacht on the night in question?"

The Greek captain with the Turkish mother seemed to enjoy it, the way a woman had put a man in his place; but only, I suspected, because it proved that Franklin was not the man he ought to be.

"Yes, your Honor; I was."

"On the night in question," she went on with measured efficiency, "approximately what time did you go out on deck?"

"It was a few minutes past midnight."

"And what was the reason you went out on deck at that hour?"

"I heard loud voices – screaming – and then I heard what sounded like a gunshot," replied Nastasis, speaking slowly and with precision. "I found Mrs. St. James standing there, with a gun in her hand. There was blood on the deck, on the railing, blood where Mr. St. James -"

Brunelli held up her hand and stopped him there.

"Yes, thank you, Mr. Nastasis."

She drew back from the front corner of the bench and turned to Franklin whose face had turned seven shades of red. It did not matter that he was prosecuting the case, it did not matter that he had prosecuted hundreds of cases before; trial was combat, even if words were the only weapons, and in her courtroom you had only yourself to blame if you thought the rules too formal, or too antiquated, and that you could pick the ones you wanted. If you could not ask the right questions of your own witness, thought you could trifle with the rules of evidence, then, by God, she would do it for you and let the jury draw its own conclusions about whether you should be trying cases in a court of law. When she gave the witness back to Franklin she looked at him as if she wondered how he had ever gotten through law school, much less become a member of the bar.

Franklin was not going to take it. He turned to face the witness but his eyes never left the woman who had just humiliated him.

"I'd ask you a question, Mr. Nastasis," he said with cold, deliberate indifference to what he knew would be the consequences, "but I'm not sure I know one that the defense attorney would not object to and the judge would not sustain!"

Alice Brunelli shot out of her chair.

"Are you suggesting collusion between the court and a party to this case?" She fixed with him a lethal stare that would have made a weaker man tremble, but only seemed to increase Franklin's defiance. "If I were you, Mr. Franklin, I would think very seriously about my answer."

Alice Longworth Brunelli had finished near the top of her class at Yale; Robert George Franklin had gone to night school and finished somewhere in the great amorphous middle of his class. She could have joined any law firm in the city; he could not have gotten so much as an interview. They came from completely different worlds and they knew it. Without meaning to, she looked down on him, a night school lawyer who, from her perspective, cared only about winning and nothing about the law; while he, on the other hand, resented the way she and all the other Ivy League lawyers thought what was taught at Yale or Harvard was more important than what he had learned on the streets. He put up with her because he had to, but he did not have to like it. He had had his moment of revenge; he knew what he had to do next.

"I apologize, your Honor," he said in a voice that fairly bragged an absence of conviction. "I can assure you that it wasn't -"

With a brusque motion of her hand, so quick it might have caught a fly, she cut him off.

"Take the witness, Mr. Franklin. Let's move on – we haven't got all day."

But before he could ask a question, she cut him off again.

"Mr. Morrison," she rasped impatiently, "I trust that you're not going to raise objections just for the sake of objecting?"

"No, your Honor," I replied. "I'll only object to questions that are objectionable."

She raised an eyebrow and lifted her chin, the preface to a warning, notice that if I made another objection it better damn well be one the rules of evidence would support.

"Mr. Franklin, please continue."

Franklin had a whole set of questions; not one of them, he was certain, leading or otherwise objectionable.

"Mr. Nastasis, would you please describe to the jury what you did when you saw the defendant standing there with the gun in her hand, after she had shot and killed her husband."

I was on my feet, shouting another objection. Some of the jurors smiled to themselves; all of them leaned forward, anxious to see what would happen now..

"The question assumes facts not in evidence," I explained, shrugging my shoulders to show that I could not be blamed for the mistakes of the other side. "No evidence has yet been introduced that Nelson St. James had been shot, much less that he was dead."

Franklin nearly laughed. He had me now; he was certain of it.

"The witness just testified, under your Honor's thorough examination, that – I believe the exact phrase was, 'There was blood on the deck, on the railing, blood where Mr. St. James –' He's testified, in other words, that the victim was shot and –"

"That may have been what he thought," I interjected, "that may have been his impression, but the fact has not yet been proven. The prosecution cannot ask a question that assumes, and by that assumption suggests to the jury, that it has."

Brunelli did not need to think about it.

"Sustained. Rephrase the question, Mr. Franklin."

And so it went on, hour after hour, testimony that should have taken twenty minutes lasting three or four times that long. I used everything I knew about the law of evidence and when there was not a rule I could use, made one up. I would not give an inch, and neither would he. There were no more cries of outrage, no more scornful looks. He asked a question, I objected; he waited for the ruling and, if he had to, asked the question a different way again. He never made the same mistake twice, and like a sullen, but determined student, he filed away each lesson for his own, later use. By the end of it, his direct examination of the prosecution's first witness, he had so far regained his confidence that he was close to the jury box, talking to Mustafa Nastasis as if they were two old friends, almost smiling whenever, through my frequent interruptions I tried to join the conversation. Then, when he was finally finished, it was my turn.

Nastasis had been kept on the stand for hours, forced to wait while the lawyers argued among themselves, but he had not seemed to mind. Perhaps it was the novelty of the situation, his first time inside an American courtroom; or perhaps, like the other spectators who sat, transfixed by the proceedings, he was intrigued by what had happened, the violent death of Nelson St. James and the question whether Danielle St. James was going to get away with it. As I rose to begin cross-examination, he regarded me with more respect, and considerably more interest, than he had that morning we first met on the deck of Blue Zephyr.

I took a position at the end of the jury box, where, along the double line of juror's faces, I could look straight at him.

"You testified you went out on deck because you heard 'loud voices – screaming.' Where exactly were you when you heard those voices – in your cabin?"

"Yes," he replied, a polite smile on his lips.

"But you weren't asleep, were you?"

"No."

"The voices weren't so loud – what you called 'screaming' – that they woke you up?"

"No, Mr. Morrison; as I say, I was not asleep."

I looked down at the floor, smiling to myself as if what I was driving at was so obvious I should not have to ask, and only after a long silence raised my eyes.

"What was the screaming about?" I asked patiently. "What were they saying?"

"I don't really know. I couldn't hear the words."

"You couldn't hear the words. I see. You heard 'loud

voices – screaming'….Which is it, Mr. Nastasis: loud voices or screaming?"

He did not grasp the distinction. With a puzzled expression he shrugged.

"It's not a difficult question, Mr. Nastasis. People sometimes speak in loud voices to make themselves heard; sometimes they do it to make a point. In either case, they have control of themselves. When they're screaming, on the other hand, they don't. So, again, Mr. Nastasis – which is it? Screaming, wasn't it? The cabins on the yacht are nearly soundproof, aren't they?"

Now he understood.

"Yes, screaming; shouting, if you prefer. They were angry – I have no doubt."

"Angry, out of control, irrational – are those the words you would use to describe what you heard?"

Nastasis agreed immediately. I nodded emphatically and turned to the jury.

"Angry, irrational – not the voice of someone about to execute a calculated plan of -"

"Objection!" thundered Franklin as he bolted from his chair.

I threw up both hands.

"That's right, I shouldn't have," I admitted before Judge Brunelli could rule. I turned back to the witness.

"You said you heard screaming, and then heard a shot – what you thought was a gunshot. How much time passed between the moment the screaming stopped and when you heard the shot? Seconds, minutes – how long?"

Pinching his lips together, Nastasis stared into the middle distance, trying to remember. As the silence lengthened, I began methodically to tap two fingers on the jury box railing. Finally, Nastasis gave up.

"I don't know. Not as long as it seemed."

My mouth dropped open.

"Not as long as…? Yes, I see. The screaming stopped, then there was nothing – not a sound – and then you heard it. Is that what you mean?"

"Exactly, just as you describe, with only one addition. The silence, which may have lasted only seconds, seemed so much longer because it served to underscore the violent noise both before and after it."

He paused to consider what he had said. Satisfied that it was just the way he had said it was, he nodded once more. He was ready for the next question, but instead I walked back to the counsel table and Danielle. I stood there a moment, looking down at her, as if we both knew something of great importance. A shrewd, knowing smile edged its way across my mouth as I turned again to the witness.

"The gun that Mrs. St. James was holding in her hand – How long had she been holding it?"

Nastasis shook his head in confusion.

"I don't…."

"Had she just picked it up?" I asked sharply as I took a quick step forward. "You testified that you heard what you thought was a gunshot. That was the reason you left your cabin, the reason you came out on deck. You didn't actually witness the gun being fired, did you?" I insisted. "As a matter of fact, you didn't see who fired that gun, did you? I'll repeat – Had she just picked it up when you came out on deck?"

"I don't know," he replied, taken aback by the sudden violence of my questioning. "I just -"

"You don't know. Thank you. Now tell me this," I went on as I began to pace in front of the counsel table. "You had been the captain of the St. James yacht for…." I stopped, looked up and smiled. "Since Nelson St. James had it built, correct?"

"Yes, that's correct; since the day it was christened."

"Blue Zephyr. How did he happen to pick that name, do you know?"

"He came across it in some book he read: A novel, I think; something about a murder in Hollywood. He said it was much more than that, and that he identified with one of the characters, a director falsely accused of murdering his movie star wife. Blue Zephyr was the name of a movie.

That's all he told me."

"You got to know Mr. St. James fairly well, then?"

The response was cold, measured, and, I suspected, utterly dishonest.

"I worked for Mr. St. James. That was the nature of our relationship."

Apparently, Mustafa Nastasis was not interested in helping the dead. Was he interested in helping the living? I took a chance.

"He wasn't an easy man to work for, was he?"

Nastasis pressed his finger to his mouth, weighing in the balance, as it seemed, what he remembered about St. James and what he knew about human behavior. I tried to help him along.

"Not an easy man..., but you liked Mrs. St. James, didn't you? Nelson St. James may not have treated you very well, but you could always count on her for a kind word, couldn't you?"

He did not have to think about his answer, there were no complexities to unravel, no subtle shades of meaning to disentangle. His response was immediate and, so far as anyone could tell, utterly sincere.

"Yes, Mrs. St. James was always pleasant, not just with me, but with all the members of the crew. She always asked questions about my family, where I came from, that sort of thing. They were wealthy people, but you wouldn't have known it from the way she treated us."

My suspicion had been correct. I was certain of it now. Mustafa Nastasis might have been called by the prosecution, but he was my witness.

"You saw them earlier that evening, while they were having dinner, didn't you?"

"I looked in on them to see if there was anything they needed."

I smiled, not to put Nastasis on his ease, but to give the jury every reason to think that all I wanted was the truth.

"And when you saw them having dinner together, just a few short hours before he was shot to death, did Mrs. St.

James look like a woman planning to murder her husband?"

Franklin had to object. I wanted him to object. That was the reason I asked the question in the way I did. He was on his feet, starting on a long oration on why the question could not be asked, but Brunelli did not need to take lessons on the law of evidence.

"Sustained!" she ruled with clinical indifference before Franklin could say another word.

Now! Do it now, I told Nastasis with my eyes. Say it now! Whether he caught my meaning, or did it on his own, he did it.

"No, she didn't look like a woman planning to murder her husband," he answered with a blameless gaze.

"'Sustained,' means that you're not supposed to answer the question," explained Brunelli with a stern glance. "The jury will disregard both the question and the answer."

Then she studied me, a silent warning that she would only be pushed so far. It may have been nothing more than my imagination, which in this instance might be just another name for vanity, but just behind the formal disapproval I thought I saw a faint glimmer of recognition, quiet admiration for the skill, if not the judgment, of what I had done: elicited without a word to prove it a flagrant violation of the rules. I went back to the witness.

"I can't ask you that question, Mr. Nastasis. Let me ask you this instead: Before that night, during the entire course of that lengthy voyage, did you ever see her throw anything at him?"

"No."

"Hit him?"

"No."

"Did you ever see her threaten him with a gun?"

"No," he said, his dark impenetrable eyes wide and intense.

"Just a few more questions. After you heard the shot, after you rushed outside and saw blood on the deck and on the railing, when you saw the defendant, Danielle St. James, standing there with the gun in her hand, you thought she had killed her husband, didn't you?"

Nastasis hesitated, unsure quite how to answer. I told him it was all right, that all anyone wanted was the truth.

"Yes, I have to admit I thought that. It's what I assumed."

"But if, as I asked you earlier, she had only just picked up the gun – in a state of shock picked it up from where it had fallen – then you would have thought something else, wouldn't you? – Not that Danielle St. James had murdered her husband, but that her husband had killed himself!"

Franklin was bellowing an objection, but I did not care. I sat down at the table, more than satisfied with what I had done.

CHAPTER TEN

Judge Brunelli cautioned the jurors not to discuss the case and not to read about it in the papers, or watch any of the reported accounts of the trial on television. Aware, as always, that people had their eyes on us, I gathered up the notes and papers scattered on the table and exchanged a few brief words with Danielle. Although nothing had happened between us after that night when I had pulled back at the last moment from making what would have been a serious mistake, I had made a point of treating her with a new formality. We did not talk about what might have happened, or whether something might happen later; we talked only about the trial. The situation was forced and artificial, pretending she was just another client, instead of a woman with whom, if I were honest with myself, I was probably already in love, but there was nothing else I could do. She was a criminal defendant and I was her lawyer and I had to concentrate on that. It was a strange pantomime I went through, keeping a respectable distance as I got ready to leave the courtroom, barely touching her on her arm, the way I would have done with any other woman on trial for her life, telling her, in case anyone was close enough to overhear, that I would see her in the morning and that she should try to get some rest. Then I left her in the hands of a bodyguard, waiting just behind the railing to take her to a waiting car. Eager to get a closer look at the famous and now notorious Danielle St. James, the surging crowd followed her outside.

I was glad to be left alone, able to walk down the deserted corridor and into an empty men's room without worrying who was going to assault me next with a question they had to ask or an observation they felt compelled to share. It was embarrassing, when you thought about it, this need for attention, this desire for the acknowledgement of other people, and, when we have it, the tired hypocrisy of wishing it would all go away. It was like the difference between how we look and how we feel, what we show the world and what we know inside. Like the face I now saw in the mirror, which looked better, less exhausted, than I felt; seeing it, I felt much better than I had before.

Throwing some cold water on my face, I reached for a paper towel. Then I heard it, an awful, retching noise from one of the stalls at the far end of the narrow, white tile room. As quickly as I could, I dried my hands and face and turned to go; but just then the stall door flew open and Robert Franklin, his face white as a sheet, staggered toward the sink. He had not heard anyone come in, and the shock of seeing me was so intense, so profound, that he seemed to lose his senses. He opened his mouth, struggling to find an explanation, an excuse, for the condition in which I had found him, but three words into it he began to stutter and could not stop.

That was when I first began to understand something of the effort with which Robert Franklin had made himself into a lawyer. He had a speech impediment – a stutter as awful as any I had ever heard – and yet had somehow overcome it. That was the reason he started out at such a distance from the witness and the jury: not because he loved the sound of his own voice, not because of vanity; but because he had with a stringent discipline I could not even imagine, he had trained himself to speak the words he wanted without falling into a bottomless well of hellish repetition.

"Are you all right?" I asked, stung by a guilty conscience. "Is there anything I can do?"

Franklin took a deep breath, and then, to my surprise, laughed in a quiet, self-deprecating way and patted me gently on the arm. His eyes, so often filled with what seemed dark malevolence, were almost friendly.

"I could tell you it was something I ate, but the truth is that I always get too tense at a trial. I wish I could be more like you; you always look like you're having the time of your life in there. I envy that."

I tried to remind myself, as I walked out of the courthouse, that no one took prisoners in a trial, that it was all about winning, but I began to regret a little the way I had pushed things, objecting to nearly every question, doing what I could to make Franklin look mean tempered and insensitive. He had not just worked his way through night school, he had overcome a handicap, forced himself through God knows what difficult and painful exercises to become a lawyer; and not just any kind of lawyer, but a courtroom lawyer, a prosecuting attorney who had to speak clearly, who had to make sense, who could not afford to get all tangled in knots. We were both in it to win, but I started asking myself whether I was going too far, throwing sand in the eyes of the jury, turning the serious business of a murder case into a carnival game in which, if I could get away with it, the prosecutor instead of the defendant was put on trial.

I tried to sort it all out. If you looked only at the facts and ignored what people feel, the way the mind can snap with sufficient provocation, there was no question but that Danielle was guilty. She had not been in any physical danger when she killed her husband. She could have walked away; there had not been any necessity for violence. But if you had any regard for a woman's self-respect, her right to be treated as a person with feelings of her own, and not just the muffled object of her husband's temporary lust, then what she had done was defensible at least in a moral sense. Or was I only trying to make myself feel better, invent an excuse for the lawyer's tricks I was playing in court? Danielle had killed her husband because she did not like his look, because she 'could not stand it anymore.' If she had felt humiliated, why not humiliate him in return instead of killing him? She did not have to let him have his divorce; she could have taken him to court and, precisely because he was rich and famous - and not just that: notorious, with who knew how many secrets to hide – made his life a living hell. But it was an impulse, there had not been time to think; it happened before she knew it. That is what she told me, but then she had told me a lot of things that did not always fit together.

I was almost at the end of the corridor. The glass doors at the entrance were just ahead. It was after five, and except for the uniformed guard at his desk, the only other person around was someone standing off to the side, leaning against the wall reading a newspaper.

"So, are you screwing her yet?" he said as I passed by him.

I spun around, ready to dare him to repeat it, and then I started to laugh. It was Tommy, Tommy Lane, looking at me with a cocky grin, daring me to deny it.

"No, I'm – What are you doing here?" I asked as we gave one another a hug. I forgot all about the trial, forgot about everything, except how glad I was to see him. "When did you get here – just now?"

"Are you kidding? I've been here all day, watching you work."

I could not believe that he had come all the way up from southern California and had not called me first. He explained that he had come to see the game.

"What game?"

"USC, Southern Cal. Who else? They're playing Berkeley on Saturday. You didn't know?" he remarked, shaking his head as we headed out the door and down the courthouse steps to the street. He moved with that same smooth suppressed power, his head up, his eyes darting all around: the graceful remnant of the great athlete he once had been. Watching him I felt better, younger, than I had felt in a long time.

"You didn't know?" he laughed. "That sounds like you. So wrapped up in what you're doing, you don't know what's going on. Southern Cal – remember? We went to school there once, played football, chased girls... is it coming back to you now?" he chided.

He stopped so quickly I had to take a step back to where he was standing. The sidewalk was crowded, the street full of noise, and while the sky was dark the lights from all the busy stores and the passing cars made it almost seem like day. "You were great in there – did I tell you that? Best I've ever seen. That other guy – Franklin – he's not bad; but, Christ, no match for you! You're good, not bad at all; almost made me think she might not have done it. Almost," he added significantly before he turned on his heel and started down the street again.

"Where are we going?" he asked a moment later. "Let's have dinner somewhere. You have time, don't you? I mean, even during a trial you remember sometimes to eat, don't you?"

"Ever occur to you I might have a date?"

"Great! I'd love to meet her," he said without breaking stride. "You have a date, night of a trial - what a laugh! Unless - ?" He grabbed my arm and made me face him, eager to make me try to lie about it. "With her?"

"If I'm screwing her, don't you think the least I can do is buy her dinner once in a while?"

"You're not screwing her." He searched my eyes just to be sure. "I'd be screwing her," he added with the proud exaggeration of remembered triumphs. "But you – no, you're too caught up in the trial. It's just like before, all you could think about was the game. We'd run into the stadium, the crowd going nuts, and I'd check out all the cheerleaders, but you wouldn't even notice." He started laughing, and without any idea why he was doing it, I started laughing too, knowing that, whatever it was, as soon as he told me I would be laughing even harder.

"That last year, the last game, regular game, before the Rose Bowl game. We were playing UCLA – and let's face it, they always had the best looking cheerleaders – I took the second half kickoff back for a touchdown. All the blocking was set up down the left side, and I started that way, but then went the other way instead. Everyone thought it was a brilliant decision, something I saw in the coverage – What a joke! There was this great looking blonde – a cheerleader, one of theirs – standing on the sideline on about the thirty. I wanted to run right by her, and I did, and when I got there, knew I was going all the way, I yelled at her, told her to give me her number after the game."

"Did she?"

"Did she what?"

"Leave you her number?"

Tommy threw me a blank look of incomprehension, as if it were the dumbest question he had ever heard, and then first his shoulders, and then his chest, began to rumble.

"Of course! Why do you think I ran all that way?- So she couldn't say no!"

"You're lucky your dick didn't fall off, with all the girls you had."

He did not miss a beat; he almost never did.

"It did, but that's all right, it grew back twice as big. Where the hell we going for dinner? I'm getting tired of walking." Before I could answer, he thought of something else, another way to taunt me about the different way we had led our lives, and, doing it, remind me how much we had in common. "Listen, it wasn't my fault, all those women. Look at it this way: they all wanted to sleep with me, but they all wanted to marry you."

I gave him a look that questioned both his veracity and his sense of proportion.

"That's supposed to make me feel better?"

It went on like this, back and forth, half said sentences and words heavy with our own peculiar meaning, phrases that made no sense but launched long paragraphs about our remembered and no doubt embellished past, paragraphs that were even more outrageous when they told the whole, unvarnished truth. We were half a block past the restaurant before I realized it was the place we were looking for.

It was a small Italian restaurant, started by an old Sicilian while he was still young and staffed by two aging waiters who, because of some ancient quarrel, the cause of which they had both forgotten, would only speak when necessary and only through a third party. Generally this was the owner, who would stand between them and, like a good translator, listen carefully before he rendered word for word an exact repetition of what was said. The menu was as old as the owner and just as reliable. I had been coming here for years and, no matter how many times I told him, he could not remember my name, but he always greeted me with open arms.

"Mr...., how long has it been? Too long, too long!"

"I was here last night."

"Yes, I know," he lied, the grin on his face cutting deeper until he managed to make it look like sorrow; "but even a day is too long. You weren't here for lunch. I think you never come for lunch," he added with downcast eyes. "You can imagine the grief we feel." He gestured for one of the waiters and then whispered, "One of these silent assassins I employ will take care of you. The ravioli is quite good tonight. Almost edible. Someday I'll find a cook!"

"You come here a lot?" asked Tommy after we ordered.

"All the time. I like the anonymity of the place. Tourists don't know about it, and the locals mind their own business. And despite what the owner said, it's some of the best food in the city."

Tommy was hungry, and so was I. We ate French bread and drank red wine and as we felt better, more comfortable and relaxed, we began to talk more about the present.

"I was not going to come at first. It's a free trip - the alumni association pays for everything – but I don't like living in the past the way a lot of these guys do. It was the best time of my life, but what's the point? – You can't go back and do it again. I wasn't going to come, but then you had this trial and we had talked about St. James before; and so I said I would, but only if I could come up a day or so early, instead of flying up with everyone else Friday afternoon." He wrinkled his nose in disgust. "You know what those things are like: camp out at the hotel night before a game, everybody gets drunk and tells a lot of lies, and then, because we used to be great, we stand out there on the sidelines and some idiot television reporter comes up and asks you what you're doing now that your great career is over. Last time that happened, I looked into the camera and said I was an attorney with the government and we were looking into corruption in the television industry. They didn't ask me anything after that. So, as I say, it was a free trip, and I figured at that price you were worth it."

He took another piece of bread and finished off his glass. Glancing around to make sure no one at the tables near us could hear, he asked me about the case, or rather, asked about Danielle.

"She's really Jean's sister? I met her, couple of times," he added when I seemed surprised that he remembered. "I liked her. She was great looking, in a different kind of way. I liked her a lot. Maybe too outgoing for you, too interested in what was going on. Was that it? She was a little like my wife that way, wasn't she? They both liked having a good time, being around other people."

I did not say anything; I did not need to. We both knew he was right. With a marvelous talent for summation, he cut right to the heart of the matter.

"But this one, the sister – she's the kind that makes you think she only wants to be around you. Even when she's with other people, the center of attention, she lets you know, she has that look that says she'd run off with you in a minute, if only she had the chance."

I tried to dismiss it with a laugh, but the laughter died on my lips and I gave him what might be called a second look, a closer scrutiny that admitted that what he said was nearer to the truth than I might have wanted.

"That's the real reason I came up. Don't misunderstand," he added immediately. "I wanted to see you; I wanted to watch how you handled yourself in court. But I wanted to warn you: she's dangerous. Hell, any woman that looks like that is dangerous. That's not what I mean."

Before he could tell me precisely what he did mean, the silent waiter brought our order. He wore the same expression of doubt and disappointment he always did when you had not bothered to ask him what he recommended, a lifted eyebrow, the mocking certainty that if you had only listened to him you would have ordered something else.

"It's even worse," I explained to Tommy as he tried the ravioli, "if you ask him what he thinks and decide on something else. I did that once. Next time I came in, he wouldn't serve me. He stood off in the corner like I wasn't here. Wouldn't move."

"And you like this place?"

I glanced around, as if I were seeing it for the first time, a small, unpromising place, without any obvious attractions: tarnished silverware and threadbare tablecloths, a worn carpet and dull lighting, and a clientele that for the most part came only out of habit.

"Like it? I'm used to it. I come here, I don't have to think. It's like court: everything works, once you learn the rules.

"And you're right about the food," said Tommy with enthusiasm as he lapped up another helping.

"After a while," I confessed, "you don't even notice that – until you go somewhere else. Then you realize that it's better here."

Tommy put down his fork and with a faded linen napkin wiped his mouth.

"That's all you do, isn't it? – Practice law, try cases, and eat dinner here. Did you ever think you might want to have a life?"

"I have a life," I protested mildly, and a little defensively. "I like what I do."

"What about women? After Jean – that was years ago. You ever think about…?"

"You're divorced – Do you?"

"Marriage? Again – hell, I don't know. Depends. Never know, I might. But you!" he cried, ready to taunt me with what he knew about me. "You won't – not unless…. No, that won't happen. But someone like her, someone that perfect…."

"What are you talking about?"

"Danielle St. James. Lot of guys would like to go to bed with her, but you'd fall in love with her. It's like everything you've ever done." His eyes glittered with the achievement of his own discovery, what he had finally figured out, though he had really always known it. "Nothing was ever good enough because you could always see how it could be better. Used to make me a little nuts, to tell you the God's honest truth," he laughed. "Good thing I loved you like a brother, because, Christ, you could be annoying! Remember the game against Stanford? I broke one off for eight yards just before half, and what did you tell me as we walked off the field? – That if I had kept my head up when I hit the hole, I could have cut faster to the right!"

I remembered, and it was true, and I felt like a fool because of it; but it was a long time ago and so now I could laugh and admit that I might have taken things a little too seriously. Tommy shook his head, but with affection, the way you do for someone you like who tries hard to do something at which he is not very good, and then he reached across the table and took my wrist and told me that none of that mattered.

"Listen to me. I had speed, I knew what I could do; I didn't have to work at it. But the truth is that I wish I had been more like you, that things hadn't come so easy. I might have learned something, how to get better, how important it is to work. There's something else, and I mean this: You're a hell of a lot better in a courtroom than I ever was on a football field, but you still don't think it's good enough. That's something else I found out today. I had lunch with the court reporter."

"Philip Conrad? You had lunch with him?"

"In the courthouse cafeteria. It was crowded. I saw him sitting alone at a table, asked if I could join him. I told him I'd been with the U.S. Attorney's office in L.A. That didn't impress him. I told him you and I had gone to school together. He got all excited. Told me you were his favorite lawyer, said he was the court reporter in one of the first cases you took to trial. He seemed surprised when I told him we played ball together. Said he didn't know that about you, that you had never mentioned it. He wanted to know what you were like then, and I wasn't quite sure what to tell him. He doesn't strike me as the kind who wants to hear about how you played; he's too serious for that. He wanted to know who you were. I told him how you used to watch film. You didn't care much about the plays that didn't work; you said anyone could see what was wrong with them. You only really studied the ones that worked, not to see why they worked, but what could be done to make them work even better."

Tommy rested his elbows on the table and folded his hands together in front of his mouth. A distant look came into his eyes, remembering, I think, what we had both been like, all those years ago. It lasted only a second, and then a smile flashed across his face and he started back on the story he wanted to tell me.

"His eyes – Conrad, the court reporter; nice man, by the way – got all wide and eager. He had to tell me something. The first trial, the first of yours in which he was the court reporter, a case no one thought you had a chance to win... He said he had never seen anything like it, the way you destroyed the prosecution's main witness with one of the most devastating cross-examinations he had ever seen, and done it so easily that it almost seemed as if the witness had only been waiting for the chance to tell the jury that everything he had said to the prosecuting attorney had been a lie. But that surprise wasn't anything like what happened next, after the trial was over."

Tommy looked at me with a baffled expression and then started laughing. He threw up his hands, exuberant that someone else, an anonymous court reporter, had had the same experience, and with the same reaction, as his own.

"He's sitting there in his cubbyhole office, and this young lawyer – barely out of law school, only had two or three trials – comes in and starts to ask how much it will cost to get a transcript of the trial. Tells him he knows he charges by the page, but if he tells him how much it might run, he can pay him something now and the rest when it's finished. The guy didn't know what to think. He knows you're pretty damn good in a courtroom, but you obviously don't know much about the law.

"'You only appeal when you lose, Mr. Morrison,' he explains. 'That's the only time you need to go back through the transcript: when you have to find some judicial mistake, some error of law. And the prosecution can't appeal a verdict of acquittal in a criminal case, so you see, there's no need to bother with a transcript. You won, Mr. Morrison, and the prosecution can't appeal. There's nothing more you have to do.'

"And then, to his astonishment, you tell him that's the reason you want the transcript. He still hasn't forgotten what you said.

"'I know I won; I thought I better find out why.'

"You weren't interested in any mistakes the judge might have made. That's what Conrad told me. You were only interested in mistakes of your own, things you might have done better, ways you might improve. And it wasn't just in that trial you did it; you've done it in every trial since, all the years you've been practicing. That's you, all right: nothing is ever good enough; you can always do it better. Must make you crazy, knowing no matter how hard you try, nothing is ever going to be perfect."

He moved his right shoulder back and turned his head, looking at me, as it seemed, not just from a different angle but with a new perspective.

"That's why she's got you, isn't it? It's how she looks. That's got to be about as perfect as it gets. It's probably what made St. James do half the things he did, at least in the beginning when he was first with her. Looks like…."

He paused, remembering something, or perhaps it just now came to him, the thought that brought everything together, made sense out of at least some of what had happened. He bent forward, searching my eyes in a way that told me that this was important and that it was important for me.

"That's what they both did, as near as I can tell: made themselves crazy trying to have it all. Ask the question no one takes seriously anymore: why didn't he quit, and get out when it was still safe? Why did he keep going after more? And more than the money, why did he have to have her? And why did she have to have him? The reason is that they didn't know what they wanted, only that it had to be more. That's what I was trying to tell you, the reason I wanted to see you: to warn you, if you didn't know it already. She may have been the kid sister of the girl you wanted to marry, but she isn't a kid anymore, and whatever she was like then…."

I stopped him with a look that said there was nothing he could tell me about Danielle I had not already thought about.

"I'm her lawyer. She's on trial for murdering her husband. What is it you think I don't know?"

There was now no more nostalgia. We were not reminiscing about the past. We were two lawyers, still good friends, but too experienced to yield to the illusions of younger men. We had been burned too often to take very much on trust.

"She did it, didn't she? – I know you can't tell me, but it makes sense. What was she going to do, sail around the world the rest of her life, married to a fugitive, never able to come home?"

"He might not have been able to come back, but she could have. He was the one indicted."

Troubled and momentarily disconcerted, Tommy stared off into the distance, pondering, as it seemed, some dilemma. The only thing I could tell for certain that, whatever it was, it had to do with Danielle.

"I'm not supposed to….I quit working for the government, but there are still things – open cases – I'm not supposed to talk about. But screw it, you need to know. There would have been another indictment. After they got her husband, they would have gone after her. They still might," he hastened to add. "If you get her off, if she doesn't go down on the murder conviction. It's a tougher case, with him dead, but a lot of people got hurt, and if they can't get him, they'll try to get her."

"Get her for what? She was married to him. She wasn't the one defrauding all those investors with that scheme of his."

There is a look that grows on people as they get older,

a look that gives expression to what they have done. Doctors, priests, day laborers and shifty eyed thieves all have it, badges of their professions, and while Tommy still moved like the athlete he had been born to be, he had acquired the gaze of the practiced prosecutor, the knowing glance that holds more secrets than you ever thought existed.

"You were out there, on that yacht of theirs, with their other guests. You watched them both – more than that, from what I remember – Do you really think she didn't know what was going on? You really think she didn't know exactly what she was doing? We had them under surveillance for years, tracked them everywhere they went. She was always there, on the Blue Zephyr, where he did most of his business. Every time someone came on board she was there to greet them."

Pushing his empty plate to the side, he reached for his glass, but just as he picked it up he had a thought that took him back again into the past, though not the one we had lived together.

"She changed her name, from what it was when you knew her, to Danielle. He did the same thing, a long time ago, before he ever came to New York. He grew up in a small town in Michigan, Petoskey, a little north of Traverse City. His father had a gas station; his mother ran off with someone else. Ray Williams, that was his name, about as plain as you can get, dropped out of high school in the tenth grade, lied about his age and joined the army. Then he sold insurance for a while, made enough money to buy a few old houses, turned them for a profit, and then – he had a kind of genius for this – started doing the same thing with bigger properties, office buildings, then companies, and then…. Then Nelson St. James became rich as hell and no one asked questions about how he got it, only how he could help them get rich as well. They both invented themselves. That's what they had in common. Funny, when you think about it, no one ever looked at either one of them when they were kids just growing up. I suppose that's part of what drove them, the need to do something that would get them noticed."

I wondered, from the way he looked at me, the things he had said about how nothing had ever been good enough, that I was always trying to get better, if he thought the same thing had driven me. Perhaps it had. All I knew was that one of the reasons I had always liked him, why he was the only friend I had, is that Tommy Lane had once had the great good fortune to be so much better than anyone else at what he did that he had not had to worry about anything except the pure enjoyment of what he did. If he was not lying when he said he wished he had been more like me, he should have been.

CHAPTER ELEVEN

A light rain had started to fall and the night air was cool and clean. The street in front of the restaurant was a shiny black mirror full of neon lights and changing colors. A young woman walked by, laughing as the man she was with struggled to hold an umbrella over her head while his other arm was around her waist. Across the street, two middle-aged men in dark, well-tailored suits, dashed from the front door of another, more exclusive, eating place to a waiting cab. A second taxi was just coming around the corner.

"Are you sure you don't want to stay with me? There's plenty of room."

"Next trip," said Tommy as we shook hands. "When you're not in the middle of a trial. I'll come up and we can spend a few days."

The cab driver reached behind him and opened the door. Tommy put his hand on my shoulder and gave me a serious look.

"Remember what I told you. Be careful. There are some other things…." His voice trailed off, and I did not know whether they were things he did not think he should tell me or things he was not sure were true. His eyes took on a sudden urgency. "She killed him – remember that. You may get her off, but it won't be because she's innocent."

Tommy had always known me better than I knew myself. He was worried about me because he understood my vulnerabilities. He had a habit of warning about things – women, mainly that he knew I could not resist. The warnings had never done any good, except to prove later, though he would never say so, that he had been right all along.

The cab driver was waiting. Tommy flashed that huge smile of his, put his arm around my neck, suddenly kissed me on the side of my face, and said with affection, "You're the best fuck-up I ever knew. Whatever happens, you'll always land on your feet."

I watched him get into the cab, watched the way he

began a cheerful banter with the driver, watched while the cab wove through the nighttime traffic, watched until the tail lights vanished around the corner, and then watched in my mind the things he had done when he and I were both young.

The weather, instead of getting worse, got better and the rain became a fine mist that swirled around like the thin fog that sometimes comes on summer nights and makes the visitors from out of town think its winter. I started walking up the hill, the steep ascent on sidewalks grooved like washboards to keep from slipping backward those brave or foolish enough to try it. At the top, two blocks ahead of me, across the street from the Fairmont, the other famous old hotel, the Mark Hopkins, was lit up like Christmas, with limousines and taxi cabs and shiny dark sedans and sleek foreign sports cars, all moving in slow procession through the open portals to the front entrance where a liveried footman helped each entitled passenger on either their arrival or their departure. Somewhere on one of the upper floors, Danielle St. James was probably in her room, perhaps on the telephone to her young son in New York, or perhaps trying to decide what time she would call me to talk about what had happened in court and what we could expect tomorrow. The only nights she did not call were the ones she decided she had to talk to me in person.

It had become a bizarre routine, on the nights she did it, to come in disguise. At first I thought she was doing it out of an abundance of caution, the fear of the rumors that might start if she were seen coming to my apartment too often late at night. But gradually I began to realize that it was not concern for her reputation; it certainly was not any concern for mine. She liked the game, the known risk, the chance that she might get caught; her only pride, the nights she did it, how many people she might fool. It did not require much effort; what she did was never elaborate. A wig, a different dress, a change of make-up and, of course, a change of mood; and, with it, the look she wore. It seemed to give her a strange pleasure, to dress as another woman and live, if only for a brief time, another woman's life. Once in a while, when she had nothing else to do, she would drop by the hotel bar dressed as someone else and let someone buy her a drink. She spent an hour with a man who said he lived less than two blocks from where Danielle St. James lived in New York. He insisted she was innocent; she told him that he obviously knew nothing about women. "I had to explain to him that with a woman like Danielle St. James you could never be sure of anything." She told me this as if all she knew about Danielle was what she had read in the papers.

She never wore the same disguise twice. She came as every kind of woman and had every kind of voice. There were so many of them, and all of them, usually, only late at night, that the doorman, though he never said a word about it, must have thought I had part interest in a brothel and that one of the benefits of ownership was an endless sample of what they sold. It was crazy, and strangely seductive, the way she took on a slightly different character with each change in her appearance. There was no end to the illusion. She was every color of the rainbow and it was hard not to be mesmerized by every one of them. She was always different, and always the same.

Or was she? Because there were times when I would start to wonder whether the reason she was never the same thing twice, the reason she liked to pretend to be other people, was because there was nothing underneath, nothing that could stand to go unchanged. If she was a woman who lived on the surface, perhaps the surface was all there was. Perhaps her only being, what held her together, what made her who she was, was what had made her become Danielle and leave Justine behind: the eager willingness to become whatever she thought others wanted her to be. None of that mattered, of course, when I was sitting next to her in the courtroom or talking to her late at night about the case. It was only in her absence, only when I could not see her, that my mind was ever clear enough to become metaphysical.

I tried to work when I got home, prepare for the next witness the prosecution was going to call, consider the kind of questions, the cross-examination, I would have to conduct, but I kept thinking back to Tommy and what he had said at dinner about Danielle and how dangerous he thought she was. I knew he was right, that Danielle had murdered her husband, but that did not mean that I thought she was some cold, calculating killer, a born criminal who would keep doing the same thing over and over again until she was caught and put away. It was a crime of passion, something that would not have happened except for a set of circumstances that, in the nature of things, could never be repeated. Danielle was guilty, but not dangerous; and guilty only because the law does not deal in exceptions.

Or so I told myself as I glanced at the clock and wondered when she might call. An hour later, she did, and I tried not to show my disappointment when it became clear that tonight, at least, she was staying where she was.

It was just as well, I told myself the next morning as I settled into my usual place at the counsel table and glanced quickly over the notes I had made. In the concentrated intensity of a trial the only important thing, the only thing I had time to think about, was the next witness and the next question I had to ask. Danielle, on the other hand, seemed to remember only what she wanted to and only when she pleased. She took the chair next to mine, and in a voice just loud enough to be heard by the jurors as they found their places in the box, said good-morning and called me Mr. Morrison.

Just below the bench, Philip Conrad finished threading a thick spool of tape through the stenotype machine. Remembering what Tommy had told me, what he had told Tommy at lunch, I smiled, but though he was looking right at me, there was no sign he had even noticed. He sat there, without expression, the way he always did when he was at his place in court, waiting for the proceedings to get underway. I smiled again, this time in recognition of the honest integrity he brought to his job.

With an armload of files, work she could do on other cases when it was not necessary to pay close attention to what was going on in the trial, Alice Brunelli swept into court. Serious, scholarly, brilliant and logical to a fault, her only passion was the law, and she spent weekends, which other judges spent playing golf, in the law library or in her study at home.

"Call your next witness," she ordered, as she buried her nose in a file.

There was no response, but already engrossed in what she was reading, she did not notice. Then, when it finally registered, her head snapped up and she shot an evil glance at the silent and recalcitrant Robert Franklin. He was not there. His place was vacant, the chair still shoved tight against the table.

"Sorry, your Honor!" shouted the deputy district attorney as he burst through the double doors in back and came half-running up the center aisle. He dropped his bulging briefcase on the table and with calculated indifference started pushing up his tie.

Oddly, Alice Brunelli seemed to enjoy it. A thin smile of cold revenge coiled across her solemn mouth.

"It's nice you remembered to finish tying your tie," she said in a dry, mocking voice. "Are you sure you finished with your zipper?"

She was bluffing; he was sure of it, or almost sure. He was afraid to look, and afraid not to. That hesitation, that moment's embarrassment as the courtroom tittered, was all she wanted.

"Call your next witness," she said abruptly and immediately went back to what she was reading.

Franklin took it all in stride. I half-suspected he had been late on purpose, a way to make an entrance, teach the jury that while he had to follow the rulings of the court, he had his own authority, and that what happened in this trial largely depended on him. He called his next witness with an air of anticipation, the suggestion that we were about to get to something of more than ordinary importance. Franklin was good, and he kept getting better.

Louis Britton was the police detective who had been summoned to the Blue Zephyr when she first returned to

San Francisco. He had the look of a veteran cop, someone who has seen too much of human violence and degradation to be much surprised at anything. The fact of murder did not concern him; his only interest was in the details. Shaped by what he did, his mind was rational and methodical; murder, like any other problem, something to be broken into its elements, analyzed and solved. He had not the time, and, after everything he had seen, perhaps no longer the capacity, for moral judgment. Even when called upon to describe the gruesome slaughter of another human being, an innocent victim of some utterly depraved killer, it was rare that any expression could be seen on his face, or any, even the slightest, emotion in his eyes. He answered Franklin's questions about what he had found at the crime scene, the St. James yacht, with what appeared to be almost bored indifference.

"There wasn't much to see," said Britton with a shrug of his round, sloping shoulders. He threw his hand to the side in a careless gesture of unimportance. "The captain – Nastasis – had roped off that section of the deck, but it was three days before they got back to San Francisco, and between the salt spray and the rain there had been a fair amount of deterioration."

Franklin's eyes twitched with nervous intensity.

"Yes, I understand; but there was still blood there, blood you could…?"

"Yes," said Britton. A trained and experienced witness, he turned immediately to the jury. "Blood on the railing, on the deck – more than enough to make a conclusive identification."

"Conclusive identification?"

"DNA. There is no question that Nelson St. James was the victim, that he was shot and no one else."

"And did you also recover the murder weapon, the -"

"They haven't proved there was a murder!" I objected as I bolted from my chair. "All they have shown is that there was some dried blood on the deck and that it appears the blood belonged to Nelson St. James."

"Appears?" shouted Franklin, determined to be heard. "It's his blood, his DNA!"

"Gentlemen, that's enough!" cried Alice Brunelli. Leaning across the bench, she lashed us with her eyes. "Enough!" she repeated even louder when I tried to continue with my objection.

It was instinct, the larcenous habit of what through years of practice I had learned to do; simple in the execution, effective, sometimes, in the result. I raised an eyebrow, just that, nothing more, as if, instead of chastened, I was actually amused, by her sudden show of temper. It gave the appearance, created the illusion, that, whatever strained relationship the judge might have with the prosecutor, she and I were friends. Even Alice Brunelli, as tough-minded a judge as there was, was caught off guard, and for a moment did not seem quite certain what to do. She tried to recover, but the flashing anger in her eyes had gone too far away.

"Enough," she said quietly and sank back in her chair.

Franklin moved immediately to get the jury's attention back on the prosecution's witness.

"And did you also recover a weapon?"

"Yes, a handgun," replied Britton with that same bland expression. "The one Captain Nastasis had taken from the defendant, Danielle St. James."

Franklin asked the clerk to give the witness the prosecution's next exhibit, a clear plastic bag with a revolver inside it.

"Is this the gun you recovered?"

Britton examined the identification tag.

"Yes, this is my mark. That's the gun Captain Nastasis gave me, the gun -"

"Yes, the gun he saw in the defendant's hand. We've had his testimony that he caught her with the gun in her hand before she had time to throw it overboard -"

I shot to my feet, genuinely angry.

"That wasn't what the witness testified!"

The objection was sustained, but it scarcely mattered. Franklin had made his point and there was nothing I could do about it. No one was going to remember in all the testimony that would be given that it was not a witness, but the prosecutor, who had said that if Nastasis had not stopped her Danielle would have thrown the murder weapon into the sea.

"Could you tell if the gun had been used?" asked Franklin.

"One bullet had been fired."

That was Franklin's last question of the witness and I challenged the answer as soon as I was on my feet.

"You have no idea whether what you just said is true or not, do you?"

This at least produced a change of expression. Puzzled, he squinted, leaned on his elbow, and shook his head.

"What?"

"You said that one bullet had been fired from the revolver."

"Yes, and...?"

"How do you know that, detective? You weren't there."

"There were five bullets left in the chamber. The gun holds six."

"I see. Five bullets left in a gun that holds six. Therefore, one bullet must have been fired."

I said this as if it was a simple question of arithmetic and I was only trying to clarify the point before I moved on to more important matters. He waited for me to ask the next question; I waited for him to explain. He was confused; I was patient. The silence took on a meaning of its own, though no one could guess what that might be.

"There were five bullets left. That's what you said. What makes you think that one was missing?"

He began to swing his foot back and forth, studying it with the weary contempt of a police detective who has spent a career – a lifetime! - listening to made-up alibis and stupid excuses, and none of them as bad as the questions he sometimes got asked in court. A tired smile cut across his hard, cynical mouth as he lifted his eyes and sighed.

"It holds six bullets. There were five left. You can probably do the math."

"I could, if I knew what number to start with, but it isn't clear from your testimony whether that number is really six, as you keep insisting, or only five, which is also possible."

Britton almost fell out of the witness chair.

"Only five!" he blustered. "Why would -"

"For all you know, detective, whoever loaded the gun might not have loaded it all the way. Isn't that correct, detective? – for all you know there might have been only five bullets in it!"

He began to scratch at his arm; the irritation he felt became physical.

"Why would anyone do that?"

"It doesn't matter why anyone would do that, detective. The point is that you assumed – you don't really know – that the gun was fully loaded."

He scratched harder, deeper. He bit his lip to keep from lashing out.

"The captain…members of the crew – They all heard the shot. The captain – Nastasis – he found her with the gun in her hand. The barrel was still hot."

I stepped forward, subjecting him to a close imitation of the cynical indifference with which, just a moment earlier, he had treated me.

"In other words, detective Britton, when you just now testified that the gun was fully loaded, that one bullet was missing, it was not because of anything you yourself observed, but because of what you were told by other people. Which means that your testimony that Nelson St. James was the victim of a homicide should be taken in exactly the same way: it isn't anything you know for certain, it isn't anything you observed, it's just what you assumed!"

"I didn't assume the blood!" Britton fired back. "I didn't assume the DNA!"

I was just turning to the jury. I spun around and fixed him with a withering stare.

"The blood came from Nelson St. James – you're sure?"

"Of course I'm sure!"

"From his body?"

"Of course from his body!"

"Which part?"

"What?" He was incredulous. "I don't -"

"Which part, detective? It's a simple enough question." I made a quarter turn and faced the jury. "From his leg?"

"I don't think -"

"From his stomach?"

"I don't -"

"From his head?" I demanded, my voice rising as I turned and again stared hard at him. "And if from his head, detective Britton, was it from a gunshot right between the eyes – the way someone bent on murder might have killed him? Or from a gunshot to the temple – the way someone with a gun often decides to kill himself?"

Britton could not answer; no one could have. St. James had fallen overboard, his body lost at sea. No one would ever know where he had been hit, or even whether the bullet that struck him had killed him. He might have only been wounded and then died of drowning. He was dead, but the circumstances surrounding his death were either uncertain or subject to interpretation. Everyone thought it murder, but could the evidence prove that it was not suicide? It was not much of a chance, but it was the only one we had.

Franklin asked a few questions on re-direct, doing what he could to show the absurdity of my suggestion that the gun might not have been fully loaded. He was too smart to mention anything about the real point I was trying to make: that all of Britton's testimony was second-hand.

After Britton, Franklin called several members of the crew, testimony that went on for days. While none of them had witnessed what had happened the night St. James was killed, they each helped paint a picture of a marriage full of tension and about to explode. Maria Sanchez, a chambermaid, told how St. James and his wife had slept apart.

Wearing the same dark suit he did nearly every day, Franklin stood next to the counsel table, his fingers poised above a long list of questions he had written out in advance. He did not look at it; he did not need to. With indefatigable self-discipline he had committed to memory everything he wanted to ask. He did not once glance down, but he seemed to feel better, more confident, knowing that the list was there. His eyes were fastened on the witness as he listened patiently to her testimony that Mr. and Mrs. St. James had on that last, terrible voyage, slept in different beds.

"Was that their usual practice?" he asked in a well-modulated voice full of encouragement.

"No, never; not before that voyage."

Franklin's finger, like a paid assistant, moving with what seemed its own, independent, volition, went to the next question on the page, but Franklin did not see.

"And do you remember exactly when this started, when the two of them started sleeping in different rooms?"

Maria Sanchez was young, not yet thirty, with clear dark eyes and a quick, agile mind; but English was not her native language and in front of a crowded courtroom she easily became confused. She thought she had just answered that same question.

"On that voyage," she repeated, the color rising to her cheek at what might be thought a question about her honesty.

"Yes, I understand. But at what point? Did they start out that way, from the day they left San Francisco, or did something happen that...?"

Her eyes brightened. Now she understood.

"The day we headed back; that night she asked me to make up one of the other cabins."

That was the end of what Franklin wanted; it was only the beginning of what I was after. I was out of my chair, heading toward the witness, before Judge Brunelli had finished asking if I wanted to cross-examine.

"This wasn't your first voyage as a maid on board the Blue Zephyr, was it, Ms. Sanchez? If I'm not mistaken, you had been employed there for nearly two years before this happened, isn't that correct?"

"Yes, this is true."

"So you had quite a few occasions to observe Mr. and Mrs. St. James – how they behaved toward one another…, where they slept?"

Almost before the answer was out of her mouth, I smiled at her and went on as if we agreed on everything.

"They didn't always sleep in the same room, though, did they?" I asked in a quiet voice. "Sometimes – especially when Mr. St. James had to be on the phone at all hours, staying in touch with his various enterprises all around the world – they slept apart."

A witness - and none more than Maria Sanchez, a woman without friends in a place she did not know - no matter how confident they look, often feel lonely and nervous, afraid they may make a mistake in the way they answer a question and, instead of an honest attempt, be accused of a deliberate lie. A witness, in other words, is almost always susceptible to a face they can trust. Two questions, and Maria Sanchez was confident I would not betray her.

"Yes, that's true," she replied almost eagerly. "That sometimes happened."

I smiled and moved closer.

"So when you told Mr. Franklin a moment ago that before this last voyage Mr. and Mrs. St. James never slept apart, you didn't mean that it had never happened before, only that it didn't happen very often – Isn't that what you meant to say?"

Maria Sanchez was grateful for the chance to explain, to get it right.

"Yes. Sometimes he – Mr. St. James – was up all night working, and then…."

"Yes, of course," I said, gently. "But there were other times when this happened, weren't there? – Times when they slept apart because they weren't getting along, because they argued; because, on more than one occasion, Mr. St. James became drunk and abusive."

She lowered her large black eyes, murmuring an answer no one could hear. I asked her to repeat it.

"Yes, that happened."

"On one occasion you saw him strike her with his hand, didn't you?"

"Yes, but it was late, and he had had too much to drink, and...."

"He accused her of sleeping with other men, didn't he? Wasn't that the main reason they quarreled? Weren't those the times when they usually slept in different rooms – after one of those drunken rages when he went after her, sometimes with his fists, because he thought she had shown too much interest in someone else?"

"That was what I understood."

I took two steps toward the jury box, glanced at those twelve pair of attentive eyes, and then turned back to Maria Sanchez.

"You changed the beds every day, didn't you – put on fresh sheets?"

"Yes, always."

"And you had done that, changed the sheets in both their rooms, the morning of the day Mr. St. James died?"

"Yes, of course."

"And what about the next morning, the morning after Mr. St. James died – did you do it then as well?"

"Yes, I -"

"No, Ms. Sanchez, you did not; not both of them, only the bed where Mr. St. James slept. Isn't that correct? Because no one had slept in Mrs. St. James' bed, had they?"

"Yes, that's right," she replied, angry with herself for having forgotten. "Mrs. St. James did not go to bed that night. After what happened, she.... Only Mr. St. James' bed had been used."

"Yes, - used! Not just slept in – used. Two people had used that bed, hadn't they, Ms. Sanchez?" My hand on the jury box railing, I held her with my eyes. "Isn't that what you found when you went in the next morning to clean up his cabin – blankets off the bed, pillows all askew, and the sheets not just crumpled but stained with the tell-tale signs of sex? Isn't that what you found, Ms. Sanchez – proof, irrefutable proof, that sometime before midnight when that single shot was fired, Danielle St. James was in the cabin she shared with her husband having sex with the man the prosecution claims she was just about to murder!"

The courtroom was pandemonium. Franklin was on his feet screaming an objection no one could hear. Alice Brunelli beat her gavel to no effect at all. And me? – I smiled at Maria Sanchez and went back to my chair at the counsel table and sat down next to Danielle.

When I left the courthouse late that afternoon, I felt for the first time that there might really be a chance, that despite the prosecution's best effort they might not be able to make their case. There had been a gunshot and St. James was dead and Danielle was seen holding the gun, but no one had actually seen her shoot him. Franklin would argue murder as the only possible explanation, but without an eyewitness to prove it, and without a body to show precisely how and where St. James had been shot, the case was circumstantial and, far more importantly, allowed a different explanation, a different narrative of what had happened.

That at least is what I told myself in the euphoria of the moment, after a cross-examination that had gone better than I could have expected. I walked for blocks, thinking back over it, how easily the questions had come, how perfectly the answers had fallen into place. Filled with energy, my blood still hot, manic with the thought of what I could do tomorrow and all the other days the trial lasted, I became the willing prisoner of my own delusions. I must have looked like a strange, demented creature, glowing with the memory of what I had done, talking to myself like an actor playing both parts of a dialogue, my hands shoved deep in my pockets as I stumbled quick-footed down the straight wide street, blind to everything except the jumbled images running through my fevered brain.

I was intoxicated with my own performance, giddy

with my own achievement, and suddenly embarrassed because of it. I knew better than to think like this. I had been through too many trials to get excited over anything, much less what I had accomplished with a single witness, before the trial was over. It was, I realized, as my heart stopped racing and I became aware of what a fool I must look, the false confidence of a first hope, the empty, ungrounded belief that because things no longer looked quite so desperate, success was just around the corner. But it was a belief Danielle fully shared.

She came to see me that night, not late, the way she usually did, but early in the evening, and, perhaps to raise the stakes a little, run the hazard of a greater risk, came without disguise.

"You must see your clients at home once in a while," she said as she breezed past me. Tossing her tan raincoat over a chair, she added with an impish stare, "Or maybe that nice man downstairs thinks that one of those shameless late night ladies who sometime come to see you has come disguised as me."

She was on trial for her life, but you would have thought she had just come from a movie.

"You think he doesn't know that all of them were you?"

"He may suspect," said Danielle, as she glanced around the room. She seemed to take her bearings by the proportions of things. It may have come from her years as a model, or it might have been an instinct, something she was born with, but one look and she knew exactly where she needed to be, where she would be seen to the greatest advantage. "He may suspect," she repeated, careless with the truth of it, "but he can't be sure; and besides, he'd never say anything. The risk is being seen by someone on the street. That's how rumors start: when you're seen by someone you don't know."

She sat at the far end of the sofa, her arm stretched along the top of it. I made us both a drink and sat in the overstuffed chair next to the fireplace, just the other side of the glass coffee table. The tension of the trial had vanished, and she looked as confident and relaxed, as much at ease, as she had that day I first saw her on the deck of the Blue Zephyr. She seemed almost happy.

"You were wonderful today," she said with eager eyes. "I couldn't wait to tell you – that's the reason I didn't call, why I came straight over – how great I thought you were. We don't have anything to worry about now, do we? You know you're going to win."

I took an almost boyish pleasure in her smile. She had that effect on me, bringing back a native shyness that I thought long since conquered, forcing me to laugh at little at my own embarrassment; and when she heard it, the smile on her lovely, vulnerable mouth grew brighter and she laughed a little as well.

I tried to bring us back to the only thing that mattered, the trial and what was going to happen next. Rolling the ice around in my drink, I became serious.

"It didn't go too badly today, but all I know for certain is that we haven't lost yet and we still have a chance."

But her bright eyes kept their glitter and her smile stayed all-knowing. It made me more determined. I sat on the edge of the chair and did not smile back.

"This isn't some game where all that matters is how well you played. You're on trial for murder. I don't have to tell you what's at stake."

The smile still lingered, but grew faint.

"I know what will happen – what could happen – if we lose; but I know what I saw, what you did in court, what you did with those witnesses. And I know what the jury thinks: they like you; they want to believe what you tell them."

"I was lucky," I said. I stood up and began to walk around.

"It wasn't luck," she insisted, following me with her eyes. "You were brilliant. No one is as good as you. I always knew that about you; I was sure of it that weekend."

I was not thinking about what had happened that weekend on the Blue Zephyr, that weekend we sailed down the California coast. I was thinking about the trial and what we had to do.

"It's the best chance we've got," I explained, pacing back and forth. "We have to raise questions about everything the prosecution is trying to tell the jury. They say you must have killed him because you had the gun in your hand, but they can't prove you didn't pick it up; they can't prove – not beyond a reasonable doubt – that he didn't kill himself. They said that you had stopped sleeping together, and now the jury knows that wasn't true -"

"But we both know it wasn't suicide," she reminded me. "We both know I killed him."

I stopped moving and looked straight at her. There was a hard truth involved and she needed to understand it.

"You've never told anyone that but me, and you're not going to. The important thing is that they can't prove it – at least not beyond a reasonable doubt."

Intensely curious, she searched my eyes.

"Rufus Wiley testifies tomorrow. He'll make it sound like I had every motive to want Nelson dead."

"The only one who really knows what happened is you, and you're not going to testify."

She wanted to be sure that she understood, but she was afraid to ask; afraid that she might seem to be questioning my knowledge and my judgment.

"It's all right," I told her; "whatever it is, go ahead and ask."

"You don't think the case against me is good enough. You don't think Franklin can prove I did it. But you can't be sure of that, can you?"

"No," I admitted, "I can't. I'd be lying if I said I was."

She got up from the sofa and came up to me and put her arm around my neck and kissed me gently. She started to say goodnight, and then it happened, and even if I had wanted to I could not have stopped myself. It was too late; it had always been too late, no matter how many lies I told myself; too late from the day I first saw her standing on the deck of the Blue Zephyr as it rode high in the water that sun drenched afternoon off the coast of California. We stumbled into the bedroom, and this time we did not stop. We made love with all the evil innocence of a man and a woman who had wanted each other more, far more, than anyone else they had ever known.

Later, after we were finally finished, as she lay naked in my arms, the moonlight streaming through the window, she asked if it bothered me, not that we had made love, a lawyer and his client, but something far more personal.

"Does it bother you that I killed him, that I'm not as innocent as you want everyone else to believe?"

I did not want to think about the moral implications of what I was doing. Most of the people I defended were guilty and it had not bothered me before. You did what you had to do to win, and while I may on occasion have bent them, I had never broken any rules. The only thing important, I told myself, my only obligation, was the trial. Later, when it was over, after I had saved Danielle, I could worry whether I might have been able to do it in some other, better, way.

"It was an accident; you didn't do it on purpose."

"But I did; I told you that I did. I grabbed the gun and followed him up on deck and when he started laughing at me, telling me there was nothing I could do, I shot him. I told you that. I couldn't stand it anymore."

"You didn't plan to do it," I said, staring into the vast moonlit night. "You wouldn't have done it if you had had time to think. You saw what he was doing to you, how he had lied to get you back in bed. You lost control; you didn't mean to lose control. It just happened. It was as much an accident as if the gun had gone off during a struggle to get it away from him."

Danielle lifted her head from my shoulder and gave me a look I did not understand, a look so strange that as I listened to what she said, I began to wonder if I had ever understood anything at all.

"I suppose it could have happened like that."

CHAPTER TWELVE

"The People call Rufus Wiley"

A cunning smile stole across Robert Franklin's mouth. Wiley's testimony was the missing piece with which he would complete the puzzle. Instead of a loose assemblage of disconnected facts, his case would become a flawless narrative, a story of greed and murder in which, like all the stories people like to hear, the killer has to pay for what she has done.

There was no smile of any kind of Rufus Wiley's mouth, and you had the impression that there seldom was. He had the shrewd, sober and penetrating eyes of a man trained to reduce things to their basic elements, and it was quite apparent what he believed those to be. Modern physics might describe the world in terms of matter in motion; Rufus Wiley, more familiar with human behavior, thought in terms of money in circulation. He glanced at the jury as if he were making a quick calculation of their average net worth.

Franklin was nothing but friendly.

"Mr. Wiley, you were employed by Nelson St. James?"

"Yes, I was." His voice was steady, dry, and unemotional. Rufus Wiley was a man who dealt in facts.

"How long had you been employed by him at the time of his death?"

Wiley did not hesitate.

"Eleven years, two months."

Franklin seemed to take a certain residual pride in the quick precision with which Wiley answered. Rubbing his hands together, he stepped closer.

"What exactly did you do for Mr. St. James?"

"Objection!" I shouted before Wiley could answer.

Alice Brunelli did not raise her eyes from what she was reading.

"Grounds, Mr. Morrison?"

"Vague and conjectural," I replied with a show of impatience, as if we both had better things to do than constantly point out and correct the mistakes of Mr. Robert

Franklin.

She raised her eyes, inviting me to explain.

"If Mr. Franklin wants to know what Mr. Wiley did for Mr. St. James in the course of his employment, he should ask him that, and not a question that would include whether he ever played golf with him on his day off, or had a drink with him at the Plaza bar, or once went out on a double-date with him when they were younger, or -"

That was all she wanted to hear. Waving her hand, she went back to what she was reading.

"Yes, yes; we understand, Mr. Morrison. Be a little more precise, if you would, Mr. Franklin."

Franklin had not moved, except to raise his eyes to the bench. He asked the question again.

"What was the main function you performed in the course of your employment with Mr. St. James?"

"I was his private attorney. I handled all of his personal legal affairs."

"In that capacity, did you have occasion to draw up any documents in connection with his marriage to the defendant, Danielle St. James?"

"At Mr. St. James' request, I drew up a pre-nuptial agreement."

"In layman's terms, what did that pre-nuptial agreement do?"

Wiley turned and looked straight at the jury.

"Two things. It stipulated the amount that Mrs. St. James would have during the marriage; her personal allowance, if you will: money she could spend on clothing or whatever else she wanted. The other thing it did was to set forth the agreement concerning what Mrs. St. James would be entitled to should the marriage end in divorce."

Franklin folded his arms across his chest and gazed down at the floor, preparing himself, as it seemed, for a question of crucial importance. When he finally raised his eyes, he did it slowly, as if reluctant to delve too closely into someone's personal affairs.

"Under the terms of that agreement, how much would

she have received in the event of a divorce?"

"A million dollars a year and their house in the Hamptons."

"A house in the Hamptons," said Franklin, pensively stroking his chin. "And approximately how much would that be worth in today's market?"

"In today's market – ten, maybe twelve, million."

Franklin's eyes opened wide with astonishment.

"Ten, maybe twelve, million? Plus another million a year. She wasn't exactly going to be thrown out on the street then, was she?"

I was out of my chair, objecting with all the self-righteous fury I could muster at the caustic tone and the gratuitous remark, and, in the process, doing the same thing myself.

"That's what happens when a prosecutor cares more about a conviction than he does about the facts!"

With a baleful glance that managed to take in both of us at once, Alice Brunelli issued a warning.

"No more! – Do you understand? Now, Mr. Franklin – Ask your questions and be done with it, unless you want the court to ask them for you. And as for you, Mr. Morrison – The court is fairly confident it can rule on an objection without the benefit of a commentary on what you think the prosecution's state of mind!"

Franklin immediately picked up where he had left off.

"So is it fair to say, Mr. Wiley, that at least by most standards she would have been left a very wealthy women had there been a divorce?"

"Yes, by most standards, I'm sure that's true," said Rufus Wiley in a tone that left little doubt that those were not the same standards by which he measured things.

Restless and preoccupied, Franklin paced back and forth, rubbing his chin. His downward gaze became more intense, a studied look of thoughtful confusion. Back and forth, moving faster and faster, and then, suddenly, he stopped, and, his eyes now steady and unflinching, turned to the witness.

"Do you have any reason to believe that at the time of his death, Mr. St. James was planning to end his marriage to the defendant, Danielle St. James?"

"Yes; Nelson – Mr. St. James – had asked me to draw up divorce papers."

"He asked you to do this before he left on his trip out here?"

"Yes. He said his wife had been cheating on him – seeing other men – and that he wouldn't put up with it, and that he wanted a divorce."

For the first time, Rufus Wiley looked at Danielle, a brief, sidelong glance in which, while the condescension was obvious, there was something else, something just below the surface, something I could not quite grasp, but something sinister - I was certain of that. It was almost as if he was glad she was on trial for murder.

"She had been seeing other men, and he wanted a divorce. That's what he told you before he left New York. But still, he went with her; he didn't go alone, when they came out here and then sailed away."

Wiley became cautious, circumspect; there were things he could not talk about.

"Things happened in a hurry. As you know, Mr. St. James had some legal problems -"

"He was indicted. Yes, we know that. And we know – everyone knows – that he apparently sailed off on his yacht to escape having to face trial. That isn't relevant now. The question is, if he wanted to divorce his wife, why did he take her with him – why didn't he just leave her behind?"

"All I know is what he told me. He said he had told her he was going to divorce her, and that she had not taken it well at all. He agreed to see if they could talk it through. He didn't think it would make any difference, but he thought if he did what she asked, things might go easier later."

"Meaning?"

"He wasn't going to change his mind about the divorce," said Wiley, making a dismissive gesture with his hand, "but he thought she wouldn't be quite so upset, or feel quite so vindictive, if he spent some time with her talking things over. And of course they have a child. He did not want things to be any more difficult than they had to be. And as I said before," he added darkly, "this was all at the time when things were moving very fast. He was making a lot of decisions, most of them against my advice."

Franklin had one more question, the last blank left to fill.

"How can you be certain that he didn't change his mind? Isn't it possible that out there, just the two of them – they were gone for weeks – he had a change of heart? Isn't it possible that he decided to try to make the marriage work?"

Rufus Wiley shook his head emphatically.

"No. He called me from the yacht – from the Blue Zephyr – and told me that he had made a mistake: that he wanted to come back and clear his name, and that he wanted the divorce more than ever."

"When was this? When did Nelson St. James make that call?"

"The night before he died."

Franklin tapped his fingers three times in quick succession on the jury box railing, and then, nodding to himself, started back toward his place at the counsel table.

I got to my feet, slowly, and with a puzzled expression on my face.

"When you handled Mr. St. James' legal affairs, did you typically explain to him each thing involved and what, if any, alternatives he might have?"

"Yes, I tried to."

"But that wasn't what you did with the pre-nuptial agreement, was it? You said earlier that you drafted it at his request, but that isn't true, is it? The pre-nuptial agreement wasn't his idea, Mr. Wiley – it was yours. And as a matter of fact, when you first suggested it, he was opposed to it and told you he didn't want it – Isn't that true, Mr. Wiley?"

"I was his lawyer, Mr. Morrison," he replied with icy reserve. "It was my obligation to do what was in his best interest."

"Because, in your judgment, he didn't always know what that was?"

All the features of Rufus Wiley's long patrician face seemed to close down. His eyes drew in on themselves; his mouth pinched tight at the corners. It was the look of a man who had seldom, or perhaps even never, known great enthusiasm, a man who had never felt the thrill of letting hope triumph over experience. His had always been the voice of caution and restraint.

"Mr. St. James had been more than generous to the women he had known, but he had not married any of them. I wasn't sure why he wanted to marry Danielle. Perhaps it was some kind of challenge he had set himself; it was not as if he had fallen in love with her," he said dismissively.

"Why do you say that: that he was not in love with her?"

"I meant really in love with her, because I have to say I never knew him to want anything in quite the same way he seemed to want her."

As soon as Wiley said this, there was what I can only describe as a physical reaction. You could almost feel the jury, and not just the jury, acknowledge the truth of it, that Danielle St. James could make even a man who could have everything want her that much.

"Nelson wanted her – that is certainly true," continued Wiley; "but he had an impulsive nature. When he wanted something he did not always see that he might lose interest once he had it."

Wiley had no sense of romance, he was too prosaic, to understand what being in love really meant.

"You talk about her, the woman who, by your own testimony, was the woman he wanted to marry, as if she were just an object of his temporary affection; that there was, if I can put it like this, too much passion for it to last. But isn't that exactly the reason why people marry, Mr. Wiley – because they want each other that much?"

"In the usual case, I'm sure that's true," he replied in a cold, condescending tone. "But Nelson was not the usual

case. He hated anything that even suggested permanence."
Wiley bent forward, his gaze determined and emphatic.
"That is what made him what he was: the belief that there
was always something new to get. And once he decided what
that new things was, there was no stopping him. But – and
this is very important if you want to understand what kind of
man he was – the only reason he bought anything was to sell
it later."

"And you were there to make sure that, in this case at
least, he did not overpay?"

He ignored the sarcasm; he ignored me. He talked
directly to the jury, trying to impress upon them the honest
motive of his actions.

"He decided he had to have Danielle, had to marry her.
Why he thought he had to do that, I'm not sure. But Nelson
had not changed: the game was all in the pursuit. He meant
to have her; he never meant to keep her. That's why I told
him he had to have a pre-nuptial agreement: because it was
my job to protect him against what I knew would happen
later."

He was still looking at the jury, a man who knew his
business.

"You say he never meant to keep her?" I waited until
he turned and looked at me again. "But earlier you made it
sound just the other way round: that she didn't mean to keep
him."

"I'm afraid I don't quite follow."

"You said Nelson St. James wanted a divorce! You said
he had taken her with him – on his flight as a fugitive when
he sailed off into the Pacific- only to make divorce as easy
as possible. You said he called you the night before he died
to tell you that he was coming back and that he wanted a
divorce more than ever! You said all that, didn't you?"

"Yes, that's what I said, but I don't see how that -"

"Have you forgotten what you told us was the reason
he wanted a divorce? It wasn't because he had gotten tired of
her; it wasn't because, as you put it, 'he never meant to keep
her.' It was because he thought his wife had been having an

affair! Isn't that what you said, Mr. Wiley? Wasn't that your sworn testimony?"

"Yes, that's what I said," replied Wiley, fidgeting nervously with his fingers. "But that doesn't change the fact that it wouldn't have lasted, that -"

"But it did last, didn't it? Through seven years and the birth of a child; lasted until, according to your testimony, he found out she was having an affair – didn't it?"

"Yes, but -"

"But what, Mr. Wiley? Did you misunderstand? Are you now going to tell us that he wanted a divorce, not because his wife was having an affair, but because he was having one?"

"No, that's not -"

"It's not true that Nelson St. James was having an affair? Not true that during the course of their marriage he had numerous relationships with other women?"

"I tried to stay out of his personal affairs."

"You tried to stay -! You're the one who insisted on a pre-nuptial agreement! You're the one who not two minutes ago claimed that he – what was the phrase you used? – 'never meant to keep her.' I will ask you directly, Mr. Wiley: Is it not true that Nelson St. James slept with other women during his marriage to the defendant, Danielle St. James?"

Wiley sat with his elbows on the arms of the witness chair, and hands, fingers interlaced, dangling in his lap. He was used to giving instructions; he did not much care for answering someone else's questions.

"Yes," he admitted.

"Do you think he did it because he thought each one might be the last?"

The question confused him. I tried to explain.

"Nelson St. James was a comparatively young man, in his early forties, and so far as we know was in good health. But he worried about his own mortality, didn't he?'

"Yes, he did, and to a surprising degree. There was apparently some history in his family. His father – he did not talk about him; I only learned this second hand – died of a heart attack before he was fifty."

"Each time he was with a new woman was proof of his continued virility, proof that he still had more time – Do you think that possible?"

Wiley turned up his palms. "I really would not know how to answer that."

"You just testified that what kept him going – what we needed to understand if we were going to understand what kind of man Nelson St. James really was – was the belief that there was always something new to get. That included, did it not, a new woman to take to bed?"

"Well, I -"

"He was obsessed with his own mortality, wasn't he? Obsessed with the very real possibility, given his family history, that he might die at an early age."

"Perhaps, but -"

"Didn't this fear of an early death bring with it a fear of not leaving anything behind? You said he wanted to marry Danielle because he wanted her, and that you knew that eventually he would get tired of her and want a divorce. But there was another reason Nelson St. James wanted to get married, wasn't there? Nelson St. James wanted a child."

"Yes, I suppose he did."

"You suppose he did! You know he did. He made a will when he got married, didn't he? Or rather, he changed the will he had."

"Yes, he did."

"And you drafted it, didn't you?"

"Yes, as I say, I was his -"

"Lawyer. Yes, we know. There were a number of charitable bequests in that will, were there not?"

"Quite a number, yes."

"And those amounted to approximately how much?"

"Roughly two hundred million."

"And the rest of it – which must run into the hundreds of millions, if not more – Who would have inherited that?"

"His wife, Danielle St. James."

I stood next to the jury box, holding him tight in my

gaze.

"With his death, then, Mrs. St. James would have become one of the wealthiest women in the world. I say would have, because Mr. St. James changed that will, didn't he?"

"Yes, he -"

"And he did that at about the same time he told you to prepare divorce papers, didn't he – just days before he left New York?"

"Yes, that's right: he changed his will."

I stared hard at him, letting him, and the jury, know that this was crucial, indispensable to an understanding of what had happened.

"And how much does Mrs. St. James stand to inherit now, Mr. Wiley – after the changes made to the will?"

"Nothing. He was going to divorce her, he was going to -"

"Give her what he was required to give her under the pre-nuptial agreement. Yes, we understand. But she doesn't get even that now, does she, Mr. Wiley?"

The jurors looked at one another, wondering how this was possible.

"And why is that, Mr. Wiley? Tell the jury why the woman who supposedly murdered her husband for his money doesn't benefit at all from his death!"

Rufus Wiley swallowed hard.

"He died before he could get a divorce."

"And because of that, she doesn't get anything, does she? She doesn't get the house in the Hamptons; she doesn't get a million dollars a year."

Shaking my head in derision, I shot a glance at Robert Franklin, but he had his face buried in a file, desperate to find something – anything – he could use to repair the damage. I wheeled around and challenged Wiley.

"You never told anyone about this, did you? – The fact that Nelson St. James changed his will; the fact that Danielle St. James was going to be left with nothing; the fact that, if she was after his money, the last thing in the world she would have wanted was for her husband to die!"

"I was Mr. St. James' lawyer! What I did for him was private!" he shot back, outraged and indignant. Suddenly, his expression changed. The anger vanished and a cold, cynical smile cut across his straight thin mouth. He sat back in the witness chair, full of the old confidence. "I doubt he told anyone, either. So she wouldn't have known that she had been cut out of the will, would she?"

"It was obvious the moment you took the stand that you didn't like her," I said, smiling back. "Of course he told her! How would I have known about it if I hadn't heard it from her?"

With a last, disdainful glance, I went back to the counsel table and started to pull out my chair, but I stopped and looked up.

"One last question, Mr. Wiley: That last time you spoke to him, when he told you he still wanted a divorce, did he sound like a man on top of the world, or did he perhaps sound a little depressed?"

"Understandably, it had all been quite a strain."

"Yes, not only was he about to lose his wife, he was about to lose everything else as well, wasn't he?"

Wiley had been bred to caution. He waited for me to expand upon the question, sharpen the details.

"He had been indicted by a federal grand jury; he was one of the most despised men in America. He was facing charges that could send him to prison for the rest of his life. And instead of trying to prove his innocence, he had left the country, disappeared -"

"Yes, but he was coming back. I told you that. In that last phone call, the night before he was killed, he said he had made a mistake, that he was -"

"Coming back to stand trial! We'll never know for sure though, will we, Mr. Wiley? All we know for certain is that before he disappeared, sailed away on that yacht of his, he promised he would not leave. You may take his word for things; all the people he defrauded may not be quite so willing."

Franklin was on his feet, objecting.

"Is there a question in there somewhere? If there is, I missed it!"

Brunelli started to tell me to move on, but I was ahead of her. I glared at Rufus Wiley.

"There he was, out there on the ocean alone, about to lose not just his beautiful young wife, but his money, his reputation, and if he did what he told you he was going to do – come back and stand trial – his freedom. It isn't any wonder - Is it, Mr. Wiley? - that a man in his condition would decide to take his own life!"

CHAPTER THIRTEEN

Rufus Wiley had done more for the defense than any witness I could have called. The pre-nuptial agreement Franklin had thought crucial, proof of what Danielle would have lost in a divorce, proved instead what she would have won. The murder of Nelson St. James was supposed to have been all about the money, but in terms of money, the worst thing that could have happened to Danielle was to have her husband die. His death had cost her everything she would have had in a divorce.

In one of the great ironies, the question of money, instead of a motive for murder, had suddenly become our best defense. The prosecution could not prove motive, and without motive Franklin could not prove his case. It was true that the gun had Danielle's fingerprints on it, but Nelson's prints were there as well. The physical evidence was just as consistent with suicide as it was with murder, and Rufus Wiley, the prosecution's own witness, had been forced to admit that Nelson St. James had been depressed.

We were almost home. Rufus Wiley was the prosecution's last witness and there was no one I could call, no one who could testify that anything said by any of the prosecution's witnesses was wrong; no one who could give Danielle an alibi, insist she was not there when her husband died; no one who could make a credible claim that Nelson St. James had been killed by someone else. I could scarcely put Danielle on the stand to tell the jury how she had done it, how it was not suicide at all, that she had done exactly what the prosecution said she had done: killed her husband with a gun. I did not have a case, but, then, I did not need one. The burden was on the prosecution to prove that Danielle had done it, and I was as certain as I could be that Robert Franklin had failed to do that, and that the jury, whatever they might really think about her guilt, would have to acquit her.

I explained this to Danielle that evening, but she had heard it all before. The distance I normally kept between

159

myself and a client had long ago ceased to exist. I had held nothing back, telling her everything I thought about what happened each day in trial, and what I planned to do next. But more than that, I told her things about myself I had never told anyone, the kind of secrets all of us have, the ones we keep hidden except when we find ourselves desperately in love. I trusted her, but only, or mainly, because I knew how much she trusted me. Her life was in my hands, and she was perfectly content, I might even say eager, to let me decide everything we did in court. The next morning, as we waited for the judge to enter and the day's proceedings to begin, I felt relaxed and confident, as certain of the outcome as I could be.

"Mr. Morrison," said Alice Brunelli, after she settled herself on the bench, "Is the defense ready to call its first witness?"

Lawyers, honest ones, will tell you that there is always a sense of relief when they know the case is over, when they know the last witness has been called and there are no more questions to be asked, no more answers to be dissected and analyzed on the spot. There is still the closing argument, still that terrible, endless wait for the verdict, but with no more witnesses there are no more surprises, nothing that can catch you unawares. Rufus Wiley, the last witness for the prosecution, had been the last witness in the trial. Everything that remained, the long summations both Franklin and I would make, the lengthy instructions Judge Brunelli would give to the jury, the jury's slow deliberations behind closed doors, all of that would be based on what was now completed.

"Your Honor," I said with perfect self-assurance, "the defense rests."

There was a collective sigh as the courtroom crowd realized that Danielle St. James, the woman they had all come to see, would not be taking the witness stand in her own defense. You could almost feel the disappointment, the chance missed to listen for themselves to this notorious woman that, through the mouths of others, they had heard so much about. Then, almost immediately, there was a second reaction, a puzzled silence as for some reason Danielle had risen from her chair and was looking directly at Alice Brunelli as if waiting for the chance to speak.

"Your Honor, don't I have the right to testify should I choose to do so?"

My legs went weak, my stomach started churning. The blood rushed to my face with such rapid force that for an instant everything went black.

"Danielle!" I whispered in a harsh, strident voice. "We decided this."

Alice Brunelli was all attention. Her lips parted and pushed forward, like someone about to exhale after holding their breath. With a deeply worried look in her eyes, she tapped two fingers on the bench, considering what she ought to do, and then, the decision made, she nodded once to seal it and turned quickly to the jury.

"Ladies and gentlemen, there is a matter that has to be discussed outside the presence of the jury."

The moment the jury was out of the room, Brunelli started to ask Danielle a question, but then, changing her mind, she asked me one instead.

"May I assume that you have advised your client of her rights in this matter, Mr. Morrison?"

"Yes, your Honor; I have."

"Specifically, her right to testify in her own defense?"

"Yes."

"You told her that a defendant in a criminal trial does not have to testify, that no one can compel her to testify, but that she can testify, if she so chooses?"

Alice Brunelli was making a record, getting my testimony about what I had done before she asked the defendant, my client, if what I said was true. Alice Brunelli did everything according to a strict interpretation of the rules, especially when it involved a potential question about a lawyer's conduct.

Was that what Danielle was up to? Was it regarding my conduct as a lawyer? It was an old game, usually played by street-wise criminals who had been in and out of the system for most of their lives: make the lawyer the issue, claim ineffective assistance of counsel as the reason why they should get a new trial. Danielle had better grounds than most of them ever had. She could claim that I had not spent as much time as I should have done on her defense because I was too desperate to spend time with her in bed. It was ludicrous, idiotic, insane; but it would have been all she needed.

Alice Brunelli adjusted her spare, thick glasses and placed both hands on the bench. For a long moment, and without a trace of sympathy to break the severity of her countenance, she studied Danielle closely.

"Mrs. St. James, you've just heard what your attorney said. Is all of it true? Has he advised you that you have the right to testify or not as you choose, and that no one, not even your attorney, can make that decision for you?"

To my great relief, Danielle nodded emphatically. She was not going to turn on me after all.

"Mr. Morrison has done all that and more. He's explained everything to me. I know I don't have to testify; I know no one can make me. And, yes, he's told me that the decision whether I do or not is mine to make. This is my fault, your Honor. Mr. Morrison went through all of this with me again yesterday after court. I told him I would follow his advice, and perhaps I should; but now that I have to make that decision, now that there isn't any more time, I suddenly realize that, whatever happens, I want to tell the truth. I want everyone to know what happened. I want to clear my name."

There was no change of expression on Danielle's eager, innocent face, not the slightest doubt or uncertainty about what she meant to do, and I now realized that, despite what she had just told the court, this was no spontaneous, last minute decision. She had made up her mind a long time ago to take the stand and testify. If she had not come right out and lied to me about her intentions, her silence had done it for her.

"Would you like a few minutes to confer with your

client, Mr. Morrison?" asked Brunelli after Danielle had finished.

Confer with her? I wanted to kill her! What could I talk to her about now? – What a liar she was, what a fool she had made out of me? She thought she knew more than I did about how to win at trial? – Let her try!

"No, your Honor," I replied with an angry, tight-lipped smile. "If I had known the defendant wanted to testify, I would have called her. I apologize for the confusion."

Brunelli motioned toward the bailiff and ordered him to bring back the jury.

We had a minute, maybe two, before the jury was back in the box and I had to call the first and last witness for the defense. I moved my chair closer to Danielle.

"I've spent the whole trial trying to make them think he might have killed himself, and now you're going to get up there and tell them that you pulled the trigger instead? If you take the stand," I warned her, "there's nothing I can do to save you. It's not too late; all I have to do is stand up and say you've decided not to do it after all. For God's sake, Danielle! – Think what you're doing. Your child doesn't have a father. Don't you want him to at least have a mother?"

She was nodding her head, following every word. The nodding stopped. Her eyes became hard, cold, and determined.

"Trust me," she said in a voice that, even after everything she had done, astonished me for the almost callous certainty it carried; "I know what I'm doing."

There was no choice: I had to call her. For the first time in my career, someone else had taken charge of the defense.

Every eye was on her as she stood and without hesitation swore to tell the truth. If there was a trace of nervousness in her voice, no one heard it. The silence in the courtroom as she settled onto the witness chair echoed back on itself, the way it does late at night when the very stillness seems to speak a language all its own. Everything was up to her now.

I began as if this were just another routine examination, no different than what I would do with a witness in any other trial.

"Would you please state your full name and spell your last for the record?"

I should have asked her to state her real name, the one given her at birth, instead of the made-up lie with which she had become famous, rich, and, I was now convinced, truly lethal.

"Danielle St. James," she replied in that thrilling, breathless voice which, as I had learned, she could turn on and off at will. She turned to the court reporter and slowly spelled her last name. Philip Conrad did not bother to look, but methodically went about his business.

One question, the one that always gets asked first, and I did not know what to ask next. I had no idea what she was going to say. All I could do was invite her to tell her own story in her own words and, while I listened along with everyone else, try to pretend that it was the same story she had told me from the beginning. That was my intention, but then something happened. Whether it was the lawyer in me, the pride I had in what I did, or simply wounded vanity, I asked the question I would have asked if I had even once thought she might be innocent.

"Mrs. St. James, did you or did you not murder your husband, Nelson St. James?"

"No, I didn't kill Nelson. He killed himself. But it's my fault. He wouldn't have done it if it hadn't been for me."

It was quite simply the most stunning lie I had ever heard. Even more astonishing, she actually seemed to believe it. Her eyes were filled with anguish and remorse, her voice a soft, choking sob. I was so lost in amazement I could not quite hide my own incredulity.

"It's your testimony, given here under oath, that you did not murder Nelson St. James, that you didn't shoot him with a gun? It's your testimony that your husband killed himself?"

"Yes!" she cried with desperation, looking every bit a

woman on the verge of collapse. "But he wouldn't have done it if I hadn't said what I did!"

"Said what you did?" I asked with a blank stare.

"He told me he was going to do it," she said through bitter tears. "I told him he should!"

A shock wave spread through the courtroom, hitting everyone at once. It was such an awful, dreadful thing to admit - that she had told her husband to kill himself and that then he had - it had to be true. No one would lie about a thing like that. And she was just getting started.

"I told him to go ahead, kill himself, for all I cared!" she cried, her eyes bright with the memory of her own wicked defiance. "He may have pulled the trigger, Mr. Morrison – but I'm the one responsible. So when you ask me, did I kill him, the honest answer is yes!"

I was trapped. There was no way out. She was lying through her teeth and I knew it. I had put on the stand a witness who was committing perjury and she was doing it with my assistance. And I had no choice; I had to pick up the thread of her deceit and see where it would take us.

"Let's start at the beginning. What was the reason you went with your husband on that last voyage, when he decided to leave the country rather than face trial? You've heard the testimony of your husband's attorney, Rufus Wiley, that your husband wanted a divorce and that you wanted a chance to talk him out of it."

She had had time to collect herself, and was now ready to answer questions without undue emotion.

"There was more to it than that," she explained. "It's true that Nelson said he wanted a divorce, and he told me that he had changed his will – just as Mr. Wiley said. But this wasn't the first time Nelson had made a threat like that. The thing that was different is that this time I told him that if he didn't file for divorce, I would. I couldn't stand it anymore, all his infidelities, and then, despite that, all his jealous rages whenever he saw me even talk to another man."

The color had started to rise to her cheek, a blush of

anger and defiance I had seen before when she began to talk about something that had been done that she did not like. But she caught it coming, as it were, and quickly turned it to her own advantage.

"We loved each other," she explained to the jury with a rueful glance that seemed to admit mistakes. "We really did; but Nelson had gotten involved in some things – business things; I don't know what they were – and he became just impossible. And then, when he was indicted, when he knew he was in trouble, serious trouble, things got…."

Danielle lowered her eyes and heaved a sigh. A moment later, when she looked up, there was a new vulnerability about her, the lost look of a woman who cannot understand how with such good intentions things had gone so horribly wrong.

"Nelson was running away. With all the publicity, all the awful things that were being said about him, he didn't think he had a chance, didn't think anyone would believe him. I told him I wanted to go with him, that I loved him, and that our marriage was worth saving."

A bleak expression of irredeemable loss entered her eyes. Her lips began to tremble and only with an effort were made to stop.

"Mrs. St. James – Do you need a minute?" I asked sympathetically. And the sympathy was real, because no matter how convinced I became of her duplicity, parts of her story, the record of what at different times she must have felt, seemed all too true.

"Thank you," she said with a brave smile. "I'll be all right." She sat straight up and turned again to the jury.

"It would have been better if I had let him go by himself. All we did was fight. And we didn't just fight in private; we had to do it everywhere. That was why I walked out on him that night in the restaurant. When Nelson lost his temper there was no end to the abuse, nothing he wouldn't say. He could be so charming, so considerate, and then something would set him off and there was no stopping it."

"Rufus Wiley testified that your husband wanted a

divorce because he discovered you were having an affair. Were you having an affair, Mrs. St. James, and did your husband find out about it?"

I was standing not ten feet from her, searching her eyes, wondering if she had lied when she told me that she had not had an affair, and if she had, whether she was going to lie about it now. Her eyes, as I should have known, never gave her away. Her gaze remained inscrutable, the only change in her expression an almost imperceptible upward tilt to her chin, a reminder that the question itself was an intrusion, a violation of what she had a right to keep private. Instead of turning back to the jury before she answered, she kept looking at me, measuring, as it seemed, what my reaction was going to be.

"Yes, Mr. Morrison; I had been having an affair, and my husband found out about it."

I had not known her then; she had lived on the other side of the country, married to another man, and I still felt a pang of jealousy. Stranger than that, she knew it - that much she let her eyes reveal - and, perhaps not so strange, it did not bother her in the least. She was used to the jealousy and disappointment of men.

"And was that the reason you were fighting?"

"Yes, mainly; the affair, if you can call it that – it only lasted a few weeks."

She had an absolute genius for diminishing the importance of every sin she committed. Admit an affair, and then dismiss it as a matter of no account, arguing the length! Murder your husband, and then insist he killed himself because of something you admit you should not have said! It was the kind of logic that would have driven the Mad Hatter mad.

Now she looked at the jury, and especially the women who were on it, and appealed to what they could all understand.

"I know it's no excuse, I know I shouldn't have done it, but I did not know any other way to get his attention, to let him know that things couldn't go on this way. I could not keep track of all the different women he had been with. But he refused to think that was any excuse for what I had done. It didn't matter what he did, so long as he was discreet; it mattered what I did because I was his wife and the mother of his child. I told him he was a hypocrite and a fool, and that he was crazy if he thought I was going to stay married to him if he kept doing the things he did."

She fell into a long, thoughtful silence, and the courtroom became deathly quiet, so quiet that a muffled cough seemed a jarring noise. I wondered what she was going to say next.

"It got so bad," said Danielle finally; "we said so many hateful things. We couldn't be in the same room without this constant, savage screaming. Nelson told me that I still belonged to him, that I couldn't leave him. Then, to show me that he meant it, he took me, made me do what he wanted. He thought that settled it, that because he had had me I was still his. But I wasn't still his, I wasn't going to live like that, be his dressed up whore! I got dressed, told him I was leaving him, that I didn't care where it was, the next place we landed I was getting off the Blue Zephyr and I was never coming back! And then I told him something else, something cruel and hateful and unforgivable. I was so angry I could not help myself! I told him I was in love with someone else, the man with whom I had been having the affair. It was a lie, but I wanted to hurt him as much as he had hurt me. I told him that the whole time he had me in bed I was pretending he was that other man, the one I was in love with, and I told him that it didn't matter anyway, his life was finished. He was going to prison and he was never going to get out!

"He was out of his mind with anger and rage. He told me I couldn't leave him; he begged me to stay. He took the pistol we carried for protection and started waving it in the air. He said he didn't give a damn what happened, he didn't care about me, he didn't care about anything anymore, that he might as well be dead. And do you know what I said to him – the words that keep echoing in my mind, the words

I would give anything to take back? I told him to go ahead and do it, that no one would miss him when he was gone!"

Her eyes were wild with the terror she still felt, the awful thing that haunted her and would never let her go.

"I tried to stop him! I ran after him, out on deck; I screamed at him, pleaded with him not to do it. But it was too late! He put that gun to his head..., and then that awful noise..., and then all that awful blood. And then nothing mattered anymore. Nelson was gone and I knew my life was over."

CHAPTER FOURTEEN

"You lied!" I shouted into Danielle's cold, belligerent eyes. I wanted to take her by the shoulders and shake her until her teeth rattled, shake her until she came to her senses, shake her until she understood what she had done. "You lied!" I yelled again, but the only effect was a thin, ironic smile. Her eyes were cool, distant, and brazenly analytical.

"How was the story I told any different from yours!" she dared to ask. "You told them it could have been suicide; I told them that it was!"

I could not fool myself anymore: Danielle lacked all conscience. Tell the truth or do not tell the truth, the only question which would help her most; honesty or rank deception, nothing but interchangeable means.

"You lied," I repeated, but quietly and in the tones of defeat. Her only reaction was a kind of measured neglect.

"It isn't any different than what you were doing."

Watching out the window at the people on the street below, hurrying home under a sea of umbrellas raised against the cold December rain, wishing I were one of them, I did not bother to look at her, sitting in front of my desk the other side of the room, elegant and undisturbed in the pale shadows of the evening light. Instead, I listened like a detached observer, a courtroom spectator, to the useless monologue of my own defense.

"I was talking about what the evidence proved or failed to prove. I told the jury that on the evidence they had in front of them, there was as much proof that your husband killed himself as there was that you had murdered him."

Slowly, and as it were, reluctantly, I turned my head just far enough to see her. The look of self-satisfaction, the utter indifference to what she had done; the absence of even the slightest remorse for the deception, the lies she had told me; the blatant refusal to think she owed me anything, even honesty, for what I had done for her, was like being kicked in the face. I struck back.

"Listen, lady – I knew you were a liar, but I didn't

think you were a fool! Because only a fool would think that what I was doing was the same thing as swearing under oath that he killed himself and that you tried to stop him when he did it. Jesus Christ! - Do you have any idea what you've done?" I demanded as I stalked back to my desk.

"I helped you win your case! I helped make sure I won't go to prison for something you said wasn't murder!"

I threw up my hand and bolted forward, glaring hard at her.

"You lied under oath! That's called perjury! And worse yet, you got me to help you do it!"

"So what!" she shouted, glaring back with contempt. "I told you everything; you knew what happened. I told you why I killed him, how he drove me to it; but that wasn't something you wanted the jury to know about – was it? What was the last thing you got Rufus Wiley to admit? – How depressed poor Nelson was the night he called him? I remember what you said – what you made damn sure the jury heard – that it wouldn't be very surprising if someone about to lose his 'young and beautiful' wife, someone facing a life in prison, might decide he didn't want to live! Yes, damn you – I lied! But just because you went three years to law school to learn how to lie within the rules doesn't mean you have the right to lecture me on what I should or shouldn't have done to save myself!"

It was a schoolgirl's logic, the argument to cover every sin: that nothing was very bad if the difference between good and evil was only a matter of degree. It was the argument that nothing had ever settled except the very thing she said I did not have: the power to tell her what she could or could not do. I slammed my open palm so hard down on the desk that it made her blink.

"Get out!" I screamed at the top of my lungs. I sprang out of my chair and pointed toward the door. "I don't ever want to see you again! I don't want to talk to you! I don't want to have anything to do with you! I swear to God, if you're not out of here in two seconds, the only closing argument I'll make tomorrow is to tell everyone the truth of what you did!"

She slammed the door behind her, and suddenly I was all alone, faced with the strange and discouraging task of continuing a conspiracy to cheat. There was no other word for it: cheat, lie, stand in front of those twelve anonymous faces, a so-called jury of her peers, and tell them that the prosecution had failed to make its case; stand there with all the false sincerity I could command and tell them that when they considered all the evidence, including the lying testimony of the only witness for the defense, they had no alternative, no other reasonable choice, but to return a verdict of not guilty. The only saving grace was that I did not have to tell them that they had to call her innocent.

The evidence; thank God for that. I reminded myself that that was what I was supposed to sum up - not what I believed, not what I knew to be true – only the evidence, the evidence that had been heard in court. I did not have to say anything about what I had been told in the privacy of my office, or in the intimacy of my bed. The evidence kept me sane.

For a while I remembered what it was like to be a lawyer, trying cases in which the defendant could be anyone at all, because the only thing that mattered was the prosecution's case and the weaknesses I could find inside it. That is what I was trained for, the craft at which through long years of practice I had tried to become proficient. It was what I lived for; more than that, it was who I was: a lawyer, a trial lawyer, and if I was not good at that, I was not good at anything. Gradually, Danielle disappeared and Mrs. St. James took her place. I knew every inch of Danielle's naked body; I had only on occasion touched Mrs. St. James on the arm, and then only to show the jury that I was sympathetic.

The case, my case, the case I could make to the jury, began to take on a shape of its own. My closing argument began to write itself. All the major elements - the claims made by the prosecution that they had not been able to prove – arranged themselves in the right, sequential order; the words and phrases describing what the prosecution had not done began to sort themselves out on the written page. My pen was flying as I wrote and re-wrote, not whole paragraphs or even whole sentences, but the short, fragmentary notes that would be all I needed to remember when I stood in front of the jury and spoke as if it were all spontaneous and none of it studied in advance. For a few brief hours, working away in the lamplight of my office, I forgot about Danielle and remembered myself.

A few minute past eleven, finally finished, I turned out the light and locked the door behind me. Everything was ready for tomorrow. Downstairs in the lobby, an elderly janitor, his eyes half shut, clung to a broom the way he must have once danced with a woman, long ago, when he was young. Outside, the gray, relentless drizzle had cleared and the sky was full of stars and the air sweet and clean. There were still people on the streets, moving slower than they did in the early morning or the late afternoon, coming in and out of restaurants, falling in and out of bars. They were all strangers and yet I seemed to know them all. In San Francisco the night was always full of nostalgia.

I took a deep breath and looked all around. I felt better than I had in days. Tomorrow, and the trial was over; one more day and I could wash my hands of the whole sordid affair. One more day, and I could get my conscience back. The jury would decide what would happen to Danielle. After I finished my closing argument, my responsibilities were at an end.

Except for a few passing cars, the street outside my Nob Hill building was deserted. Two blocks ahead, at the Mark Hopkins, a small crowd of gray haired women and their well-fed husbands, waited with bright, shining faces for their cars. Upstairs in her room, Danielle was probably sound asleep. Before I reached the door, I looked one last time down the empty sidewalk. I could still see her, the way she used to walk the few short blocks from the hotel, wearing one of her crazy disguises, full of a strange, eager excitement at what my first, startled, reaction would be. I tried to tell myself that it was better that, once the trial was over, I would never see her again; that she was too dishonest, too dangerous – a woman who had murdered her husband and might get away with it; a woman who had lied to me, used me, made a fool of me in court. It was all true, and I knew it, and it did not do anything to take away the hurt I felt, the howling sense of loss.

The doorman had the door open before my hand was on it.

"She's been here for more than an hour," he said in a confidential tone as he rolled his eyes toward the two easy chairs next to the front window. Danielle was sitting in one of them. She had come as herself.

"I'm sorry," she murmured with downcast eyes. "Sorry for what I did…, for what I said." She looked at me, worried that this time she had gone too far, and that nothing she could say could change it. "I'm sorry; I was too scared to think straight. I should have done what you said; I should have listened. Can you forgive me? I hate myself for what I did."

I grabbed her wrist and held it tight.

"Don't talk about it now."

We waited in silence for the elevator. She seemed nervous, distracted; her eyes darted all around. There was an air of desperation, like that of a gambler who does not hesitate to take a risk and then, when it is too late to pull back, has second thoughts. The elevator groaned to a halt and the door creaked open. We started the ascent, but almost immediately, on the third floor, there was the sound of a bell and the elevator jolted to a stop. An elderly couple in their sixties or seventies with whom I had a nodding acquaintance got on. The woman smiled perfunctorily and looked straight ahead, but her husband recognized Danielle. With a serious, courtly expression, he said good-evening in a way that seemed to wish her nothing but good luck. Everyone was following the trial.

The elevator reached my floor and we walked slowly down the narrow hallway to my apartment. The door swung shut behind us. We stood in the shadows, looking at each other. Neither of us said a word. She started unbuttoning her blouse; I took off my coat and started unbuttoning my shirt. Then, still half dressed, we were on the floor and I was inside her and she was all I knew. There was nothing but Danielle.

"I'm sorry," she said in a gentle, soothing voice when it was over. "Sorry for what I did to you. I've never trusted anyone, but I should have trusted you."

She picked up our scattered clothing and tossed it together in a heap on a chair. She held out her hand.

"The floor was nice, but the bed is better."

A sad, wistful look entered her large oval eyes. She started to say something, hesitated and looked away, and then, her mind made up, looked back.

"I've never been in love with anyone -" She stopped, a sudden sparkle in her eyes. "If you don't count what a sixteen year old girl once felt." Then she turned serious again. "I've never been in love with anyone. You knew that, didn't you? I could see it in your eyes – when I told you what I had done with Nelson that first time in his office – that tinge of disappointment, and maybe even hurt. You didn't want to think of me like that – the kid sister of the girl you almost married – a woman who would use her sex to get what she wanted. You thought I deserved better than that; you thought I should have found someone I wanted as much as he wanted me. That never happened to me; I never wanted anyone that much. I've never been in love, Andrew Morrison," she said plaintively, "but I think I may be, or could be, with you."

I put my arm around her and held her close and wished I never had to let her go, that I could just hold her and feel her heart beat next to mine and know that for all the heat and violence of what we did together there was something more than that, and that there was at least a chance that it might last.

"Let's go to bed," she whispered in the soft, enchanted voice that made me forget everything except the moment and what I felt.

We made love with a kind of first time innocence, gentle, at times awkward, full of hesitant anticipations and small apologies, a carnal ignorance neither of us had known for a very long time. A dance of our own invention, it ended as slowly, and as easily, as it had begun.

"What are we going to do?"

We looked at each other in the night time darkness. She smiled at me with her eyes.

"What are we going to do?" she asked me again, her voice become a sweet, sad lament.

"I don't know. Get through tomorrow; get through the trial. See what happens then, I guess."

"Why don't we just stay here, after the trial, after it's all over. I could – if you wanted me to."

"Yes, I want you to. Would you?"

"Yes, I want to."

"You have Michael."

"Yes, I have Michael. Do you mind that – that I have a child?"

"No, of course not; why would I?"

"Maybe it isn't a good idea; maybe it wouldn't work."

"It will work if we want it to. Do you want it to?"

"Yes, but let's see how we feel – how you feel – when this is all over. You feel a certain way now, but when it's over, when the trial stops, you won't have the same responsibility, the same sense of obligation."

I told her what I had not told her before, what I had known, deep down, from the beginning; what I had known from the first moment I saw her.

"I'm in love with you; obligation has nothing to do with it."

She pressed her finger against my mouth and with a fragile smile tried to warn me.

"I'm not what you think I am. I'm not what I used to be. I wish I were; I wish I were still sixteen. I wish I could give you all you want, all you need, but I can't! So don't be in love with me, not like that, not so much that you can't forget all about me when you find out how wrong I am for you."

It may have been the only completely honest thing she ever said to me, but it was too late. I was in love with her; more in love than I had ever thought I could be. Everything that was going to happen, everything that was going to happen to me, all the heartache and tragedy, was written from that.

I did not sleep that night, not because I could not sleep, but because I did not want to miss a moment of what it was like to hold her in my arms. And so I held her while she slept, until morning came and I could not hold her anymore. The trial was not finished.

CHAPTER FIFTEEN

Robert Franklin wore a new suit. It had been bought off the rack at a department store, and it was less than a perfect fit, but the effort to look his best had itself a favorable effect on the jury when he stood in front of them, ready to begin his summation. He began by reminding them of the mistakes he had made.

"I've prosecuted a lot of cases, but this was the first time in a long time that I was nervous at the start of a trial." He looked at them with shared sympathy. "Most of you, I imagine, felt a little the same way yourselves: all those people watching, knowing that everything was going to be reported all around the country, all around the world." Remembering what he had done, a modest, rueful smile flashed across his face. "And then, not two minutes into my opening statement, I couldn't remember what I was supposed to say!" The smile grew broader, and more emphatic. He shook his head at his own misfortune. "Tell you the truth, for a moment I couldn't even remember where I was."

The only jurors who did not smile were the ones who were nodding their encouragement. They liked him for what he was doing. As much as any lawyer I had known, and far more than most, Franklin understood that jurors, like the rest of us, are far more likely to admire, and to trust, someone honest enough to admit his own deficiencies. Perhaps it was the lesson of his own handicap and what he had done to overcome it. America was the land of second chances.

"I made a fool of myself, I'm afraid; not only forgot what I wanted to say, but probably said some things I didn't mean to say. It was not just the crowd; it was not just the coverage of the media, all the attention the trial received, that made me so self-conscious and ill at ease. That might not have bothered me at all if I had been up against someone else," he said as his gaze drifted from the jury box and came to rest on me. "I have faced other lawyers before, some of them quite good, but none of them as formidable and well-prepared as Mr. Morrison, the attorney for the defense."

He looked at me, sitting just a few feet away, with what seemed genuine respect. With a brief nod, and a business-like smile, I acknowledged the gesture as coming from a respected adversary. The jury noticed, and approved, what it thought Franklin's sense of fairness. It was a victory for the prosecution.

"But this is not a trial about the lawyers," said Franklin, turning serious. "This is a trial about whether the defendant, Danielle St. James, murdered her husband, Nelson St. James. And on that issue the evidence is entirely on one side: Danielle St. James is guilty. Let me remind you what I told you at the beginning; what, despite my own mistakes, the prosecution was going to prove. I told you that this was not some crime of passion, an act of violence when an argument got out of hand; I told you that it was cold-blooded murder carried out for financial gain.

"The defendant came here, to San Francisco, with her husband, and they argued all the time. They were arguing when the plane landed, arguing at dinner to the point that she walked out of the restaurant, arguing when they left on that last deadly voyage on their yacht."

Franklin's eyes moved in a slow, methodical arc from one end of the jury box to the other. Shoving his left hand into his pocket, he dipped his forehead as he made a long, sweeping turn toward the table where Danielle sat next to me. It drew every eye toward her, serving as reminder that for all the courtroom fireworks, she was the one on trial and that he at least did not have the slightest doubt that she was as guilty of murder as anyone could ever be.

"And I told you that just moments after the shot was fired that killed Nelson St. James, the defendant, Danielle St. James, was found with the gun still in her hand, and that there was blood all over. That's what I told you. Has it been proven? Was Nelson St. James shot on his yacht in the middle of the Pacific? Yes, of course: you heard the testimony – there isn't any doubt about it. Was his death caused by a gunshot wound? Yes, everyone – even including the defense – agrees that was how he died. Nor does anyone dispute that the gun that killed him was found in the defendant's hand or that the gun had the fingerprints of the defendant all over it."

With his hands held loosely behind his back, Franklin began to pace, short, wandering steps, first in one direction, then another. The lines in his forehead deepened and spread farther across his brow. He was concentrating, as it seemed, on some problem of enormous difficulty and importance.

"All of the evidence – all of it! – points to her. No one else was out there, on the deck of the Blue Zephyr, when it happened. Her gun was the murder weapon – Yes, I know that it was purchased under her husband's name, but she doesn't deny that he bought it for her. It was her gun; she killed him with it; and before she could get rid of it – toss it overboard into the sea – she was caught with it, still holding it in her hand. All the evidence points to her, evidence about which there is not even the possibility of a doubt. But the question, the question the defense has tried to raise every chance it could, is why? Why would Danielle St. James have murdered her husband?"

Franklin stood at the end of the jury box, resting his left hand on the railing. A thin line of perspiration glistened on his forehead.

"I told you in my opening statement, as I reminded you just a few minutes ago, that it was 'cold-blooded murder carried out for gain.' Perhaps I should have said, 'cold-blooded murder carried out because of money.' The defense has tried to argue that Danielle St. James had every reason to want her husband alive. He was going to get a divorce, but so what if he did? She would get the house in the Hamptons and a million dollars a year. Now, because he's dead, she doesn't even get that. The death of Nelson St. James, in other words, costs her everything. But that leaves out all the anger, all the rage, the humiliation, she must have felt at being forced to submit to a pre-nuptial agreement that, no matter how large it may seem to you and me, was nothing compared to what she would have gotten in a divorce had that agreement never been signed. She murdered him, ladies and gentlemen – shot him to death – not because of the money she was going to get, but because of the money she was going to lose!"

Folding his arms across his chest, Franklin stepped back from the jury box and cast a baleful glance at Danielle.

"The evidence against her is overwhelming. What is her defense?" he asked, turning back to the jury as if they already knew the answer. "Does she claim that someone else on board took the gun and killed him? Does she claim that it was an accident, that the gun went off while they were in the middle of another one of their arguments? Does she claim that it was self-defense: that he was attacking her and it was the only way she had to stop him? No! She tells us that he killed himself! He was depressed, she tells us: depressed that he was losing her, depressed that he was in trouble. And the evidence offered for this? – Why, the testimony of the defendant herself. All the evidence proves she did it, and what does she say? – 'I didn't do it – he did. I didn't kill him – he killed himself!'"

Pausing, Franklin cast a long, knowing look at the jury, a look that told them they should treat Danielle's testimony with all the contempt lies like that deserved. When he began to speak again, he was cool and methodical, calm and efficient, all the outrage gone as he became the voice of reason and responsibility.

For the next hour, Franklin reviewed with textbook precision the testimony of each witness, listing every relevant fact in a bare-bones outline of everything that had been said in the course of the trial. My mind on other things, I barely heard a thing he said. With everyone watching him, I looked at Danielle. Odd as it may seem, I felt grateful just to see her, a woman that beautiful with a face that perfect. And then, suddenly, I realized what I had been missing; what, of all things, I had not understood. That face – her face – was the best defense she had! Hurriedly, I scribbled a note to myself, not that I thought I could possibly forget what, had I only noticed, had always been obvious, but for the pure pleasure of seeing it in tangible form down on paper.

Franklin was nearly finished. I gave him my full attention and, because I now knew not only what I was going to do, but the effect it was likely to have, began to enjoy it, the way someone enjoys the performance of a play they have seen once before.

"All the evidence points to the defendant, Danielle St. James – and what does she tell us?" he asked, repeating with studied cynicism the question he had raised at the beginning. "That she did not do it, he did. It was suicide, and she feels bad about it because when he threatened to do it, she told him no one would miss him if he did."

His hands on his hips, he thrust his chin forward and glowered defiance. He stared at Danielle, daring her, as it seemed, to rise from her chair and deny the truth of what he was saying.

"All good lies have some basis in truth. You wanted him dead, and by these words of yours you admitted it! But kill himself!" he asked, incredulous, as he wheeled around to the waiting eyes of the jury. "Why? Because he was about to lose his 'young and beautiful' wife, as Mr. Morrison would have us believe? But wasn't it the defense that kept insisting that Nelson St. James was habitually unfaithful: all those other women and Nelson St. James kills himself because he is about to lose his wife? If this weren't a case of murder, we'd all be laughing!

"But forget all that; forget that Nelson St. James was one of the wealthiest men in the world and, whatever you or I may think of how he lived, could do pretty much as he pleased; forget that he was in trouble with the law. Nelson St. James had a son, his only child, the child he wanted, the child he had married his wife to have. The defense wants us to believe that he killed himself because he was depressed? He had everything to live for, and the only reason he isn't home with his son somewhere is because his wife could not stand the thought that she was about to be cast aside, replaced by someone else, cheated out of the fortune that in her mind should have been hers! Danielle St. James is guilty of murder, ladies and gentlemen of the jury, and guilty is the only verdict you can give!"

Robert Franklin sank into his chair, exhausted, having gone to the limit of what he could do. He sat there, staring straight ahead, physically spent, but with a sense of his own achievement. Danielle St. James was guilty, and he had proven it.

The voice of Alice Brunelli broke a silence so profound that had you been sitting there you would have sworn you could hear your own heartbeat.

"Mr. Morrison, are you ready to make your closing argument?"

Instead of rising from my chair, instead of moving quickly and with a sense of purpose to the jury box, I crossed one leg over the other, threw my arm over the back of the chair and stayed where I was.

"Nothing that was said here, none of the testimony that the prosecution has spoken at such length about, is nearly as important as something Mr. Franklin did not mention at all. You never heard it from any witness, you never heard it from anyone; but it was always there, right in front of your eyes, the single undeniable fact that explains everything, and changes everything. The prosecution wants you to think that it was murder, but cannot prove it was murder at all."

Slowly, almost casually, I got to my feet and with my hand on the corner of the table shook my head as if I had only now come to understand something that, though they did not yet know it, they knew as well. They were waiting for me, all twelve of them, when I raised my eyes; waiting for me to tell them what it was, quite without their knowing, they had always understood. I pointed to Danielle.

"Look at her. Have you ever seen anyone who looked like that, looked that beautiful? And yet no one has even mentioned it, not one of the witnesses called by the prosecution." I stepped closer to the jury box. "What did they talk about instead? – Money. That's all you heard about: how she married her husband for his money, how she murdered him because she wasn't going to get all the money she thought she deserved."

I looked at Danielle as if I were seeing her for the first time, and in a way, that was true. I had been so enamored of the way she looked, she had had such an astonishing effect on the way I felt, that I had lost the distance necessary to understand what it meant; not for me, but for everyone else, all the other people who, drawn by the way she looked, had feelings of their own.

"Assume that everything you've been told by the prosecution is true," I continued, my attention back on the jury. "Assume she was greedy, calculating, interested only in what she could get; assume that more than anything she wanted the kind of wealthy, privileged life Nelson St. James with all his money could give her. That might tell you why she married him; it doesn't tell you why he married her. But that's obvious, isn't it? Look at her! Everyone in this courtroom knows why he married her. You knew it the moment you walked in her and saw her for the very first time. Rufus Wiley must have known it, too, the first time he saw her. Rufus Wiley knew why Nelson St. James wanted to marry her. It wasn't because he wanted a child – he could have had a child with anyone. It was because she was quite simply the most beautiful woman Nelson St. James had ever seen!"

Every eye in the courtroom followed mine as I stepped back from the jury box and gazed across at Danielle. She looked at me as if we were all alone, the only two people in the room. It did not bother her that a crowd was watching: she was used to everyone staring at her, the most beautiful woman any of them had ever seen. Something sad and wistful in her eyes, luminous and not immodest, seemed to acknowledge the truth of what others saw. With a pensive expression, I walked behind her and placed a protective hand lightly on her shoulder. The jury had to look at her while I spoke.

"If the reason – the only reason – she married Nelson St. James was because she wanted money, why would she worry about what she might be left with after a divorce?"

The question, absurd on the face of it, had a different

meaning applied to her, a meaning just below the surface
of conscious thought, one of those possibilities that, once
you are made to see it, become suddenly the only thing that
makes sense. I put it to them directly.

"If she married him for money – if what the
prosecution says is true – how long do you think it would
have been before she found someone else, someone just as
rich? The money was supposed to have meant everything
to her. What did the prosecution tell us? - That she killed
him because of all the money she was going to lose! – But
how could it have meant anything, when there were always
so many other men with money, all of them as eager, as
desperate, as Nelson St. James had been to have her for their
own? Or is the prosecution going to insist that a divorced
woman, even one who looks like this, has no prospects
in this day and age?" I asked with a smile on my lips and
laughter in my eyes.

My hand fell away from Danielle's shoulder. I
stepped to the side, not far, but enough to move her into
the background so that nothing would distract the attention
of the jury from the last thing I had to say to them. If they
remembered nothing else, I wanted them to remember this.

"The prosecution insists it was murder. The defendant
testified under oath that Nelson St. James took his own life.
The evidence brought by the prosecution proves suicide
every bit as much as it proves murder. And that means that
the prosecution has not proved murder at all. Danielle St.
James told you what happened, and not one witness called
by the prosecution can prove that she was lying."

I could have proved it, but I was not a witness for the
prosecution: I was the lawyer for the defense. Caught up in
all the emotion of the moment, the single-minded intensity
of a closing argument in which the words had taken on a life
of their own, I was almost convinced I was telling the truth.

CHAPTER SIXTEEN

Danielle did not want to go back to the hotel, but I insisted. There was no point waiting at the courthouse: the jury might be out for days. She would be comfortable in her suite at the Mark Hopkins, and, more importantly, no one could bother her there. I promised I would call her the moment I heard anything. I went back to my office and tried to pretend that this was just another trial and that while I waited for the verdict I could start working on the next case, and the one after that.

Alice Brunelli had finished giving the jury their instructions and sent them off to begin deliberations a few minutes before three in the afternoon. There was nothing more to be done, and I had another trial scheduled to start next week. I grabbed a cup of coffee and opened the voluminous file that had been gathering dust for weeks. Three pages into it and the words became a blur. I was too worried to think, though I am not sure I could have said exactly what it was I was worried about. The verdict, of course, but no matter how many trials I had had, I always worried about that. What would happen to Danielle if the jury found her guilty – but not with any wrenching sense of anguish or despair. The possibility was too vague, too abstract, to concentrate my attention. No, it was something else: a sense that in some yet undetermined way, I would have to pay a price for what I had done.

I had known from the beginning that I should have refused when Danielle asked me to defend her. I had been seduced, literally seduced, made to act against my own, better judgment, by the effect she had on me. The effect was physical, the pain of longing for something you want almost more than you can stand, an effect that was all the greater for having known her with the kind of fondness you have for someone's younger sister. That was it, of course - the fact I had known Justine. It was easy to believe, to convince myself, that because I had known her in a way no one else had known her, before she was the woman everyone knew

and wanted, before she was Danielle, she belonged, or
should belong, to me. Others had known her only later; I
knew her, so to speak, from the beginning.

None of that excused what I had done. I should have
kept my distance, treated her like any other client, once
I agreed to take her case; I should never have become
involved. She would not have dared do what she did, take the
stand after agreeing that she would not testify, and then tell
a story full of lies. I would not have let it happen. I would
have stopped the proceedings, told the judge in chambers
that if the defendant testified I would have to withdraw
as her attorney. All the judge had to know was that I was
faced with an ethical conflict. Alice Brunelli - any half way
competent judge – would have known immediately what
that meant. The trial would have been delayed while other
counsel was found to take over the defense. It would have
been an extreme step to take, but one which I was not only
entitled, but, strictly speaking, obligated to take. There are
a lot of things a lawyer is supposed to do, but few are as
serious as calling a witness you know is going to perjure
herself.

The trial was over, and there was nothing I could do.
I could not even confess! The prohibition against revealing
the communications of a client was absolute, binding even
after death. No one would ever know what she had done,
or how I had helped her. I could not tell anyone, and she
had every reason not to. There would be no punishment,
no sanction - no possibility that I might face disbarment.
Danielle might or might not get away with murder, the crime
she had committed; there was no question that I would
get away with mine. That only made me more certain that
sooner or later a price would have to be paid. I was already
paying it in a loss of self-respect, the howling protest that
came from somewhere the back of my mind at the way I
had been used; the voice that I heard late at night, taunting
me with the ease at which I rationalized everything when,
passion spent, she lay naked in my arms. She had murdered
her husband, but that was almost more forgivable than the

blind-eyed eagerness with which I had become her after-the-fact accomplice, breaking all the rules so that she could, without penalty, break them too. I was a fool, and I knew it, and there was nothing I could do: I did not have the strength - I did not have the courage - to walk away and forget I had ever known her. I hated myself a little for that; I hated that I had become a coward.

I tried to go back to work and managed to get through a dozen more pages before I threw the case file to the side and swore softly under my breath. There was nothing to do but wait, wait for the jury's verdict, wait for what would happen after that. It was quarter past six, but we were in the short days of winter and the only light at the window was from the street below. Switching off the lamp, I stared into the shadows, watching as they danced on the ceiling and down the walls, graceful and insubstantial, a reminder, as if one were needed, of what Danielle and her beauty were all about.

The telephone rang, breaking the silence with its lonely, insistent call. I knew before I answered who it was.

"You didn't think they would be out this long, did you?" asked Danielle. She tried to sound cheerful, confident, full of hope, but the strain was evident and I knew that, like everyone else who had ever been in her position, she was anxious, scared, dying by inches inside. I tried to sound professional and matter of fact, not overly concerned by what was going on.

"I never know how long a jury is going to be out. It's impossible to predict."

She wanted more than that: she wanted certainty.

"You didn't think it would take any time at all," she insisted in a soft, breathless voice. There was a tapping noise, a pencil, or perhaps a fingernail, beating time, a nervous habit she did not know she had. "Maybe it was just me," she said, confused by things she could not control. "Maybe I just thought that after what you said, after the way they seemed to hang on every word, that it wouldn't take them any time at all."

I started to fall back on my old, settled routine, explaining that in a murder trial a jury might be out for days, or even weeks, but we had talked about all this before. She was not calling because she wanted me to tell her about it again; she was calling because she did not want to be alone. But I could not think of anything to say, words of encouragement, which would not sound hollow and contrived; and so I sat there in silence, helpless and defeated, listening to the constant nervous drumbeat coming from the other end.

"When did you decide to do that – what you said to the jury about what I would have done after a divorce?" she asked, eager to escape her own thoughts. "Do you really think that's what I would have done, if Nelson had gotten a divorce – married someone else, someone with money?"

"Don't," I said quietly, as I leaned on my elbow and stared into the darkness, my eyes heavy with fatigue. "There's no point to it."

"Marry another wealthy man? – That's what you said: that every wealthy man would want me and I could pick and choose among them. Like some whore! - you should have said." There was a frantic quality to her belligerence, the sudden onset of something close to panic. The tapping noise got louder, and more insistent. "'She's a whore, and a whore can always get money from another man!'- You should have said. Marry another wealthy man! I may never marry anyone; I may be going to prison - I may not live!"

Fatigue gave way to depression. The room began to turn, the shadows moving quicker on the wall, moving faster in a spiral, a black whirlpool pulling everything down behind it. I slammed my hand hard on the top of the desk, shining with my own reflection.

"You're not going to prison!" I shouted, as much to keep me from falling into the abyss as to give her comfort. "The jury isn't going to find you guilty: I could see it in their eyes. And I didn't call you a whore, and you know it....But isn't that what you think? – That because you're beautiful and you can choose whomever you want, he might as well be rich?"

Before she could answer, make some reply in her own defense, I went for the jugular: I told her the truth. "It's what you told me – remember? That whole long story of duplicity and sex: what you did when you decided that you wanted to be the wife of Nelson St. James! It's what you told me just the other night – remember? That you've never been in love with anyone, that you married him because you wanted what he had!"

The relentless, incessant tapping abruptly stopped. There was nothing, not a sound, not so much as the whisper of her breath. And then, suddenly, she began to cry, softly at first, but soon a wild, wailing lament.

"Why are you doing this, Andrew? Why do you want to hurt me – now, while I'm terrified - out of my mind with fear! I told you things about me…, I trusted you – No, I was falling in love with you! And you think I'm a …! Don't you understand? If I could do whatever I liked, marry anyone I wanted – what you said to the jury – I wouldn't have married another Nelson – I would have married you!"

The shadows stopped moving; the darkness slipped away.

"Then why don't you? – Why don't you marry me? You know I want to. Do you?"

"Yes. No. I can't. Oh, God – I don't know." There was something in her voice I could not quite place, a kind of bittersweet nostalgia, as of a feeling, a condition of her youth, that she would have given anything to get back and knew she never could. "Let's not talk about it now – I'm too confused. Take me somewhere to dinner, some place private, where people won't stare; some place I can just be with you, where I can forget the trial and what might happen."

Another phone line flashed. Danielle waited while I took the call.

"It was the court clerk," I told her when I came back on the line. "They have a verdict."

"Is that good?" she asked after a long silence. "That they decided this fast."

I did not know.

"Yes, I think so."

An hour and a half later, at eight o'clock in the evening, in a courtroom filled with reporters, I walked down the center aisle with Danielle on my arm. It struck me odd, how often on the most serious occasions of our lives – weddings and funerals and the verdicts of juries – we make the same entrance, the formal beginning of the rituals that, in some measure, mark the moment that will change everything. We could have been entering a church, ready to begin a new life, instead of a courtroom where we might be ending an old one.

Robert Franklin was already there, his hands folded carelessly on the hard polished counsel table in front of him. He did not look around when we came in, nor did he turn to the side to glance at us when I pulled out a chair for Danielle and then took the one next to her. He stared at a space on the table between his wrists, and did not raise his eyes to look at anything until, just minutes after Danielle and I had settled into our places, Alice Brunelli burst through the door at the side.

Before the trial, during the trial, after the trial, Alice Brunelli was all business. She sat straight as a board on the front edge of the chair, her thin, almost emaciated face stern and implacable.

"I have been informed that the jury has reached a verdict," she announced in a brittle, metallic voice. She cast a warning glance at the burgeoning courtroom crowd. "There will be no demonstrations of any kind, not a word!" Then she looked at Franklin, and then she looked at me. "Let the record reflect that counsel both are present, as is the defendant." She turned to the bailiff. "Bring in the jury."

With long, solemn faces and tired, downcast eyes, the twelve citizens, drawn almost at random from the obscurity of their private lives, filed back into the jury box. Careful not to look at anyone, careful not to make a gesture that might give a hint of what they had done, the decision they had come to after only three hours of deliberation, they sat in their chairs like twelve parishioners come to do penance for their sins. Three hours of deliberations! – I could not get over it. Weeks of testimony, and only three hours! A murder case, a woman on trial for her life, and that was all the time they had spent! Three hours! – What did it mean? Had I missed something? Was it really all that one-sided? Was it that simple, in a case like this, to reach a verdict, whatever that verdict might be?

"Has the jury reached a verdict?" asked Judge Brunelli with a tight smile of purely formal politeness. Her lashes beat like butterfly wings.

The second juror from the left on the bottom row, the youngest member of the jury, not more than thirty, with a crooked nose and eyes set too close together, stood up. I was surprised, and alarmed. There were other jurors better educated and more articulate that should have been chosen foreman instead. He seemed weak, indecisive, during voir dire; someone more likely to go along with what others might think rather than have, much less express, any strong opinion of his own. When he spoke now, however, he did not seem to have any reluctance to be out in front. No matter how many questions you asked during jury selection, you never really knew what you were getting. It was all guesswork in the end.

"We have, your Honor."

Danielle's fingers close tight around my hand.

"Would you please hand the verdict form to the clerk."

Alice Brunelli examined the verdict form with no more change of expression than if she were reading the weather report. Through the clerk, she gave it back to the foreman. The silence in the courtroom was massive and intense. The footsteps of the clerk as she walked the short distance from the bench to the jury box echoed with a harsh staccato. The verdict form, that single piece of white paper, seemed to make a violent, cracking sound as the foreman unfolded it. And then, when he began to read, it seemed to take forever, each word a gate that had to be opened, and then closed, before the next gate, the next word, came into view and could be approached. A lifetime could have been lived between the beginning and the end of that single interminable sentence.

"We, the jury, in the above entitled case, on the sole count of the indictment, murder in the first degree, find the defendant, Danielle St. James…"

He stopped, did not say another word, folded up the verdict form as if, knowing the secret, he had decided not to share it. He looked around the crowded courtroom, everyone waiting. The moment belonged to him and he was not going to lose it. Slowly, and with astonishing presence, he turned and looked straight at Danielle.

"Not guilty."

The courtroom, despite the judge's warning, erupted into a bedlam of confusion and noise. Danielle threw her arms around my neck, thanking me through her tears.

"They did it because of you," she murmured, digging hard with her fingers. "They believed you, believed what you said; believed that you believed me."

Still clutching my shoulder, she wiped her wet eyes with her other hand, tried to smile at the jury, and started to cry again.

Alice Brunelli thanked the jury for their service, and with one quick stroke of her gavel brought the trial to a final end. Robert Franklin started to leave, but then remembered that there was one more thing he had to do. He came over, looked me straight in the eyes, and offered his congratulations. He did not once look at Danielle.

"Horrible man," said Danielle under her breath, after Franklin disappeared into the crowd.

"Actually, one of the best I know," I remarked, remembering what I had learned about what, against all odds, he had done. But Danielle was not interested in anything but her own feelings of relief. And who could blame her? It was over, and she was free; and if the meaning of that was not what it once might have been, years earlier, before she had met Nelson St. James, it was still far more than she could have hoped for the night she killed him.

Because whatever we might tell each other, however we might excuse it, the truth was that, with my help, she had just gotten away with murder, and we both knew it.

"I owe you everything," she whispered frantically. "My life, my...."

There were too many people pressing close, eager to get one last look; too many reporters trying to ask one last question. Maybe that was the reason it happened – the sudden panic in her eyes, the sudden, urgent need to get away –all those people pulling, pushing, grabbing at whatever they could get their hands on, all of them trying to get at her.

"Get me out of here!" she cried. "I can't breathe!"

Wrapping my arm close around her shoulder, I bowled my way through a frenzied gauntlet of flying arms and grasping hands. It was bedlam, pure and simple, the noise deafening, overwhelming. An elbow, hard and sharp, struck me in the eye; a knee jabbed my thigh and nearly crippled my leg.

"Out of my way!" I shouted, scowling fiercely at the contorted faces pressing all around me. "Get out!" Other faces, other bodies, jumped in front. I shoved through them and we kept moving, fighting our way, stumbling out of the courtroom into the harsh lights of a dozen glaring cameras and a dozen waiting microphones. The crowd behind us, the mob that had been clawing at the chance to get closer, to touch Danielle, suddenly lost interest in her and lost itself instead, every sweating red-faced one of them, in the thought that they might get on television. They would not have stopped moving so quickly had they run straight into a brick wall. Now we all had different parts to play. The crowd could not stop us, but those cameras could.

"The trial is over," I announced with the fastidious air of someone about to say something quite profound. Danielle let go of my arm and, perfectly calm, stood next to me. "The jury has returned its verdict. Danielle St. James is not guilty. All she wants now is to be left alone."

This said nothing at all, but it seemed to be enough.

The news people had the shot they wanted, the one that would be shown on the late night news and seen in all the morning papers: Danielle St. James, minutes after her acquittal on a charge of murder, looking somehow even more beautiful than she had before.

"Danielle!" shouted some reporter I could not see. "Isn't there something you want to say?"

Danielle looked at me as if to see if it was all right and then took a half step forward. The silence was sudden and complete.

"This has been a tragedy from start to finish. My husband killed himself and, as I said at the trial, I will always blame myself. Now I want to go home to New York and take care of my child."

She stepped back, a signal that there was nothing more she wished to say, but all it did was make each of the other reporters more determined to get in a question of their own. The place was half-mad with noise. I tried to stop it.

"There is nothing more to be said. The jury reached the only verdict it could have reached. Mrs. St. James is going home."

With my arm around her shoulder we started walking, moving quickly, trying to reach the door before the reporters and the cameras could catch up. The lights from the traffic in the street outside made a crazy, changing, crisscross pattern on the white marble walls.

"The jury may not have found her guilty, but everyone else thinks she did it!"

I stopped in my tracks and spun around, searching the pack of reporters clinging to our heels.

"Who said that?"

"I did!" shouted a woman with lacquered hair and vapid eyes.

"You'd substitute your judgment for the judgment of the jury?" I yelled back, angry and looking for a fight. Danielle tugged at my sleeve, reminding me that the car was just outside and that we were almost there.

"They may not have been able to prove it," said

the reporter, staring at Danielle with a thin, caustic grin.
"Your lawyer may have convinced the jury that there was a
reasonable doubt. But do you really think anyone is going to
believe that Nelson St. James committed suicide?"

Danielle pulled on my arm, determined to get me
out the door, but I would not move. I glared at the reporter,
defying her smug belligerence.

"What an ugly thing to say, but then, that's what you
get paid for – isn't it? – To say really stupid things! It's nice
you've found something you're so good at!"

Then we were out the door and across the sidewalk to
the waiting car.

Her eyes closed tight, and her small fists pressed hard
on her knees, Danielle doubled over and began to sob. My
hand went to her shoulder. She threw herself against me, and
her tears fell hot and wet against the side of my face, and for
a few moments I held her close and let her cry.

"It's never going to be over, is it?" she asked
plaintively when the crying stopped. "That's what they'll say
about me – what everyone will think – that I murdered him
and that I got away with it."

There was not much I could say to give her comfort
against what, despite the verdict, we both knew to be the
truth. It was only now, after it was over, that she had finally
to recognize that getting away with murder was not the
complete victory she might have wished.

"I know you thought you had to do what you did," I
said in a voice that sounded even to me lifeless and without
conviction. "I know that you -"

"You don't know anything!" she cried. She pushed
away from me and looked at me with something that seemed
almost like hatred. "You don't have the slightest idea what
happened – what really happened! No one does; no one
ever will." She made a gesture with her hand, as if to ask
forgiveness for what she said, or rather, the way she had said
it. "I'm sorry…, I didn't mean…." She waved her hand again,
and then stared out the window, helpless and vulnerable and
all alone.

THE SWINDLERS

The driver had just turned onto California Street, on the way to Nob Hill. The city was all lit up, the stores, the windows, full of decoration, painted in the bright cheerful colors of Christmas, December scenes of falling snow in a place where it never got cold enough for anything but fog and rain. We passed a cable car, full of giddy tourists, chugging up the shiny iron tracks to the top. Danielle tapped on the glass.

"I'm not going to the hotel. You can drop us both at Mr. Morrison's building."

It was only after the car was gone, after we had slipped through the lobby and the elevator door had closed behind us, that I started repeat what in my lame attempt to make her feel better I had tried to say before. But now I did it because I was confused and worried, and more than little angry, that she had waited until after the verdict to tell me that apparently nothing she had told me had been the truth.

"You said it happened because of that look he had on his face, that look he had after he finished with you in bed; that look that said he could do whatever he wanted and there was nothing you could do about it! Are you telling me that wasn't true? – That it wasn't the reason you killed him, that it was something else?"

Every conceivable emotion – anger, defiance, pride, and then hurt, regret, fatigue, and even sorrow – ran one after the other through her marvelous eyes in a losing race to dominate, take control, give her, if only for a moment, a clear sense of who she was and what she really felt. I could not escape the feeling that some part of her was almost desperate to tell me the truth, but that another part of her, stronger and more disciplined, and I think more instinctive, would not let her.

"What was it?" I pleaded. "What really happened that night? You owe me that much, after what I've done."

The elevator shuddered to a stop. She did not say anything – she did not even look at me – until we were inside the apartment, and then it was only to tell me that she was not going to answer.

"Let's not talk about anything. Let's make love and then sleep and then make love again." She looked at me with a strange, wounded expression, like someone forced into an ordeal that was still not over, that might never be over. "Whatever happens, when I told you that I might be falling in love with you – that was true. I am falling in love with you. Remember that," she said as we started toward the bedroom door. "Whatever happens later, remember that."

CHAPTER SEVENTEEN

The next morning, before I left for the office, we agreed to meet that night for dinner. In a few days, Danielle would be going back to New York to spend time with her son, but after I finished the next trial I had, we would meet somewhere and decide then what we wanted to do next. It seemed a very good idea, given everything that had happened, to take our time and let things take their course. We would find a place - Danielle mentioned an island in the Caribbean – where we could have all the privacy we needed. For the first time in a long time - since, really, the day she asked me to defend her - I felt confident and relaxed, certain about the future, or as certain as anyone can be. I was almost looking forward to the trial that was coming up, getting back to my normal life.

An hour after I started I had finished going through the case file, the same one that just a few days earlier I had not been able read even two pages without losing concentration. Everything fell into place. I began to make a list of witnesses, prosecution witnesses, with a short summary of what they could be expected to say and what I thought would be the weak points of their testimony by which I could discredit them. My mind was clear. I could see in advance everything that was going to happen: every question I was going to ask and every answer I could turn to advantage. I worked without any awareness of time, lost in what I was doing, the next trial, the only trial that mattered. I did not hear the buzzer on the telephone, and did not know my secretary had something to tell me until her hand was on my shoulder.

"There's someone here to see you."

Tall, taciturn, with a strict devotion to work, Stella Summerfield knew my habits better than I knew them myself. When I was getting ready for a trial, there were no phone calls, no appointments, nothing that would interrupt what I was doing. Telling me that someone was here to see me made no sense at all.

"I told him you were busy and that he needed to make an appointment," she explained when my only response was a blank, incredulous stare. "He says it's about the St. James trial."

The blank expression on my face turned to one of puzzled annoyance. That was the last reason I would see anyone, and she knew it.

"He was a witness, a witness for the prosecution," she said with her usual calm efficiency. "He says he has something to tell you he thinks you should know."

"Did he tell you his name?" I asked, vaguely interested.

"Rufus Wiley."

"Rufus Wiley!" I exclaimed, astonished as much that he was here, in San Francisco, as that he had something to say to me. "Yes, all right; send him in."

There was none of the smug complacency, the irritating condescension, which had so much marked Wiley's demeanor when I had first watched him take the witness stand in court. He moved with a cautious, almost hesitant, step as he came toward my desk and took the wing back chair in front. I did not get up, did not reach out my hand, as perhaps I should have done. I was too surprised that he was here, too intrigued by why he might have come to see me this soon after the trial, to remember courtesy; and besides, I did not like him. Whatever the reason he was here, it was not likely to be pleasant.

"You said you wanted to see me," I said, watching him, as it were, from a distance. "Something about the trial?"

Wiley bent his head to the side. There was a pensive, and oddly troubled, expression on his round, smooth face.

"Yes, about the trial..., that business about Nelson killing himself." He tilted his head farther to the side. A nervous smile started onto his mouth and then as quickly disappeared. "You didn't know she was going to say that, did you? – until she said it on the witness stand."

It was none of his business, but that was not what got

my attention.

"You were there – in the courtroom - watching the trial?"

He seemed to study me for a moment, searching my eyes to see if I meant it. He smiled, not like before, narrow and cramped, but broadly and with what, if I understood it right, seemed like relief, though at what, or for what reason, I could not have guessed. Suddenly, he glanced around my office and made a sweeping gesture with his hand.

"It's like this room. If you closed your eyes and I asked you to describe it, I'll bet you couldn't tell me the color the walls are painted." That thought seemed to lead to another, an escalating sense of analysis. "You wouldn't notice if you came in one morning and all the paintings had been removed, all the furniture taken away, and all the books stolen, so long as you had that desk and chair, a place you could work. That's why you're so good at what you do, Mr. Morrison: perfect concentration, or as close to perfect as I have ever seen. I admire you for that. It's a gift I wish I had. Yes, I was there, watching the trial; seldom missed a day of it after I was finished as a witness. But you didn't see a thing, did you? - didn't even notice me there in the crowd. As I say, I'm not surprised."

"But why did you?" I asked, deeply curious.

"Because of you, Mr. Morrison. You see, I was certain she was going to be convicted, but then – well, I saw what you could do, and I wasn't so sure anymore."

He was older than I, twenty years or more, a lawyer all his life and a man not given to praise. One leg crossed over the other, his hands held together in his lap, he spoke with the tempered judgment of a senior partner drawing on a vast, accumulated experience.

"That question you asked right at the end, whether Nelson, the last time I talked to him, had not seemed depressed: that was brilliant – a stroke of genius, really. Everyone said you were good, but I had no idea you were as good as that. One question, and you had everything you needed; or rather, all she needed."

He laughed, as at some private joke, a low, muffled laugh followed immediately by a rueful smile. He seemed certain I would understand.

"That must have been when she first thought of it – when you suggested it as a possibility – the story she could tell, the one that gave her the best chance to save herself. You didn't know, did you? – You didn't know, and then you had no choice when she took the stand and started telling that made-up story of hers."

I could not see the point to this. Why was he here? It had been obvious from the moment he had taken the stand as a witness for the prosecution that he disliked Danielle. I did not need to listen to him tell me that again.

"You wanted her to be convicted, didn't you? Was that the reason you stayed around: to see the look on her face when the jury found her guilty?"

He ignored me, dismissed my remark as somehow irrelevant to the reason he was there. He was so intent on what he had come to say I am not even sure he had heard me.

"That was a brilliant performance," he went on; "not just yesterday – though that closing argument of yours was as good as anything I've seen, - but all the way through. I thought you might win, after what you did with me on cross-examination, but until she took the stand and told that lie of hers, I have to confess I wasn't quite sure how you were going to pull it off. Even with what she said on the stand, if you hadn't been her lawyer, if she'd had anyone else…."

Wiley fell into a long, brooding silence. Streaming through the curtained window on the other side of the room, the morning light made the slightest movement of his eyes seem furtive and full of secrets, as if he knew more than he wanted to; more, even, than he should.

"You made quite a point of the legal difficulties Nelson was in," he said presently; "that being indicted must have weighed heavily on his mind, added to the depression he must have felt over the failure of his marriage. Did you really believe that she knew nothing about the kind of business

Nelson was in? I was his lawyer," he added, quick to put some distance between himself and what his client had done; "I was not his accountant. I didn't know what he was doing with all his different financial schemes and transactions. But she was married to him, and she's much too intelligent – much too shrewd – not to have known what he was up to. Every time someone visited the yacht, every time Nelson brought someone on board to discuss what they were going to do next, she was there to greet them. You were there, Mr. Morrison, on the Blue Zephyr – you met Nelson, and you've now spent months with her. Which of them do you think was smarter? Do you really think she didn't know?"

Wiley searched my eyes, subjecting me to a scrutiny suggesting culpability on my part. Either I was a fool for not having believed she could be involved in her husband's criminal acts, or a liar for denying it.

"I don't know anything about the things St. James might have done – or what his wife may have known. But even if I did," I added, wondering why I felt the need to explain myself to him, "you know as well as I do that I can't discuss anything my client may have said."

"She never mentioned it, never said a word about how he got all that money – nothing about how he stole it?" he persisted, ignoring what I had just told him. "Never told you how the money was the real reason she killed him? Never said anything about how killing Nelson was the only chance she had to keep it all for herself?"

This was crazy; none of it made sense. Wiley had been at the trial; he could not have forgotten.

"'The chance to keep it all for herself'? - She doesn't get anything! He changed his will – you did it, you made the changes! There was no divorce, so she doesn't even get what she would have had under the pre-nuptial agreement you insisted she sign! If money was what she wanted, the last thing -"

"Was to have him dead – Yes, I remember what you told the jury. But you left something out: the will. Almost everything now goes to their son, but he's just a boy and his mother will be the trustee. Yes, that's correct: the woman you convinced the jury would get less from her husband's death than she would have gotten in a divorce ends up in control of everything. Why do you think she's going back to New York? Because now that she's been acquitted of Nelson's murder, there are certain papers – papers I have to draw up – transferring ownership from his name to hers."

"She's going back to New York to see her son. She probably doesn't even know she's going to be trustee for the money he inherits."

Rufus Wiley rose from the chair. He looked at me, pitying the deception of which he seemed certain I had been the victim.

"Is that what she told you: that she was going to New York to be with her son? He's been in a private boarding school in Switzerland for the last two years. And as for not knowing she would become the trustee, with full power to do with the money what she likes, she called my office first thing this morning and made the appointment to sign the papers. It's really quite ironic. If Nelson had lived, it would not have mattered if he had stayed out there on the Blue Zephyr, a fugitive from the law, or come back and been convicted at trial: the government would have taken everything, all the houses, all the money, even the yacht. There wouldn't have been anything left for Danielle, not the house in the Hamptons, not the million dollars a year, nothing. I rather imagine she knew that, understood right from the beginning that Nelson was finished, and that her only chance was to make sure he died before the government started proceedings against everything he owned."

I had listened to everything Wiley said, concentrating on every word; I had studied his face, peered into his eyes, watched each gesture, each small change of expression, trying to learn if there was something else, something he was holding back; but if there was, I could not discover it. He stood with his hand resting on the top of the wing-back chair, his eyes somber and filled with regret. I wanted to tell him he was wrong, that Danielle could never have been that calculating, that ruthless, but it all was too close to what I had known was true and had not wanted to believe.

"I'm sorry I had to tell you this, but I thought you would want to know the truth. I owed you that much. I meant what I said earlier: you're the best trial lawyer I've ever seen. We've all had clients who lied to us, and you and I have had two of the best at that. They were two of a kind that way, Nelson and Danielle. Even when you knew they weren't telling the truth, you wanted to believe them. That's always the danger when you're dealing with beautiful and charming people who have a gift for making you think they are whatever you want them to be. We all seem to need someone or something to worship, don't we?"

As soon as Wiley was gone, I picked up the telephone and called the Mark Hopkins. I wanted to confront Danielle, tell her what Wiley had just told me, and let her try to lie her way out of it, but when I asked to be connected to her room I was told that she had checked out an hour earlier. Danielle was gone. Everything had been a lie, everything; not just all the different versions of what had happened the night she killed her husband, but everything that had happened between us.

Something snapped inside. I had lived like some cloistered monk, trying to get better at what I did, and then Danielle had come and shown me something closer to perfection than anything I had imagined, the beauty I had seen not just on her face, but in her eyes when we lay together a breath apart and whispered to each other.

Folding my hands together I lowered my head, blind to everything except the memory of what we had done the night before, when we made love and then made love again. That at least had been no deception, that look I had seen in her eyes, when I was deep inside her and she did not want it to stop. No deception? She had no need to disguise a feeling that would not last! If I had learned anything it was that the only thing constant about Danielle was her incessant need to change. That tender, bittersweet request, that echo of a long farewell, that promise she made me give her to remember, whatever happened, that though she had never been in love with anyone, she was in love with me. In love with me! She had played me like the fool I was, made me her all too willing accomplice in what the world now thought the perfect murder. I did not know what I was going to do, only that I had to do something. I could not let it end like this. It hurt too much for that; because despite everything she had done, I was still in love with her. I hated her for that, hated that she had that kind of hold on me, hated that I could not shake free. There is a reason why we only kill the ones we love.

For the next few weeks I went through all the hollow motions of my life. With a kind of manic energy I prepared for the next trial, and, according to Philip Conrad, who was again the court reporter, seemed to take an even greater pleasure in the give and take of the courtroom. I ignored everything but what I was doing. Tommy Lane called several times, but even though the messages he left said it was important, I told myself I would do it later and did not call him back. I had gone into hiding, from the world and from myself. The immediate moment occupied all my attention, and neither the past nor the future was allowed to intrude. I suppose that is what they mean when they say that work is the best therapy. There was certainly no time for idle, harmful thought, no time for old memories, in the middle of a jury trial in which the stakes were high and the evidence close. I lived on euphoria, the inner thrill that comes with the consciousness of doing something well, and doing it with all your powers. Instead of dreading the long, sleepless nights with my mind racing through all the possible things that might happen the next day in court, I started looking forward to all the vain imaginings, the invented spectacles of what might happen next in court. Some might think it private madness, but it gave me the only relief I knew from thoughts of Danielle and the awful, aching loneliness that kept tearing at my heart. The trial kept me going, and with every passing day drove what had happened farther back into the past. But, finally, the trial was over, and though there would soon be other cases and other trials, I knew I had to find out what had happened.

I had heard nothing from Danielle after the morning she left San Francisco and walked out of my life. She had not written; she had not called. I assumed that she had gone back to New York and, as Rufus Wiley had told me, made the arrangements that gave her control over everything Nelson St. James had left to their son. But what she had done after that, where she might have gone, unless it was to visit her son in Europe, I did not know and had no way even to guess. I would not have known how to find her, or, when I thought about it, what I would do if I did.

I did not know what I was going to do, and then, late one afternoon, a few days after that second trial was over, Tommy Lane called and for a brief moment I forgot about everything except how much he could make me laugh.

"Jesus Christ!" he cried; "I call, and you don't answer; I call again, and you don't call back." He was laughing hard, a piercing, high pitched cackle. "Jesus, I sound like some woman who let herself get laid on the first date: 'You don't write, you don't call,'" he mimicked in a sing-song voice, the start of a manic dialogue in which he played not only both parts but the audience as well. "'I would have called, but I never got your number – or your name!' Oh, Christ, listen to me: I'm down here all alone and as soon as I have someone to talk to I can't remember why I called. How are you? - Everything okay? I tried to reach you soon as I heard the verdict; tried to reach you before that, as soon as I found out…."

The boyish enthusiasm had left his voice. Whatever he had to tell me, it was serious, and even disturbing.

"What is it? What did you find out?"

"What she's been up to – your client, Danielle St. James. I started asking around, some of the people I got to know when I was investigating her husband. She's been seeing someone. It's not clear when it started, but at least six months before she killed St. James. Yeah, I know," he added quickly; "you got her off. I'm glad you won, but only because it's you; because she did it, murdered him out there on that yacht of his, and we both know it. I don't know why she did it – this guy she's seeing isn't exactly poor!"

"Who is he?" I asked, as a cold shiver ran up my spine.

"An Italian, a Greek – I'm not sure. I don't even know his name. One of those shadowy types; lives in different places; supposed to come from some old family; lots of money, almost never seen in public. People here with money want everyone to know it; over there they don't want anyone to even know who they are. He has a yacht – like St. James – but he doesn't go very far with it, just around the Mediterranean. That's where they are now."

"Where?" I asked. "Where exactly?"

CHAPTER EIGHTEEN

I watched out the window as the black Mercedes raced through the dark shadows of a tunnel and then followed the highway that ran close to the sea. Mount Pellegrino, rising straight up like Gibraltar, loomed in the distance, guarding the coastline and the narrow, fertile valley that twisted inland from the shore. I had not been able to sleep at all on the long plane ride from San Francisco to Paris and then from Paris to here. Perhaps that was the reason why my mind began to wander back to things I had learned in college and, or so I had thought, forgotten about as soon as I left. I began to imagine what Sicily must have looked like, a three-sided island a mile from Italy and in the middle of the sea, to the long line of invaders who had come to conquer and, having conquered, stayed. It had been the constant, unchanging motive for all the violence and all the wars, the forced impositions, the revolutions, the new religions, all the changes brought first by the Greeks and then the Romans, then the Arabs and the Normans: the haunting sheer beauty of the place. Like the face of a gorgeous woman, the face of a Helen, or the face of a Danielle, it had driven men out of their senses and made them crazy with ambition.

The driver gestured toward a small concrete monument on the side of the road.

"This is where Falcone was killed, where the Mafia blew up his car. That's when everything started to change, after they killed the judge; that's when everyone had had enough." A cap pulled low over his eyes, the driver glanced in the rearview mirror. "Falcone," he repeated with respect. "He had no fear. They killed him – But you know what? – They couldn't kill his example."

We drove in silence for a few minutes before he again glanced in the mirror.

"You're American – yes? Have you been here before?"

"No, my first trip."

"Business, or vacation?"

"Neither one, really; I'm just here," I said, staring out

the window, wondering now why I had come.

We reached the outskirts of Palermo and the driver turned off the highway and started down a city street jammed with cars. Honking the horn, swearing under his breath, he inched along until, twenty minutes and a few miles later we reached the open gates of the hotel.

"The best we've got," said the driver with pride. "You heard about it in America? Someone recommended it?" he asked, as he pulled to a stop at the bottom of the front steps. I paid him and took my bag.

"There's a marina just around the other side, isn't there?" I asked him. "Some people I know keep a boat there."

The Hotel Villa Igeia had the look of a Moorish castle, with sand colored walls and a flat, crenellated roof. It had been built, as I later learned, as a seaside villa for the only daughter of an Italian nobleman, a private sanatorium in which, it was hoped, the ocean air and quiet surroundings would remedy the chronic ill-health which all the science of some of Europe's most famous physicians had been unable to cure. Whether her health improved, or she died an early death from an undiagnosed disease, remained hidden behind a veil of obscurity, subject, like much of Sicilian history, to interpretation and doubt.

Sometime near the end of the 19th century, the villa was turned into a hotel and quickly became a favorite gathering place for European royalty. A century later their photographs, as large as life-size paintings, decorated at discreet intervals the long and elegant corridors that ran the length and breadth of the hotel. Kings and queens of countries still famous, kings and queens of countries that no longer exist, came here, to the Hotel Villa Igeia, to take the sun in the warmth of a Sicilian spring or winter, oblivious, or so it seemed from the world-weary look caught on their faces, to how near they were to Armageddon, the Great War, the first world war, that would sweep many of them off their thrones, and in the case of some of them, like the Russian Czar, into their graves.

It seemed to me, as I glanced at their photographs on the way to my fourth floor room, that even though they could not know that war was coming, they had a sense that they were all living in a vanishing age, that the world was changing and there was nothing they could do about it, that no one could. The forces at work, the machinery of modern life, had gotten too big, too powerful, for that. Or perhaps I was only seeing in their faces what I myself had started to feel: that I was caught in a downward spiral, playing a part written by someone else that I did not yet quite understand.

His back bent with age, the porter opened the curtains and pushed the blue wooden shutters back inside the window casement.

"One of our finest rooms," he said, gesturing toward the palm lined gardens below and to the marina just beyond. A yacht, the size of the Blue Zephyr, and close enough to be its twin, but painted black instead of white, lay anchored a couple hundred meters outside the breakwater of the small harbor. There was nothing else even half its length.

"The Midnight Sun," explained the porter. "The owner keeps a suite here."

I gave him a tip, the same as I would have given in an American hotel. It was larger than the Sicilian custom and his aging eyes lit up with friendly gratitude.

"Keeps a suite here – you mean all the time, whether he is here or not?"

"Yes, of course; all the time. Señor Orsini is -"

"Orsini – that's the name of the owner?"

I gazed out the window at the Midnight Sun, shining long and sleek and black as night. Several people, members of the crew probably, were moving about on deck. I glanced over my shoulder.

"There's a woman with him – a young woman, quite beautiful?"

A look of quiet admiration and subdued enthusiasm for a woman impossible not to notice flickered at the wrinkled corners of the old man's sad and gentle mouth.

"Señor Orsini is seldom without her."

The porter finished showing me the room and then, alone, I tossed my jacket over a chair and kicked off my shoes. Leaning against the deep stucco casement I adjusted the focus on the small pair of binoculars I had brought with me until I could see quite clearly anyone who ventured out on the deck of the yacht. From time to time I put the glasses down and peered into the courtyard below. The tables had begun to fill up with men and women who had decided to have a drink outdoors and enjoy the weather. In the soft echo of Italian voices, I felt a comfortable stranger, come to a place I did not know, surrounded by a language I did not speak, but still somehow drawn to it, as if the scented Sicilian air itself carried the timeless promise of betrayal and revenge.

I kept looking through the glasses, but I did not see Danielle. If she was on board, she was staying below. I did catch a brief glimpse of her new lover, the private and reclusive Señor Orsini, as he passed along the starboard side. Shirtless, wearing only sandals and tan shorts, he had jet black hair and a black mustache. He was about my age, or perhaps a few years older, as near as I could tell. His skin was burned the deep, rich color of mahogany, and he carried himself in the way of someone who lived his life, at least his daytime life, outdoors. Had he just come from Danielle – was he going there now, to the cabin they shared? She was there, all right; I was sure of it. The Midnight Sun was now the only home she had.

The apartment in New York, the house in the Hampton; all the places they had – all the places Nelson St. James had owned – had been sold. Danielle, Nelson's widow, the woman who had murdered him and gotten away with it, the woman who had committed, so they said, the perfect crime, had taken all the proceeds, along with all the other wealth her husband had accumulated during his long career as a financial genius and a brilliant swindler and left the country. According to the rumor circulating among some of her former friends in New York, she had gone to Europe to be closer to her son; gone to Europe to get away from the prying eyes of the paparazzi and the lying tongues of tabloid journalists who refused to believe that her husband's death had been a suicide. Gone to Europe, according to another rumor circulating just below the surface of the first, to be with the man she really loved, a European of mysterious origin who could offer her protection and seclusion from the rabid scandalmongers who would not leave her in peace. No one knew exactly where she was, or precisely whom she was with; only that she was gone and would almost certainly never be back; gone, and for that reason, sure to be forgotten, a name no one would remember once her face was no longer seen on television.

Forgotten by everyone but me. I lay on the bed, staring up at the ceiling while I waited for the time to pass. More tired than I thought, I closed my eyes, remembering, or trying to remember, why I had come. To see her, see her one last time; to tell her that I knew what she had done; to see what she would say: whether she would try to explain it all away, invent another set of lies, or for once tell the truth and, with that, let me make a final break, walk away with no more doubts about whether there might have been something I could have done, something that would have made her stay. It was hopeless, pathetic, a search for reasons where none existed. Had it been anyone else instead of me, I would have called it madness and been absolutely certain that with that there was an end to explanation, because that fact alone explained everything. I would have been wrong, of course: madness is just the beginning of what there is to know.

I woke with a start in almost perfect darkness. I jumped off the bed and went to the window. The Midnight Sun was still there, a dark silhouette against the eastern sky, broken by the running lights along the level of the deck. I checked my watch. It was nearly nine o'clock. If Danielle and Orsini were not have dinner on the yacht, they might be in the dining room downstairs.

Showered and shaved, wearing a dark suit and tie, I rode the elevator to the ground floor. The head waiter, in white tie and tails, welcomed me with easy formality. The dining room, which doubled as the ballroom, was bathed in the brilliant golden light of crystal chandeliers. On a hardwood floor, polished to a gleaming iridescence, several couples moved to the slow rhythms of a small orchestra. A second waiter, on orders from the first, showed me to a table next to the windows that looked onto the palm lined courtyard and, beyond it, the moonlit sea. I ordered a glass of wine and then, moving methodically from one table to the next, I began to look around the crowded, palatial room. I did not see Danielle. The music stopped and the floor cleared and suddenly I found her, Danielle, sitting with a half dozen other people. She did not see me coming until I was standing right in front of her.

And even then she did not seem to know me. I could not believe it; of all the things I had expected, imagined might happen, the possibility that she would not recognize me had never entered my mind. But there it was: a blank look of incomprehension as she stared at a perfect stranger who for some reason seemed to know her. Then, suddenly, she knew. She jumped to her feet, her eyes wide with wonder and something close to fear.

"What is it, Gabriella?" asked someone at her table.

Gabriella? I looked to see who said it, and realized that the man I had seen earlier on the deck of the Midnight Sun, the man called Orsini, was not there. Danielle quickly recovered her composure. The color came back to her face and the quiet confidence to her eyes, though the smile that ran across her mouth still seemed brittle and forced.

"This is an old friend of mine," she said, as her gaze remained fixed on me. "Someone I haven't seen in a very long time."

She did not tell the fashionable people with whom she was having dinner my name, much less stay to introduce us. Instead, she came around the table and took me by the hand, as if the reason I had come over was to ask her to dance.

There was music and muffled noise all around us. My heart was pounding, blood rushed through my veins. The very nearness of her as she followed my lead, the sweet scent of her as I held her again in my arms, brought everything back: the deception, the betrayal, but more than anything, how much I still wanted her, how much I missed what I had in my ignorance once thought I had.

"Gabriella? Someone called you Gabriella."

She did not reply. We kept dancing, swaying to the soft sound of the music, moving with the easy carelessness of lovers who can remember only each other. Holding her close, I forgot why I was there. I knew by heart everything I had wanted to say; I had rehearsed over and over again in my mind. How often had I seen it, the shattered ruins of that perfect, mannequin face, when I told her what I thought of her cunning treachery and criminal duplicity. Finally, I started to speak, to tell her, but my throat went dry and before I could start again on my long practiced invective, she whispered that she knew what I was thinking and that she did not blame me.

"But it wasn't a lie," she insisted, "when I told you I loved you. That was always the truth."

My resolve began to weaken; all my clarity of purpose disappeared. I could not trust her, but I could not hate her, and revenge, if I could have had it, seemed suddenly stale and stupid and enormously cruel. I began to notice things, small things I had not noticed at first. Her hair was a different color, or rather a different, lighter shade, cut much closer than it had been before. There was something else, something that at first I could not quite grasp; something that worked even more of a change. Then it hit me.

"Your eyes! – They're not the same color."

In the middle of the dance floor, less than a foot apart, I watched in amazement as she tossed her head back and laughed.

"I was Justine when you first knew me, and then I was Danielle. And now…."

The color had changed, but her eyes were still capable of that strange combination of open defiance and wistful regret, as if she were proud of what she had done but wishing she could have done – what? Perhaps she did not know, except that once she had made a change, she could not go back.

"And now," I said, ready to finish for her. "Now you're Gabriella?"

She raised her chin in an attitude of formality. Her eyes became distant and remote, banishing, as it seemed forever, anything that had happened between us. Whether she had really loved me, whether that had been true, it had become, like everything else, part of a replaceable past.

"Yes, Gabriella – Gabriella Orsini."

She said it as if she were just getting used to it, a line in a new part she was learning to play. She seemed to test the inflection, looking for just the right ring. She moved her lips a silent, second time, making certain of the effect.

It was so unexpected - I was so stunned by her easy assumption of a wholly new identity - that it took a moment before I understood the full significance of what she had done.

"You're – married! You married Orsini already?" I could not conceal my anger, the sense of outrage at what she had done. If I had had a knife I might have used it; instead I fixed her with a piercing stare. "That was the reason you killed him, - the reason you wouldn't talk about: You were in love with someone else!"

The couples closest to us on the dance floor looked to see what the trouble was. Danielle darted a worried glance at the table where her friends were watching with puzzled faces. I pulled her closer and held her tight, forcing her to pay attention.

"You murdered him – Why? – Because Orsini was not rich enough: you had to have Nelson's money too!"

"No, that's not...." She shook her head, afraid to finish what she had started to say. "You don't understand; you don't understand anything," she said, throwing me a look that seemed a warning, though a warning about what I could not have guessed. "I didn't lie to you – about what I felt; about you and me!"

"That's right!" I replied with an angry, caustic laugh.

"You loved me so much the first thing you did – after you got your hands on everything St. James ever owned – was to run off to Europe and marry someone else, the man you had been seeing for months before you committed murder!"

I looked around, across the dance floor, to the table where Danielle – Gabriella! – had been dining with a half dozen well-dressed and obviously well-heeled Europeans. The women had long noses and too much make-up and affected an air of indifference; the men had hooded eyes and jaded mouths and the look of easy tolerance by which money and experience conceal arrogance. They were exactly the kind of crowd I would have expected to see her with when she had been married to Nelson St. James. Other than speaking a different language, they could have been the same people I had been with the weekend we sailed down the coast of California on the Blue Zephyr. Change the color of her hair, change the color of her eyes, change her name, change the name of her husband, change the place she lived or the yacht she sailed on, it was not change at all – it was endless repetition, like the constant itching of an old wound, one that would never heal: the illusion that life was full of chances and that if only you kept trying, you would finally have it all.

"How did you know where to find me?" she asked as the music came to an end. "Never mind; it doesn't matter. You shouldn't have come. You should have left things the way they were."

She smiled at me as, along with the others, we applauded the orchestra, but only because we were being watched. We walked toward her table, but before we got there, she turned and, loud enough so that her friends could hear, told me how glad she was that I was here, in Palermo, and how anxious she knew her husband, "Niccolo," would be to see me.

"Tomorrow, then, at lunch," she added, as she extended her hand and wished me a formal, and quite final, good-night.

CHAPTER NINETEEN

The motor launch was waiting at the bottom of
the seaside steps behind the Villa Igeia. Under a broiling
mid-day sun, the far horizon lost in a choking haze, the
sea had become a smooth metallic mirror. The light was
unendurable; the air heavy, still, and ominous. There were
boats all around, the marina full of them, but there was no
movement anywhere. They might have all been abandoned,
their owners fled to safer places, afraid the sea itself might
catch on fire, for all the life you could see in them. It was
silent, quiet as death, the only sound the muffled echo of
the motor as the launch cut through the glass water, heading
straight for the blinding black hull of the Midnight Sun.

I put on dark glasses and leaned back in the leather
seat, remembering the last launch I had seen, the one that
had taken Danielle and her husband from the Blue Zephyr
to Santa Barbara the morning they left on their way to New
York. I could still see her, the moment she turned around
to take one last look, and I could still feel the hope, the
sense of excitement, at the thought that she might be trying
to catch one last glimpse of me. I remembered everything
that happened that weekend, and nothing so much as how
the meaning of everything had changed. What had seemed
a harmless flirtation had been in reality the beginning of
a heartless, lethal seduction. Or had it? Had I been invited
along because Nelson St. James thought he might soon need
a lawyer, or because Danielle had already decided she was
going to kill him and might need me to defend her? Had I
been invited because Danielle wanted to show me what I
had missed seeing years earlier in Justine, a final end to a
schoolgirl fantasy; and then, only later, after she had done
what she did, came to me because, having known me all
those years before, she thought she could trust me? The
questions were endless, and even if she had wanted to tell
the truth, I was not sure Danielle could have done much
more than guess at the answers. There may not have been a
reason for anything that happened. There frequently is not

one, when all we are doing is reacting to events. It is only afterward, when it is all over, that it seems to make sense.

A steward in a white jacket and Bermuda shorts was waiting for me when I climbed up a three step ladder from the motor launch to the deck of the Midnight Sun. There was no word of greeting; nothing but a dumb, acquiescent look, as of one who knows his narrow function and not much else besides. For all the chattering he must have done with members of his own race and language, he remained silent and inscrutable as he led me up a flight of stairs to the upper deck where, under a dark blue canopy, a table had been set for lunch. There were, oddly enough, only two chairs.

The steward nodded toward one of the empty places, held the chair while I sat down, and then, before I noticed, disappeared, vanished so completely that it left a doubt whether he might have been a mirage, an insubstantial thing created by the heat.

A chilled bottle of wine sat uncorked in the middle of the table, and, right next to it, a golden bowl filled with purple grapes. On opposite sides of the table, the two places were set with crystal glasses and the finest china, alive with color, I had ever seen. The silverware, engraved with the letter O, the insignia for the House of Orsini, had the feel and the luster of a priceless, ancient heritage. The linen napkins felt like silk to the touch. I picked up a knife and turned it around in my hand, marveling at the perfect balance and the perfect fit. Everything was perfect, one of a kind, and nothing more expensive.

"I'm glad you were able to join us," said a voice from just behind me. Taken by surprise, I jumped to my feet and turned to meet Danielle's new husband, Niccolo Orsini.

And then, to my amazement, I was face to face, not with Niccolo Orsini but with an impossibility.

"You - !" I cried, staggered by what I saw.

It was the same man I had seen the day before, a brief glimpse through a pair of small binoculars - the same jet black hair, the same mustache, the same bronze skin – but how different the impression, how different the effect, seen, not from a distance, but close enough to touch. I was staring into the eyes of a dead man, murdered by his wife, his body lost at sea. Nelson St. James was alive! And the sight of him almost killed me. I struggled to catch my breath, to somehow get my bearings, to find some stability in a world that had gone insane.

"You're alive - ! But how? Why?"

He treated me like a convalescent, which in a sense I was, having lost the ability to distinguish what was real from what was not. He placed a comforting hand on my shoulder and smiled sympathetically.

"I know it must be a shock, seeing someone you thought was dead. But I'm afraid I'm very much alive. I'm only sorry you had to find out."

"Sorry...that I had to...?"

He guided me back to my chair and stood next to me for a moment, as if in doubt how he wanted to proceed.

"Danielle won't be joining us," he said finally.

There was no explanation given for her absence, nothing said in words; but the look in his eyes suggested that there were important matters to discuss and that the discussion should be between the two of us alone.

"Perhaps later," he added vaguely.

The same steward who had met me earlier, reappeared, waiting unobtrusively off to the side. The moment St. James reached for his chair, he was there, pulling it out for him. With a deft movement of his smooth, dark hands, he placed a napkin on his lap. St. James then said something to him in what may have been Arabic. Immediately, the steward looked at me.

"What would you like to drink?" asked St. James. "I'm having ice tea, but there's wine on the table, and anything else you might like, I'm sure we have it on board."

I heard the question, but I could not think of an answer. I don't mean that I could not decide; I could not get beyond the words to what they meant. I knew what he said, I knew what he asked, but I had the uncanny sense that I was observing something that was happening to someone else. I did not say anything; I did not know how. Nelson St. James seemed to understand. He dismissed the steward with a few more words in that exotic language that was almost as unintelligible to me as English had suddenly become.

"I thought we might talk for a while before lunch – unless you're hungry, of course; in which case we can...." His voice trailed off and he glanced down at his manicured hands clasped together in his lap. Dressed all in white –his pants, his jacket, even his shirt and shoes – his face looked even darker than it had before and his eyes more alive than I remembered them. Though he did not make a sound, he seemed to be laughing at some colossal, private joke.

"Tell me," he said, slowly lifting his eyes, "how exactly is it that you come to be here?" But almost before it was out of his mouth, he dismissed the question with an abrupt and emphatic movement of his head. He bent forward, his hands on the table. "You didn't know I was alive, did you? No, I could tell from your reaction. You came looking for Danielle. Yes, of course; that makes sense. Or did you have a suspicion, a doubt, that the story she told you wasn't quite true; something she may have let slip late one night while the two of you were in bed?"

I began to recover my senses; the world began to take on a definable shape. St. James was only guessing about what had happened.

"Is that what she told you?" I replied, pretending indifference as I sipped on the ice tea. "That we slept together?"

I wondered if he would press the point, admit his ignorance and ask directly. He said nothing, and we sat there, in the breathless silence of the summer heat, trying to read what was going on in each other's minds.

"You must be angry, Morrison - given the way you were treated. But then, it wouldn't have made any sense to tell you the truth, would it? And really, when you think about it, what do you have to be angry about, except perhaps a little injured pride."

"Injured pride!" I exclaimed bitterly. "You and

your wife made me party to a fraud, a massive deception; destroyed everything I believed in – and for what?"

"For what?" he laughed. He looked at me to make sure I was serious. "Don't you understand? They're still talking about it – 'the perfect murder' – How Danielle St. James murdered her husband and, thanks to that brilliant attorney, Andrew Morrison, got away with it. But it's really much better than that, isn't it?" he asked, with a knowing, ruthless grin. "People have gotten away with murder before, but no one has ever done this – no one ever had the wit or daring even to try! Try? – No one in their right mind would even think of it. That's why it worked – Because it's the last thing anyone would ever suspect. Think of it, Morrison – You can't help but admire the sheer audacity of it!" He was full of excitement, thrilled by his own achievement. "Have your own wife stand trial for a murder that never happened, stage your own death, and do it all in a way so that after she's acquitted everyone will be so certain that she really did it, so convinced that she got away with murder, that no one will ever think to wonder whether you might still be alive!"

Pushing back from the table, St. James folded his arms across his chest and stared down at the deck. He swung his foot, back and forth, over and over again, until, gradually, the triumph in his eyes began to give way to a different judgment. When he finally looked at me he seemed almost apologetic.

"No one was hurt; no one was killed. You defended a woman charged with a crime she didn't commit – and you won. Are you going to quarrel with the result?"

He lifted an eyebrow in tribute to what he wanted me to admit had been a perfect scheme: no one killed, no one punished, and the whole world fooled into thinking he was dead.

"And instead of going to prison, or spending your life a fugitive, you get to keep all the money you ever stole!" I spat out in contempt.

"Sent to prison, made a fugitive, for doing nothing but what everyone does every day!" he said with scorn for what had, unfairly as he thought, been done to him. "They call it a Ponzi scheme, but what is that except what everyone on Wall Street – everyone in business – does: paying what you owe to some with money you get from others? You don't believe me? – What do you think would happen if everyone owed money by a bank asked for it back? The bank doesn't have that much money – most of it has been loaned out. That's what no one seems to understand: in business you either grow or die! As long as I kept making profits – as long as I brought in more business, more clients – as long as they stayed happy with the money I made them – no one complained."

I took off my dark glasses so I could look St. James straight in the eye. I wanted to preserve at least that much of my self-respect.

"I was used, and I don't like it; I don't like it one bit."

With a knowing shrug, St. James threw up his hands.

"Everyone gets used, Andrew! It's the way of the world." Furrowing his brow, he bent his shoulders and searched my eyes, looking for something he was convinced I could not quite hide. "And if you were….I wonder – did you really mind it?"

It hung in the air, this second allusion to what he suspected, but apparently only suspected, I might have done with Danielle, while he continued to watch, daring me to search my own conscience for how much I may have been the willing victim of deceit.

"Used," I insisted, staring back hard. "Lied to, told something that never happened."

St. James would have none of it. His eyes gleamed with eager malice.

"You can't tell me that it's never happened before, that no one has ever asked you to take their case because they're innocent and you're the only one who can save them. How many times? How many times did you believe them, and then because you were the only one between them and a life in prison – or their execution – work yourself into a state of sheer exhaustion, only to realize, after you had won, after the jury had set them free, what you had really known all along: that they were guilty and that because of you they had gotten away with it, got away with murder! Used? – I think not.

"Danielle told you she was innocent, told you she hadn't committed murder; and she was telling the truth – she didn't murder me, she didn't murder anyone. You did what you always do – what you were paid a great deal of money to do – you defended someone charged with a crime. She was charged with a crime, remember, before she ever asked for your help. Your job was to hold the government to account, show that the evidence wasn't sufficient for a conviction. And you did that; you did it very well. You aren't going to complain that the verdict wasn't the right one, are you? You surely aren't going to say she should have been found guilty!"

I turned on my hip, shoved one leg over the other, and wrapped both hands around the wooden corner of the canvas chair and held it tight. What he had done, the way he now tried to defend it, was so outrageous, so astonishing in its open duplicity, I was afraid I might hit him.

"What would you have done if she had?" I asked suddenly. "What would you have done if this well-planned fraud of yours hadn't worked, if she had been convicted? – Let her go prison? Waited until you read in the papers about her execution and then dismissed it as just another deal gone bad!"

His eyebrows, dyed black like his hair, shot straight up, acknowledging the possibility. He lowered his head, and with the back of two fingers scratched the side of his smooth shaven cheek, considering, as it were, whether in retrospect he might have underplayed the risk.

"There was never any real chance of that – not with you as her lawyer," he said with the blithe assurance of someone who knew nothing about the real hazards of the courtroom.

"I haven't always won."

"You've never lost with someone innocent."

"The whole world thinks she's guilty," I reminded him.

That was the last thing he cared about. The world could think what it liked.

"The whole world thinks I'm dead," he remarked, with an impervious sneer. "But I'm still alive. And Danielle, the woman the world thinks is so guilty – she doesn't exist anymore. We've both become other people. Nelson St. James is somewhere the bottom of the Pacific; Danielle St. James has disappeared. Niccolo Orsini and his wife Gabriella now sail around on a yacht – the Midnight Sun, the Blue Zephyr painted black – making rich people even richer, those lucky enough to invest in one of the Orsini enterprises, the profitable parts of this new, global economy of ours. Yes," he added with gloating satisfaction, "thanks to you, my friend, Danielle and I now lead new and different lives."

"Lead different lives! – You're living the same life all over again, the same game with different players."

I meant to offend him, call him the hypocrite he was; but he took it, if not as a compliment, then as a reasonable description of the only reality he knew. It was, for him, what it had always been: a game about money; or rather a game about winning and losing in which money was a way to count. It was, when you got right down to it, when your eye was not dazzled by all the beautiful people and all their fine clothes, by their shiny fast cars and their expensive houses, nothing but the ancient and much despised war of all against all, but without the violence, and with none of the courage.

St. James snapped his fingers, the steward materialized out of thin air and we ordered lunch. For the next hour, as course after course was served, St. James spoke with ruthless candor about what he had done; not just how he had staged his own death, but what he planned to do next. He seemed to enjoy it, the chance to tell someone, to have an audience. He thought he was the only one smart enough to figure out that the perfect murder would be the one in which the murder itself was a fiction. It was sleight of hand, the cunning trickery of a great magician. The analogy was his, and a source of pride. Everyone he had dealt with, whether the Wall Street tycoons he had forced into bankruptcy or the government officials who had come after him with a vengeance, all were a type he despised: privileged and overeducated, the kind who hung their framed degrees and credentials on the walls of their offices and thought them proof of their competence.

"I didn't finish high school – Did you know that?" he asked, shoving his plate to the side. He laughed when he said it, but there was a hard edge, an undercurrent of injury and resentment. "A tenth grade education, two years in the army, and lots of crummy jobs. Funny thing is, when I was a kid – I wasn't any good at sports – I used to read a lot. Adventure stories, mainly – things like that."

He put his hand to his head and held it there, smiling at what he remembered, the threadbare books which, as he told me, he used to check out by the armload from the one room local library. "Sleight of hand, making everyone concentrate on one thing while you do something else. It was a book about Houdini. He would have them sew him into a big paper bag. A screen would be put up in front it. And then - twenty, thirty minutes later – when the screen came down, there would be Houdini, standing next to the paper bag, but the paper bag had not been opened. He had a second bag, exactly the same as the first, which he kept under his clothes. He simply cut his way out of the first one and replaced it with the other one. Then he would sit there – for twenty, thirty minutes; maybe even an hour – reading a book, but making the kind of sounds someone would be making if they were struggling to get out of something that held them prisoner. That was the genius part – not getting out of the bag, but making everyone think that he was trapped, that he could not get out. That's what held everyone's attention and made it believable. I could have just pretended to fall overboard, an accident at sea – but that would have concentrated everyone's attention on my death, on me, and that would have led to questions. But if instead of an accident, I'm murdered, then everyone concentrates on the question of who did it and why. It was perfect – you have to admit that, Morrison. Harry Houdini would have been proud," he laughed. "A high school dropout, and I beat them all!"

The more he talked, the more it seemed he wanted to. He was all puffed up with himself, recounting with smirking certainty how he had beaten everyone who had stood in his way. He told me story after story, ending finally with what had started when we first met, that weekend off the coast of California.

"It was Danielle's idea, by the way, that we invite you along," he added. He could not quite conceal a curiosity, an irritation that he did not know whether, or how often, she might have cheated with me.

I was curious about something else.

"Her idea I come along? Was it her idea that she go on trial for a murder that never happened – or was it yours?"

He shrugged as if it were a distinction without a difference. It was not important who first thought of it, only that it worked. He could not quite understand why I did not see that.

"It might have been her; it might have been me. I don't really remember. I knew I might need a lawyer; she said she had heard you were one of the best. But that weekend – when we met – I had not thought of it yet, what I was going to do, become a victim of a homicide."

He tugged at his sleeve and, shifting position, craned his neck to stare up at a blank, cloudless sky. There was not a sound anywhere, nothing to break the eerie silence that was even more oppressive than the heat.

"Remember what I told you, that first time we met - ? For some reason, even then, I felt comfortable telling you things I haven't told anyone. It's a gift you have - ." He laughed suddenly, and to no apparent purpose; but then his expression changed into the eager satisfaction of having just discovered the secret of another man's success. "Even when someone is lying, they look at you and want to tell the truth! Poor Danielle!" And he laughed again.

We were finished with lunch. The steward began to clear away the dishes. St. James checked his watch.

"Tell Mustafa to get underway," he said to the steward. Then he turned to me. "We took the liberty of having your things brought on board. We're going to sail around the island – around Sicily – and I insist you come along."

Mustafa Nastasis, the witness to St. James's murder, the lying witness to Danielle's guilt, had been waiting for the order. The deck began to vibrate with the motion of the ship's engine. I was a guest, that meant a prisoner, on the Midnight Sun, and there was nothing I could do about it. I do not know if St. James had decided what he was going to do, whether he thought he had to kill me to keep his secret safe, but he now had me in his power, and yet I did not feel any fear at all. Call it what you will – and I suppose madness must be the first thing that comes to mind: that I was crazy, driven half insane by what they had done to me – but I was glad I was back out on the Blue Zephyr, eager to see where we were all going and what would happen when we got there. When St. James told me I was going with them, I told him I was looking forward to the voyage. Perhaps I really was crazy.

CHAPTER TWENTY

As the Midnight Sun raced along the northern shore of Sicily, I leaned against the starboard railing, remembering from my long vanished youth Homer's description of the 'wine-tinted sea.' Somewhere ahead in the crowding darkness lay the straits of Messina and, as I had once read, the unenviable choice of the swirling whirlpool of Charybdis and the jagged rocks of Scylla, a choice that, as I thought of it, seemed not that much worse than the one I knew I would eventually have to make. There were three of us tangled together in this web of deceit, this murder that never happened and a trial that had from start to finish been a fraud. I had a feeling bordering on certainty that sometime soon there would be only two of us left.

Perhaps it was that sense of danger that made me start to sense things before they happened. I knew, for example, without turning around, that Danielle was coming, that in another moment she would be here, leaning against the railing next to me. Our shoulders touched; her arm pressed against mine. I stared out at the sea, growing darker in the last light of dusk, waiting for her to speak, but she said nothing and the only sound I heard was the slight breeze that brushed past my ear.

"It was your idea, wasn't it?" I asked quietly and without a hint of anger. I felt tired, weary of the whole charade; tired, really, of who I was, of what I had become. "Husband murdered, wife accused, and all the evidence – if you have a lawyer smart enough, or dumb enough, to see it – that there's as much a proof that her husband shot himself as that she killed him." Finally, I turned my head just far enough to see her. "Because, after all, the point is to have everyone think he's dead."

She started to deny it, but I would not listen. I changed positions, moved my back against the railing, so I could catch each new expression, each new reaction, in her eyes.

"You played your part too well not to have written it yourself. You made him think it was his idea, but it was really yours. You're good at that: making people think they're only doing what they must have thought of first. You've convinced him that he's Harry Houdini, making fools of everyone; you had me convinced that I had to let you lie under oath because it was the only way to save the woman who wanted to spend the rest of her life with me."

She looked at me with what, if I had not known her, or if I had known her some other way, I would have taken as injured innocence. The innocence, I knew, did not exist; but the sense of injury, of something lost, somehow seemed real.

"I didn't have to sleep with you to get you to take the case," she reminded me in a low, mournful voice.

Had I injured her pride? My injury went much deeper than that.

"You had to 'almost sleep with me' – that weekend on the yacht – to make me think that you were scared of him, afraid of things he might do; to make me believe, later on, that if you killed him, you had a reason for what you did."

I was scared of him," she insisted. "I'm still scared of him…more than ever."

A bitter smile whipped across my mouth. I stood straight up.

"Scared of him, but willing to risk your own life to keep him out of prison!"

She took hold of my arm.

"But I didn't have to sleep with you – don't you understand?" she asked, pleading with her eyes. "If we'd never gone to bed together, that wouldn't have changed anything you did at trial. You would have tried just as hard to win."

The shadows darkened. A warm wind, restless and chaotic, came from first one direction, then another. I felt my gaze weaken, and instead of weariness I began to feel lost. Nothing seemed worth doing.

"It would have changed how I felt…" I whispered into the night.

She heard the bittersweet nostalgia in my distant voice, the sense of my own innocence lost, innocence of a kind I had not known I had until Danielle had taught me how to abandon all inhibition in the intimacy we had shared. She seemed to teach me freedom and, as I only later understood, she made me more a slave.

Danielle's grasp moved from my arm down to my hand.

"I slept with you because I wanted to sleep with you. I wanted to the very first day we met, that day off the California coast when I saw the way you looked at me and I knew you didn't remember me. I felt something, something I had not felt before. It wasn't some schoolgirl fantasy, the crush I had on you when you were engaged to my sister. It was more, much more, than that."

I pulled my arm away from her.

"It didn't stop you, though – did it? It didn't change a thing. You went right ahead with everything – just the way you had planned!"

Angry and hurt, she stamped her foot in frustration.

"It was too late! Don't you understand? There was nothing I could do."

"Nothing you could do?" I fixed her with a piercing stare. "You could have told the truth: that he wasn't dead, that it was all a hoax!"

"And if I had done that – who would have believed me? I wasn't the only one involved. Mustafa…!"

"I was there, remember? Were you the one who rehearsed him? He lied with such effect!" I taunted her. "He heard yelling, came up on deck, saw you with the gun in your hand; saw blood all over the railing, all over the deck." My voice was full of scorn, my gaze full of contempt. "But he didn't see you pull the trigger, didn't see you shoot him, didn't see your husband fall overboard into the sea…." I bore in on her as if she were a witness on the stand, throwing back in her face every false, deceitful thing she had ever said. "You knew how important that would be, that Nastasis tell the story just that way. There couldn't be any doubt that Nelson died, only room for doubt that you did it. The gun is in your hand, but for all he knows – which he is eager to admit the moment I ask him – you could have just picked it up from where it had fallen after Nelson shot himself."

She shook her head in anguish, as if even now she wanted to convince me that I was wrong, that whatever she may have done, however wrong it may have been, what had happened between us had been separate and apart, unexpected, and regretted as something she could not keep.

"Do you think he would have changed his story if I had changed mine? Told the truth – that Nelson wasn't dead? Why? – To save me? Mustafa is a lot of things, but he isn't stupid. He was paid a lot of money to do what he did."

"Yes, precisely: a lot of money! That excuses everything, doesn't it? Only stupid people think the truth is something that can't be bought and sold!"

A slight shudder, as of something painful, passed through her and for a moment she seemed desolate and alone.

"Why did you come?" she asked after a long silence. She searched my eyes for the answer. At least that is what I thought at first, because an instant later I was certain it was the other way round: that she wanted me to see in her eyes the answer to a question I had never thought to ask, a question which in its shocking simplicity made me wonder if I had not seriously misjudged her.

"Do you want to know what I really wish, what I started wishing that first night we spent together? I wish that everything the prosecution said had been true, that I had killed him just the way they said, shot him over there," she said, nodding toward the railing on the other side. "Shot him so his body would fall overboard and could not be found, shot him after yelling loud enough to bring Mustafa so he could find me holding the gun. The same thing would have happened then, except that Nelson would be dead and the trial wouldn't have been a fraud. I could have lied myself to an acquittal, but instead of living in a different place with a different name, I could be home, in San Francisco, living with you. Don't you think I wish I had, wish I had -"

"Wish what, my dear?"

Nelson St. James had come up behind us. We had not seen him in the darkness. Danielle spun around.

"Wish I didn't have to spend all my time on this damn boat!" she cried as she stormed past him.

With a raised eyebrow and an indulgent smile, St. James watched her go. But more, I thought, to shield his embarrassment than from any real feeling of affection for the occasional and forgivable outbursts of someone he loved and understood. He began to rub his upper arm, something I had seen him do once or twice at lunch, and behind the shining surface of his eyes I thought I saw something like discomfort and even a little fear.

"I'm afraid I lost my temper this afternoon," he said unexpectedly. "I came to apologize for that, and to tell you that whatever our differences over what happened, I'm sure we can work things out. But we can talk about all that later," he remarked as he took me by the arm and started to lead me away. "In the meantime, why don't you join us for dinner?" With a shrewd, knowing look, he added, "It's what I liked about you the first time I met you: you're never boring, Morrison. Of course I have a certain bias in that regard. I'd hate to think that someone who wanted to kill me wasn't an interesting man."

Dinner that evening was nothing like what I had experienced the first time, months earlier, when the Midnight Sun was still the Blue Zephyr and a dozen people had sat at the table. There were just the three of us and St. James did most of the talking. None of it, however, was about what they had done or what might happen because of it. If he was worried about whether I might expose him, tell the world he was still alive – if he was planning how he might stop me from revealing the fraud the two of them had committed – he kept it to himself. He spoke instead as if we were all great friends, on our way to a splendid little voyage which he could not wait to preview in advance. In another side of the resentment he felt toward all the overeducated fools, as he had described them, whom he had beaten at their own game, he could not rid himself of the insecurity he felt at his lack of a college education. He talked about Sicily and what we were going to see, but only after he had made a point of explaining that while he seldom read much anymore, he always found people who could tell him about the places he visited. He said it in a way that left no doubt that he believed you could always learn more from hearing it directly from someone who knew what they were talking about than getting it second hand from the writings of someone you had never met. And the truth was that he seemed to have learned quite a lot.

The next day, he told us, after we passed through the Straits of Messina and turned south past Taormina and Catania, we were going to stop at the harbor in Syracuse, or Siracusa as it was properly called, where one of the great battles of the ancient world had taken place. St. James was intrigued. He leaned on his elbows, his eyes glistening, as he explained that it was not just that the Athenian fleet had been destroyed, and with it the hope that Athens might triumph over Sparta in the Peloponnesian War, that had struck his imagination so forcibly, but that the battle had been watched by an Athenian army that knew that without ships to carry them back they would never see home again.

"Some of them did, of course – a few managed to get back to Athens alive – but most of them perished in an agonizing captivity. But I've often thought, since I was first told about it, that worse than dying was watching while your fate was decided by others." Folding his hands together, he studied me in the way of someone reasoning from an analogy, finding in some event from the distant past an example that might be repeated. "Imagine thinking one moment that you are going to win, and then, a moment later, knowing for certain that you are going to lose." His gaze drifted down to his hands, and then he sat back. "On the other hand, I suppose it isn't so unusual to have your life in the hands of someone else," he said in a tone with a different significance. He glanced at Danielle and then looked back at me. "We're all dependent, at some time or other, on what other people do. It's all in knowing who you can trust; that, and what they're really capable of. Don't you agree?"

Despite the strange fascination the story of the abandoned Athenians seemed to have for St. James, we stopped the next afternoon not at Syracuse, where he had said we were going, but at Taormina. He said it was nothing more than a slight change of plans, a pleasant diversion, and a chance for Danielle to get off the yacht. Taormina had the best shopping in Sicily, and Danielle was always looking for something new.

"That was a lie," said Danielle. She reached into her purse for a cigarette. She tapped the end of it against the back of her hand and snapped open a gold lighter. "He wanted you off the boat. Someone is coming and he doesn't want them to see you."

We were sitting at a table at an outdoor café. The plaza was crowded with tourists - Germans and Scandinavians, mainly, from the blonde, blue-eyed look of them – standing along the stone balustrade from which, high above the narrow Strait of Messina, they could see across to Italy on the farther shore. Danielle looked around as she took a long drag. Wearing dark glasses and a green silk scarf wrapped around her head, she drew constant, puzzled stares from passersby who thought she must be famous, an actress, a movie star, but could not quite place her. I sipped on a glass of red Sicilian wine and pretended not to notice.

"I imagine Niccolo Orsini has many guests," I remarked. Bending the half-filled glass to the side I watched the way the sunlight danced on the surface and changed the color. "Though I imagine whoever he has coming today will be disappointed not to see his wife, the beautiful and mysterious Gabriella."

Danielle took a quick, hard drag on the cigarette and then stamped it out.

"You really despise me, don't you? You think I'm lying when I tell you that I only slept with you because I wanted to; you think I'm lying when I tell you I was falling in love with you."

There were people all around, bunched together at

tables with barely room to move between them. Danielle bent closer. Pulling her white blouse a little to the side, she exposed a deep purple bruise at the base of her throat.

"The other night, the night you showed up at the hotel, the night you took me out on the dance floor – this is what he did when we got back, this and a few of his more twisted perversions!"

She fumbled in her purse for another cigarette; but then, as she started to light it, she changed her mind.

"I slept with you because I wanted to. You don't believe me, but Nelson knows, or thinks he knows, and he's furious." She shook her head in disgust. "I meant what I said. I should have killed him instead of doing what I did."

"Leave him!" I took her wrist and held it tight. "Leave him – right now! We'll get up from this table and walk out of here and never look back. Come with me. There's nothing that can stop us."

A wistful smile floated over her lovely mouth.

"Wouldn't it be nice to think that we could?"

I did not understand at first what that smile really meant. And then I did, and my heart went cold. I let go of her wrist and looked at the face of a stranger, a beautiful woman I did not know.

"I've put too much into this," she was saying, trying to explain. "I've spent too many years, too much has happened. I've…."

But I was not listening. I had heard all I needed to hear.

CHAPTER TWENTY ONE

"They stood right there," said St. James, gesturing toward the vacant hills of Syracuse that circled the harbor. The evening sun had slipped down from the sky and left behind a brilliant scarlet glow. "Thousands of Athenian troops, come to conquer Sicily, forced to watch as their navy lost the battle and Sparta won the war. The Athenian fleet tried to break the blockade – probably over there," he said, pointing toward the narrow strait that led to the smaller, inner harbor. "It was 406 B.C. and none of it should have happened. The Athenians would have won, if they had been willing to do everything they needed to do to win."

He turned and looked at me, standing with my back to the railing a few feet away. He expected me to ask what he meant. I jiggled the ice that was left in my glass and took another drink.

"Because they recalled Alcibiades and left Nicias in charge?" I said indifferently when I finished swallowing.

St. James was surprised. His mind worked in categories and he had me down as a lawyer; and lawyers, in his experience, knew nothing outside the narrow confines of their craft. He was surprised, but not disappointed. It made what he had to say easier. His eyes lit up with anticipation.

"You know about this – good. Then perhaps you'll see the point I'm trying to make. The Athenians loved Alcibiades, but they could never quite trust him: he was too brilliant, too much better than the rest of them. They knew he was the one who could conquer Sicily, but at the last minute they held back, decided they had to send someone along more cautious – more respectable, if you will. So they sent Nicias, old, God-fearing Nicias. Even with that joint command, they might still have won; but then they charged Alcibiades with impiety, with desecrating the statues of the gods, and sent a ship to bring him back to stand trial -"

"But instead of going," I interjected, irritated at the way in which with his smattering of passed on knowledge he tried to make himself sound important, "he went over to the Spartans and helped them in the war. Is that your point? – That you're like Alcibiades because he refused to go back and stand trial?" I gave him a cold, dismissive look. "But no one chose you to lead anything; and if your tour guide didn't bother to mention it, the story didn't end with what happened here in Syracuse. Alcibiades eventually went back to Athens, helped give it the best government it ever had, and almost won the war."

A smile full of danger creased St. James' mouth. His eyes became hard and unforgiving.

"My point isn't just that Alcibiades reminded me of my own situation, but that he reminded me of yours. I can't go home again, but neither can you."

He moved away from the railing and pulled up a deck chair. He sat there, rubbing his upper arm, though more from habit than from any pain he might be experiencing, and for a long time did not say anything, considering, as it seemed, what he was going to do.

"Can't go home," he said, almost as I was not there and he was thinking out loud. "We've gone to too much trouble; there's too much at stake…." He paused, a puzzled expression in his eyes. "It was a stupid thing to do, Morrison. For the life of me, I don't know why you did it. What did you think was going to happen when you found her? She left – right after the trial ended. Didn't that tell you…? You thought you were in love with her; that much I can understand – But you couldn't have thought she was in love with you; at least not after she left." Suddenly, he understood, or thought he did. "Yes, of course: You couldn't help yourself, could you? Couldn't let go of it, couldn't forget her; couldn't get her out of your mind?"

He made a slight abrupt motion of his head, confirming the devastating effect she could have on anyone too reckless, or too foolish, not to keep their distance. Narrowing his eyes, his gaze drew in on itself in the way of someone nursing a grudge, or rather, as in this case, a deep resentment at his own weakness. He was in love with her, and he hated her for that, because he knew that she could never feel the same way. She was too beautiful, too perfect, to need anyone else to make her feel whole. She was a changeling, always eager to see, and to hide behind, another side of herself. You went running after her, but she was too elusive to ever let you get close to knowing who she really was. Even in the act of submission, when she let you have her, you never knew, as I had discovered, if she was really there; whether she was not, in her imagination, making love with someone else. It must have made St. James every bit as crazy as it made me, and he was married to her. I think he would have divorced her, if he had not gotten in trouble and decided to fake his own death. Better to get rid of her, and do it all at once, than to lose day by day a little more of your self-respect, knowing that the last thing the woman you had to have ever thought about was you.

St. James slowly rose from the deck chair. He put his hand on my arm, but looked past me toward the far horizon, marked now by a single narrow band of light, a scarlet remnant of the vanished sun.

"You think that if it were just the two of you, everything would be perfect, that nothing would ever change."

I was not sure at first if he was saying this about my assumption, or his experience; but I suspect he meant both, and something even more than that.

"But then, after a while, you begin to get the strange feeling that, without quite knowing how it happened, you have disappeared, that you're not anything anymore except what at any given moment she wants you to be. That is the mistake everyone makes. You can't change Danielle; she changes you. And you do it, become whatever she wants, because you think it's the only way that she might still want you. You know the story of Medusa – a face so awful, so terrifying, that it drives men mad. The same thing happens when it's the face of a woman you can't resist."

We left Syracuse and its ancient memories the next morning, sailing around the southeastern corner of the Sicilian triangle and then west along the southern shore.

That day, and the day after, while I was free to roam the ship, I was left alone, without contact with anyone. I did not see St. James again, and I did not see Danielle. Something was going on, I could feel it; the two of them, sequestered in their own, private part of the yacht, eating their meals in their cabin, while I sat by myself in that elegantly appointed dining room served by a single, silent waiter. Several times I thought I heard loud voices, but whether raised in anger or to emphasize a point I could not tell. I was almost certain they were talking about me, but that did not answer anything. The question, the only one that mattered, was how my sudden and unexpected appearance would either end their marriage or begin a new, and final, conspiracy in which the object would be a real murder instead of fraud.

I did not see St. James or Danielle and I began to wonder if I would. For two days we sailed west, following the sun, in no great hurry to get anywhere, until we reached Agrigento and word was sent that Mr. and Mrs. Orsini wanted me to join them on a tour of the Greek ruins in the Valley of the Temples. They were waiting for me when I stepped into the motor launch, Danielle radiant in a pale green summer dress, and St. James, dressed in casual clothes, relaxed and full of easy confidence. He chatted amiably about nothing in particular as we headed toward the shore and the sand colored columns that marked the shape of what had once been a place of ancient worship. Danielle seemed distant, distracted, her mind on other things. She smiled at me once, but without significance. I was not even sure she had been aware she was doing it.

We walked through the Valley of the Temples, the best preserved Greek ruins anywhere. Starting near the top we followed the narrow road downward on stones worn smooth over thousands of years, down past hollowed out tombs of ancient burials, down past the jagged remains of shrines and tributes to lesser, local gods. St. James, though far from old, seemed younger than his age. Instead of plastered down, slick against his round, well-shaped head, his dyed black hair flowed clean and loose over his collar; and his eyes, so often sharp and penetrating, full of calculation or half-shut in boredom, were eager and alive. I had not noticed it before, but when he talked about ancient things - like the night he described the route around Sicily, or the day he spoke about what had happened in the harbor of Syracuse – there was none of the cynicism, none of the contempt, that you saw on his face when he talked about money and the people who talked about nothing else. He might have been a young man in his twenties, a graduate student in archeology, or even classics, seeing for the first time – and hungry for all of it – the last remains of the ancient world he had come to love.

"In America we think ancient history is anything that happened before we were born, but here…!" He gestured toward the great temple on the hill just ahead of us. "The Greeks came here almost three thousand years ago. Syracuse, the first Greek colony in Sicily, was founded in 745 B.C.," he said, as proud that he knew this as if he had been the first to discover it.

He turned his face to the sun, basking in the warmth of it; and then, remembering something else he had learned, another fact he was eager to share, he began to describe the dimensions, the perfect proportions, by which the Greeks had built such monuments of classic beauty.

"Basic geometry, really; but more than that, a sense of what…."

A strange, puzzled expression came into his eyes, and then, clutching his arm, he staggered to a nearby bench. Danielle started toward him, but he shook his head.

"It's nothing," he insisted. But the color had drained from his face and he suddenly looked years older. His breath was slow, methodical, and shallow, as if he knew not to exert himself even in this. "Go ahead. I just need to sit here a minute. I'll catch up."

"His heart," explained Danielle when we were far enough away not to be heard. "It isn't anything serious." Her eyes narrowed into a harsh, bitter stare. "Worse luck! If only he'd just die."

She started walking faster, the leather soles of her

shoes scraping on the sand-covered stones, as if she were determined to put as much distance between them as she could. Suddenly, she stopped, spun on her heel and pointed out to where the Midnight Sun stood at anchor, a tiny speck on the shimmering blue surface of an endless sea.

"Look at that! I'll never be able to go home; I'll be a prisoner on that damn boat until the day I die. Or until the day he dies," she added with an angry shudder. "Instead of wishing that I'd killed him, I should just do it!"

She gave me a sharp, questioning glance, and I knew immediately that it had to do with what they had been discussing, the two of them, behind closed doors.

"He's going to kill you, you know. Or rather, have someone do it for him. He wouldn't have the guts to do it himself. That story he told about the Athenians – or whoever they were – watching while their fate was decided and they couldn't do anything about it. That was meant for you! He knows what happened between us. He wasn't sure at first," she said, snapping her head to show that no one, least of all Nelson St. James, could presume to pass judgment on anything she had done. "But then I told him, and not just that we had slept together, but that you had made me feel things I'd never felt before."

Her eyes were wild with excitement. She grabbed my arm.

"He's jealous – he's insane! He's going to have you killed, if I don't kill him first!"

"Would you?" I asked, with as much detachment as if I were putting the question to a witness, or someone I did not know and did not care to meet.

I turned and started walking, but slowly, like a tourist who had all day. The question, lethal in its implications, had been asked with so little hint of moral judgment that it might have been a question about what color she preferred or what she thought she might like for dinner. 'Would you, or would you not,' the simple formulation for a choice so finely balanced that the slightest, the most temporary, whim might be not only decisive, but all the justification ever needed.

Danielle took hold of my arm and made me stop.

"And I could, too – couldn't I? I've already been tried for his murder; they couldn't try me again. Double jeopardy – isn't that what it's called?"

I pulled free and, ignoring her question, began to remark on the tumbled wreckage of some columns lying haphazard in an open field. She grabbed my arm again, harder than before.

"It's true, isn't it? Once you've been acquitted, they can't try you again – can they?"

She had learned it all from the movies. But double-jeopardy was not a license to kill. Time was always one of the provable elements of a crime. She had been acquitted of a murder committed a year ago; the fact she killed the same man she was supposed to have killed before would not stop a prosecution for murder a year later. She was interested in whether she could get away with it; I wanted to know if she would really do it.

I kicked at a pebble on the ground, not hard, but enough to start it rolling down a thick, time-worn stone.

"There would still be the question of your conscience. Could you live with that: the knowledge that you had killed someone in cold blood?"

I waited for an answer, but she kept her answer to herself. Smiling at the ease with which things could be set in motion, I kicked at another pebble and watched it bounce onto the next stone and roll a little after that.

"The man you married, the father of your child?" I continued. "You could do that: murder a man who was father to your child?"

Again there was no answer, just that same deathlike silence. I looked up and found her waiting, her eyes cold, dismissive, and impatient.

"Once you're acquitted, they can't try you again – can they?"

It was nearly word for word, as if it were the only question that could possibly matter: not whether murder was wrong, but could she get away with it.

"Double jeopardy – That's what you want to know?"

She pressed her lips together and raised her chin in an attitude so imperious, so superior to what the world in its simplicity called morality, that it fairly took my breath away. She had told me one lie after another, she had been guilty of every kind of deception, but I had not until now understood how utterly amoral she really was. She was all instinct, and the instincts were those of a child: selfish and immediate, without any thought of the consequences. And, like a child, almost blameless because of it. I say almost, because of course she did not have the excuse of her age. But she had something else that made it even more tragic. She had the power, often seen in children, to make others want to give her what she wanted; the power to make you believe that what, in someone older, would have been nothing short of criminal had, in her case, all the charm of innocence. It had taken me a long time to realize my mistake, to understand that behind those bright, eager eyes that made you feel so wanted, so alive, there was nothing real; that what you saw was only a mirror made to reflect your own private hopes and secret dreams.

"Why would you want to kill him?" I asked finally. "You're both so much alike."

But nothing could stop her. I could have screamed at her and it would have made no difference. She had to have an answer; she had to know.

"They can't, can they?"

I was just about to tell her the truth, that not only could they try her again, but, given what she had done before – made a travesty of the solemn proceedings of a court of law – would come after her like a pack of jackals, when, suddenly, my eyes moved past her. St. James was coming toward us, moving slowly through the crowd, every step a burden. Sweat glistened on his forehead and there was a troubled, dangerous expression on his face. He grabbed Danielle, digging his fingers into her arms, demanding to know why she had tried to run off. She pulled hard, trying to get away, but she could not break his grip.

"Let me go! What do you think you're doing? Are you crazy!" she cried as she continued to struggle. "I wasn't running anywhere!"

He held her in both hands and began to shake her. His face was all twisted up, demented and full of rage, as he screamed at her.

"You think I don't know what you're doing, what you'd like to do – run off with him! You were sleeping with him – Goddamn you, you admitted it!"

Flushed, breathing hard, he shut his eyes and shoved with all his strength. She stumbled backward and nearly fell.

"Go ahead – leave! You think I give a damn what you do!"

He glared at her; and then, as if he were seeing her for the first time and did not like what he saw, shook his head with disgust. Slowly, but with an unmistakable air of finality, he turned and left.

Danielle stood there, watching, angry and defiant. It was over; she was done with him, now free to do what she wished. I started toward her to tell her that nothing mattered but us. The anger, the defiance, all the bitterness which just moments earlier had led her to utter dark words of hatred and murder, vanished from her eyes. She was ready for a new life, ready to give up everything and go away with me. The reservations, the doubt that she was capable of thinking of anyone but herself, had no chance against that hope. I could see it in her eyes, an instant's intuition that she was going to tell me she loved me and would go anywhere I wanted.

The next moment, faced with the reality of it, that he was leaving her, leaving her without anything except the clothes on her back, leaving her without any way to get even what she would have had in a divorce, she was seized by panic. Without a word of explanation, without a word of any kind, she went running after him.

"I told you what happened," I heard her say as she caught up with St. James and walked alongside him. "I told you it was a mistake. If I'd wanted to run off with him, why would I have come back? Everything we planned has worked perfectly. Don't ruin it all because one night I got too lonely and did something I wish I hadn't."

One night! I could not hear the rest of their conversation, I don't know what else she might have told him, except that, whatever it was, it was not the truth; not the whole truth, anyway. That was the really remarkable thing about her, even more than the way she looked – this ability she had to make you want to believe her no matter how many times she had lied to you before. There was a certain intimacy in that; the knowledge that if she lied to you it was only because she still wanted you to think well of her. St. James knew that about her, and so did I, but we both wanted her too much for it to make any difference.

It was crazy; I admit it. I have asked myself why I did not put a stop to things; why I did not just check into a hotel and the next day fly home. I did not have to keep following them; I certainly did not have to go back to the yacht. St. James may or may not have been planning to get rid of me, but he was too upset, too distracted, to worry about anything except how to work out some manageable arrangement with his wife. He would not have noticed I was gone. The only answer I can come up with is that I was trapped in a spell of uncertainty. I did not know what was real and what was not, whether Danielle loved me or whether even that had been a lie. It all seemed too unfinished, and I had to see it through to a conclusion, though I knew, with a kind of terrible certainty, that however it ended, it would end badly. Call it a premonition, call it fear, but it assumed an importance – a test, if you will, of what I was made of – that I could not resist without admitting to cowardice, a refusal to see things for what they were. It was stupid, irresponsible, and I know it; but it did not feel that way. I had crossed a boundary, stepped over a line; I had become almost as instinctive, as free of restraint, as Danielle.

Two more days went by in which I did not see either of them. We had left the coast of Sicily and started sailing toward Algeria, though why we were headed there instead of continuing around the island I was not told. The weather changed, hot as blazes in the day and still hot at night, the wind from Africa warm on my face in the evening, the air clean and good to breathe.

It was close to midnight on the second day that I was summoned up on deck. I had not been told who wanted to see me, but I did not need to ask. I had always known, I think, that it was going to happen. Nelson was waiting for me. He had been drinking, drinking quite a lot. He was not drunk, but his face had a reddish tinge and instead of looking straight at me, the way he usually did, his eyes darted back and forth with a strange, inexplicable excitement. Then I saw Danielle.

Two days they had been together, two more days in which, whatever else they had talked about, they had talked about me. Something had been decided, I was certain of that; I was not quite so certain what it was, except that it was final, and none of it good. Danielle was standing just a few feet away, the third point, if you will, of the triangle we formed. I had never seen her look like this: nervous, intense, her face drawn and almost rigid, something wild and half-crazy about her eyes. I was so struck by how different, how almost deranged, she appeared, that at first I did not notice the revolver, pointed downward toward the deck, that she was holding in her hand.

"Danielle will do anything for me, Morrison," said St. James with a grim, triumphant smile. "It's what you never understood. Look what she did for me at the trial: put herself under that much at risk, willing to have everyone believe that she committed murder! How many women do you know would do a thing like that? She slept with you – I know that – and I'm sure she told you things, and she might even have meant them when she said them," he added, for a moment strangely sympathetic. "But she never forgot what she was there to do. You should have left it alone. I really wish you had. There's no choice now. We have to do this. Danielle has to do this," he said, glancing at her as she slowly raised the gun. "It's ironic, isn't it? That you should end up the way everyone thinks I did: shot to death, your body lost at sea, murdered by the same woman who murdered me!"

He turned away, choosing not to look.

"Do it, Danielle. Do it now!"

CHAPTER TWENTY TWO

Tommy Lane was curious. He looked at me, expecting me to go on, but I retreated into a long silence.

"What happened then? Tell me," he said patiently.

I crossed my arms and sank lower in the rocking chair. The light in mid-morning gave a silver sheen to the water sprinkling the lawn. The gardener, bent with age, knelt at the edge of the flower bed on the far side of the cottage, removing with a surgeon's touch every tiny weed.

"I've told you before. Why do you want to hear it again? It's been two years and every time I see you, you ask the same thing. Why? Don't you believe me? You think I'm making it up – you think I'm crazy?" I laughed.

"No, of course not," replied Tommy. Sitting next to me in one of the wooden chairs scattered along the front porch, he patted my arm in reassurance. "I've always believed you."

"I know you have," I said after another long pause. It was not because I needed time to think about it; I just did not know what else I could tell him about what had happened or why.

We sat there, listening to the rhythmic clicking noise as the sprinklers moved back and forth, shooting plumes of water across the long, sloping lawn.

"How is it for you here," asked my old friend. "Do you miss the city, do you miss…?"

He had become diplomatic as of late, approaching certain questions with a delicacy that anyone who had known him in college would never have suspected. We were young then, and full of ourselves, and certain that everyone else was full of us as well.

"Do I miss the law, do I miss the courtroom? Yes, all the time; no, hardly ever. Hell, I don't know."

I shook my head in confusion. It was hard sometimes to think too clearly about questions that, as I now understood, had no real answers. Then I remembered something, or rather a new thought came from somewhere and made me think it was my own creation.

"You quit, too. Do you ever miss it – being a lawyer? Do you miss football, the Saturdays in the fall – days like this – when the air was crisp and clean and there was that smell of new cut grass? Yes, no, sometimes, all the time, almost never? Depends what else you're doing, doesn't it?"

We lapsed into a long silence. Tommy sat with folded hands, trying, as I knew, to think of something that might cheer me up. I felt sorry for him. I knew how difficult it was for him. Sometimes the only way to tell the truth, especially about how you feel, is to tell a lie.

"No, I don't miss it much," I said with a quick, confident grin. Clutching the arm of the chair I began to rock back and forth. "Sometimes, especially late at night, I miss the city, the sense of excitement, the mystery; but I needed a place like this, away from all the madness and the noise. I suppose I'll go back one day, live in the city again, but for now Napa is a better place for me." I gestured toward the oak trees and the sloping green grass lawn, out to the tan colored hills. "It's a peaceful setting, don't you think? Nice cottage, nothing much I have to do. Some days I don't even bother getting dressed; I just lounge around in the same pajamas I wore to bed."

Tommy listened and nodded and did not say very much. He kept staring out at the long private drive, wondering perhaps how things had come to this, two old friends trapped in a past one of them could not understand and the other could not escape.

"She made me crazy, you know – Danielle, what happened that night, what it taught me....It wasn't just that night of course; I mean, none of it would have happened if.... If everything! If she hadn't been the kid sister of the girl I almost married, if she hadn't changed into the woman she became; if she hadn't met St. James, if he hadn't cheated half the world; if he hadn't gotten caught, if they hadn't figured out a way to commit the perfect murder that wasn't murder at all; if she hadn't known she could seduce me into becoming a party to a fraud -"

"You weren't an accomplice in anything!" insisted

Tommy with some heat. "A woman, a client – someone you're defending – takes the stand and tells a different story than what she's told you. It's the middle of the trial. There wasn't anything you could have done." He put his hand on my shoulder, forcing me to look at him instead of staring off into space. "She was right when she told you she didn't need to sleep with you to take the stand and lie!"

"And I was right when I told her that it changed how I felt!"

Tommy was still insistent. I do not know how many times now he had told me that it was not my fault, that there was nothing in my conduct as a lawyer of which I had to be ashamed. I looked back at the sloping lawn and the fence at the bottom where it ended.

"Danielle's mother – Justine's mother – told me I should move out of the city, find a place with privacy, tennis courts and a swimming pool, all the things that make life worth living – that kind of thing," I said, smiling to myself at the memory of Carol Llewelyn and the endless eagerness with which she praised the virtues of every home she sold. "She and her daughter weren't that much different," I remarked, struck by a similarity I had only just grasped. "The different sides of the great American dream: A house that everyone will envy, a house you can exchange for a better one when you have more money, and a new life, one you can invent for yourself, when you get tired of the one you have. They were both selling something, but it wasn't what you imagined; they were both selling you an image of yourself."

With my hands in my lap and my fingers intertwined, I beat my thumbs together in rapid, birdlike, repetition, and blinked my eyes to keep them company. It is a habit I have now developed, a nervous habit I suppose; though I don't feel the least bit anxious when I do it. Quite the contrary, if you really want to know. There is something actually very soothing about doing the same thing over and over again, the only variable the speed.

"Could you stop that!" said Tommy, unable to repress

his irritation.

"Sorry," I mumbled. "I seem to be getting all sorts of bad habits. Where were we?"

"That night. Tell me what happened."

"What happened? We were all the same – the three of us, I mean. I didn't understand that for a long time, but it's true. I didn't want to understand that. He was a thief, a charlatan, a man who stole billions and did not think he had done anything wrong. And Danielle – beautiful beyond description, and incapable, or unwilling, to think of anyone but herself. And I was just like that, too: unwilling, or incapable, of thinking about anything except what I thought I had to have. Don't you see? It's what each of us believed: that whatever we didn't have was more important than what we had. It was not enough to be rich, or beautiful, or good at what you did; we always, each of us, always had to have more. It's what makes this country great – this restless drive to keep moving from one thing to the next, always getting more – and that's also the reason why we're all so miserable."

I got up from the rocking chair and stood at the porch railing. Far to the north, at the end of the valley, a gray haze lay along the ridge top of the hills, the sign of a distant wildfire, the price of summer in a rainless season.

"It's going to be hot today," I remarked. "Not hot like Sicily, but hot enough."

Both hands on the railing, I spread my legs and bent forward. I could feel the motion of the ship, the Blue Zephyr turned Midnight Sun, and the smooth vibration of the engine; I could hear the sounds of the waves slapping hard against the hull. I could see Nelson turning away, choosing not to watch; I could see Danielle and her gorgeous, fevered eyes, the gun held firmly in her hand, the barrel shining smooth and silver in the moonlight. Two years, and it might have all happened just last night – it might be happening right now! – That was how vivid it remained in my mind.

"What happened that night?"

It was the only question he knew how to ask; the only

one that had a meaning. Was it because he did not believe me, thought it was some kind of delusion of mine that, forced often enough to talk about it, I would eventually reject as my own fabrication, or because he thought I was still concealing something, that I still refused to tell the truth? Or was the real reason simply that the truth was too difficult, that it did not correspond to what he wanted to believe? Tommy was the only friend I had, and I liked him even more for that, for how reluctant he was to take at face value what I had told him, for insisting so often that there must be some other explanation. But I also liked him too much, trusted him too much, to lie. There had been enough, more than enough, of that.

"You want to know what happened that night? Everything happened that night," I said as I turned around to face him. "And all of it in just a few seconds. It's strange how your whole life can be defined in a single act. Did you ever wonder what you would do if you saw someone about to be hit by a car, wonder whether you would jump out in front, push them clear, knowing that you would get hit instead, save someone and die yourself? I used to imagine that, wonder about it. Would I do the brave and noble thing, or freeze instead: watch helpless while someone – a child, perhaps – got run over. No one would blame you if you didn't do anything, but you would always blame yourself, or at least question what you had done, or rather, hadn't done. But suppose – just suppose – those weren't the two alternatives; suppose that it wasn't a question of whether you would put your own life at hazard to save another. Suppose – just suppose – that you have another choice, a choice to do nothing, or to make that other person die!"

I was almost used to his reaction, the way, quite without his meaning to, his mouth tightened at the corners and his eyes went dead, as if he had given up hope, as if he knew that there was not any use, the story was not going to change. No matter how many different ways I told it, the ending stayed the same.

"You don't want me to tell you the rest?" I asked,

ready to give up myself.

Tommy got to his feet and with that athletic step of his crossed over to the railing, a few feet from where I stood. He blinked into the morning sun, reminding himself to stay patient.

"No, tell me. I want to know. But the way you started – it's all wrong. There wasn't any choice like that. You were out there, all alone, in the middle of the night, off the coast of North Africa, and they were about to kill you. St. James had just turned his back; Danielle had the gun in her hand."

I could not help myself. It made me angry, this refusal to remember - or remembering, believe – what I had told him so many times before.

"Yes, damn it! She had the gun in her hand. More than that, she was pointing the damn thing right at me. I thought she was going to kill me, all right. The look in her eyes! – The sheer excitement! - The thought of murder seemed like sex to her. And then, suddenly, before I knew what was happening, she gave the gun to me - shoved it into my hand - and then stepped away. She was looking at Nelson, and I could not stop looking at her, frenzied, maniacal, her eyes on fire, telling me, over and over again, 'Do it, do it - Do it now!' Nelson turned, saw her - saw that look of hatred, saw how much she despised him. He started toward her, reaching for her; ready to strangle her if he could. He did not even look at me. If he saw the gun he did not care; he did not care if he was going to die, as long as he could kill her first. That's when I fired, that's when the gun went off, because for a moment – until he staggered backward – I did not know I had done it, - murdered Nelson St. James!"

"But you didn't murder him!" protested Tommy. "They were going to kill you – He was going to kill you! He had given her the gun. She gave it to you -"

"Because she wanted me to do it, kill her husband."

"He was going after her. You just said it. He would have killed her if you hadn't stopped him."

"You think I wouldn't have shot him, killed him, if he hadn't moved; if he had just stood there, waiting to see what

I would do? You forget how much I wanted her, how much I wanted him out of the way. No, it wasn't self-defense; it wasn't the defense of another. It was none of those lawful excuses. The truth is what I told you. If I didn't think about what I was doing, if I didn't even know I had done it until the blood came pouring out of his chest, it was only because I didn't have to think about it: the decision had already been made. The decision had been made, maybe not with my conscious mind, but made by that someone I really am. You don't stop and think when you dash into traffic to save someone: it's who you are. I didn't think when I fired the gun, when I killed St. James: it's what I was – what I am - a murderer, plain and simple."

Tommy's eyes were tired, and full of sympathy. A half-hearted smile started across his mouth and then vanished at once. He started to speak but had to clear his throat; and then, when he was able, his voice had a low, husky rasp.

"If you were 'a murderer, plain and simple,' you wouldn't have done what you did next; you wouldn't have done any of the things that happened later. You would have stayed with Danielle."

I tried to smile, to pretend that none of it was of any consequence, but I felt the tears start to come and I had to look away.

"Maybe I should have," I said when I could finally look back. "Maybe it would have been better. But something happened that night, when I murdered St. James: something broke inside."

"You tried to kill yourself," Tommy tried to remind me.

"You give me too much credit. I jumped, but I wasn't trying to kill myself. I didn't care what happened. I didn't know if I could make it to shore – we were a little less than a mile off the coast – I didn't care if I drowned; all I knew was that I had to get away, get away from what I had learned about myself, the evil in my soul. I loved Danielle, more than I thought I could ever love anyone, and I hated her as well, hated her for what she had made me into. But more than anything, I hated myself for letting her do it. I jumped because in that moment I knew that if I stayed with her I was lost."

"You're not a murderer," Tommy kept insisting. He seemed to think that everything would change if only he could convince me that he was right about that. In my awkward way, I tried to cheer him up a little.

"You mean, because no one believed me when I tried to confess?"

He glanced at me with the kind of disapproval that cannot begrudge a certain degree of admiration. Though he thought that what I had done had been the right thing, he wished I had not done it. But we both knew that it would not have made any difference, that the same thing would have happened if instead of going first to the district attorney, and then, when that did not work, to the judge, I had kept it to myself. I would still be here, retired from the world, living in peaceful seclusion instead of back in the city, practicing law.

"Of course, I didn't think so at the time, but it really was quite funny. Poor Franklin. You should have seen the look on his face - I should say the looks, because he must have had a dozen of them, one right after the other, an escalating series of curiosity, disbelief, and then alarm – as I told him that the trial had been start to finish a gigantic hoax, that Danielle had not killed anyone, that Nelson St. James had not been murdered, that they had staged the whole thing, and then sailed off to Sicily, changed their names to Orsini, painted the yacht – that really made his eyes pop open! – painted the yacht and changed its name. 'It's the Midnight Sun, now; not Blue Zephyr.' That I found them, that they were going to kill me, but that, at the last second, Danielle gave me the gun and instead of becoming the victim of a homicide I became a murderer, and that I was there in his office, come to make my confession."

Exchanging a glance with Tommy, I laughed softly; remembering with what at the time had been puzzlement but was now something close to affection, the kindness Franklin had tried to show me.

"He told me he was sorry about everything I had been through, and that the best thing I could do was to go home and try to get some rest. 'After a few days,' he said as he led me out of his office, 'things will be better.'"

I shrugged helplessly, and though Tommy was right in front of me, just a few feet away, I stared right at Robert Franklin, watching the embarrassment, and more than that, the genuine sense of concern, spread across his countenance. When he said goodbye, I heard him stutter through the final words.

"And then you had to go tell Brunelli," said Tommy, bringing me back to myself.

"Yes, then I had to tell Brunelli." I shook my head with shining eyes, eager not to tell him again about my last meeting with a judge. "It's nice here, isn't it?" I asked, surprised that this passing thought just came out. I made a vague gesture with my hand, meant to take in all of it: the long drive, the stately trees, the well-tended garden. "Nice as any place, I suppose."

"Alice Brunelli."

I looked at Tommy, for a moment not sure what he meant.

"Oh, yes – Alice Brunelli. I think I was in a state of shock. Franklin did not believe me. I had told him everything, and he refused to believe it. Can you imagine? I confess to murder, and all he can say is that I couldn't have killed St. James because he had been killed a year earlier. Now, Brunelli, to give her credit, took me much more seriously. She listened – did not say a word – let me tell her everything. She didn't show any emotion, no reaction of any kind. She was just like she is in court: her face a perfect mask. Then when I was finished, when I told her that I murdered St. James, she quite calmly began to ask me questions. Questions about a lot of things, and not all of them about the things I had just finished telling her.

"We must have spent an hour in her chambers. She told me that she knew I was telling her what I thought to be the truth, but that because there was no evidence, nothing to prove that Nelson St. James had been alive, nothing to prove that I had killed anyone, she wanted me to talk to someone else, a friend of hers, who was quite good at finding out things like this. She meant an investigator, I was sure of it. And she did mean that – an investigator, though a different kind than what I thought. Anyway, after a while, after I talked to a few more people, I began to realize that no one was ever going to believe me, and that I had to make some changes, that I had to leave the city, stop practicing law, and come up here, away from all that madness, and live a quiet life."

When it was time for Tommy to leave, I asked if he had been able to find out anything about Danielle. The last time I had seen him, a few months earlier, he had told me he would look into it.

"Nothing definite. You were right about Sicily, what you said someone told you: that it's always full of rumors – rumors, secrets and lies. The new owner of the Midnight Sun is someone supposed to be rich and reclusive, a South American who, according to one rumor, won it all from Orsini one night at cards. There is another rumor that says Gabriella Orsini was in love with him, that her husband found out, and that in the argument they had she shot him to death and that his body was never found. There are even those who insist that they – Gabriella and her new lover – were in it together, and that he was the one who, in order to have her, murdered her husband one night at sea. All anyone knows for certain is that the new owner, whoever he is, painted the Midnight Sun a different color and gave her a different name. There is one other thing. They say that the new owner is married to one of the most beautiful women anyone has ever seen."

I stood on the porch and waved as Tommy got into his car and drove away. I watched as he went down the long, narrow drive and out through the gate and the two stone pillars, out past the sign for the Napa State Hospital. I watched until there was nothing left to see.

THE SWINDLERS

That night, after I had had dinner and taken my medication, I dreamed, the way I often do, of a beautiful woman and a long, elegant yacht, Danielle St. James on board the Blue Zephyr, sailing down the California coast on a sunlit summer night. I watch as it moves farther and farther away, until it becomes a tiny speck on the horizon, caught for a fleeting moment in the scarlet light before it finally and forever vanishes out of sight. And then I see myself, staring at the empty sea, wondering what will happen to me now that I am safe on land and all alone.

A Note from the Author:

Thank you for reading The Swindlers. Please let me know your thoughts about the book. You can send me email, sign up for my newsletter and get updates about new releases by visiting my web site at www.dwbuffa.net.

- D.W. Buffa

OTHER BOOKS BY D. W. BUFFA

THE DEFENSE

THE PROSECUTION

THE JUDGMENT

THE LEGACY

STAR WITNESS

BREACH OF TRUST

TRIAL BY FIRE

THE GRAND MASTER

EVANGELINE

RUBICON
(Released under the pen name
'Lawrence Alexander')

CPSIA information can be obtained
at www.ICGtesting.com
Printed in the USA
LVOW13s1214310717
543259LV00005B/708/P